fw.

‖‖‖‖‖‖‖‖‖‖‖‖‖‖‖‖‖‖‖‖‖‖‖‖‖

◁ **Y0-CBF-301**

Dear Romance Reader,

Welcome to a world of breathtaking passion and never-ending romance.
Welcome to *Precious Gem Romances.*

It is our pleasure to present *Precious Gem Romances,* a wonderful new line of romance books by some of America's best-loved authors. Let these thrilling historical and contemporary romances sweep you away to far-off times and places in stories that will dazzle your senses and melt your heart.

Sparkling with joy, laughter, and love, each *Precious Gem Romance* glows with all the passion and excitement you expect from the very best in romance. Offered at a great affordable price, these books are an irresistible value—and an essential addition to your romance collection. Tender love stories you will want to read again and again, *Precious Gem Romances* are books you will treasure forever.

Look for fabulous new *Precious Gem Romances* each month—available only at Wal★Mart.

Kate Duffy
Editorial Director

MISS McNEAL'S PIRATE

Nora LeDuc

Zebra Books
Kensington Publishing Corp.
http://www.zebrabooks.com

One

He had sailed over a hundred miles for nothing.

Captain Jack St. George glared at the hand-lettered CLOSED sign on the Oyster River library. He'd missed the meeting that would lead him to his nemesis, Gaspar.

Jack scowled at the building. What man worth his salt would conduct his business in a library? He clenched and unclenched his fist while the letters on the sign danced and blurred into the face of Gaspar.

His enemy's cold blue eyes shimmered with icy contempt, and his mouth twisted into a sneer. *You'll never catch me, Jack. Never.*

With a curse that made decent ladies faint, Jack leapt at the door. He beat on the graying pine wood.

"Up here!"

Jack's fist froze in midair. Who had spoken? It was a woman's voice. Suspicions coiling within him, he backtracked a few steps and stared into the graying blue sky. Above the white clapboard building, a territorial seagull circled and squawked. Jack lowered his gaze and saw a woman in brown waving frantically. She leaned precariously over the widow's walk.

"Great Blackbeard's Ghost!" Why was the fool woman

on a rooftop? Didn't she possess any common sense about heights?

The figure in brown bent further over the balustrade. Warning signals spiraled through Jack. She was inches from falling. With this realization, he charged to the pine door and forced down the iron latch. The weathered door swung open.

Inside, he scanned the tiny, bare hallway. Spying a narrow staircase in the corner, he bounded up it. At the top, he froze.

Before him on a flat section of the roof stood a woman of short stature. Wisps of chestnut hair framed her face, and a neat chignon held the rest. But her eyes captured him. They were green, the color of the sea. They beckoned to him, making him think of calm waters and whispering breezes. She started forward, and he spotted a two-inch spyglass dangling about her neck.

With a dimpled smile, she held out a hand. "You're Captain St. George. I'm Mary McNeal. I hoped you'd still come."

Caution held him back. He examined her small outstretched hand and welcome grin before answering. "A storm in Massachusetts delayed me."

Reluctantly, Jack accepted her smooth hand. A warm tingling spread from her palm into his. Shocked, he looked at the young lady and saw surprise reflected in her eyes. He released her hand and tried to collect himself. "I thought you were in trouble up here."

Amazement flashed in her green eyes. "Trouble? How foolish. I was simply waving at you to get your attention."

He frowned and remembered her greeting. "McNeal, you said? I'm to meet your brother or, uh, husband?"

"I've no brother or husband." She sidestepped, allowing him to join her on the widow's walk.

While confusion tumbled in his mind, a strong sea breeze brought the taste of salt and the fragrance of the lilac bush from below. "Excuse me." He glanced at the slate roof. "Why are you up here?"

"I'm the librarian," Mary said in a matter-of-fact voice. " 'There is no enjoyment like reading! How much sooner one tires of anything than of a book.' "

He narrowed his eyes in skepticism. "What?"

"It's a quote from a book."

"Does it mean something?"

She sighed. "It seems unimportant at the moment." With her index finger, she indicated the sun slipping from the sky tinged with pink. "I also write down the exact time the sun sets and when the different stars appear."

Jack quirked his eyebrows in disbelief. "Was that another quote or something? What are you doing up here?"

Mary gave a short laugh. "No quotation, and our town received money from the wealthy widow of a sea captain. She specifically requested the town's people use the money for a library with a widow's walk."

"A good story. I—"

"Wait. I have more to tell you. Apparently during her husband's absences, she spent much time looking out to sea and *reading.*"

She paused. Probably for breath, Jack thought. He tapped a finger above his lip and glanced at the disappearing sun. Time grew short. He wanted to leave and set sail to renew his search.

She followed his gaze toward the setting sun. "The heavens have fascinated people through the ages. Did you know that the earliest description of the sky came from a Greek poet, Aratus? Even Homer in the ninth century referred to the constellations."

The unexpected change in the conversation left him

gaping at her. Had he stumbled upon someone not quite right? Far from his ship and surrounded by a patchwork of pointed rooftops, he experienced the sensation of floating above another world.

Apparently oblivious to his feelings, the diminutive librarian continued with her speech. "Many people look at the night sky and see only darkness and a few lights. I gaze at it and see a world beyond our vision."

She hesitated for a moment and gazed upwards into the darkening heavens. A wistful, faraway glimmer shone in her eyes, and her full lips parted in eagerness. "Imagine sailing a ship into the stars."

Jack stared at her, caught by the expression of desire on her face. She was the most beautiful woman he'd ever seen. He took a step toward her and stopped. Damn! What was wrong with him? She was a straitlaced librarian. He clenched his teeth.

The diminishing light pulled his thoughts back to the present problem. "I received a letter from M. McNeal."

"I am M. McNeal."

Jack stared at her, distrust snaking inside him. *"You saw Gaspar?"*

Mary McNeal blushed and folded her hands demurely in front of her. "I'm afraid I took some liberties in my writing."

"Exactly what does that mean?" He ran a hand through his hair and wished she'd spit out the information.

For a second, her gaze wavered to his scuffed Hessian boots. "Three weeks ago my father, Marcus McNeal, and his friend, Harold Ramfus, set sail to visit an inventor, Thaddius Higgins. Mr. Higgins had been experimenting with refractors and reflectors and he—"

"Wait." Jack held up a hand. He didn't give a damn

about reflectors. "It's late. I'm tired. All I care about is Gaspar."

"Certainly," Miss McNeal said with a trace of coldness. "Mr. Gaspar delayed my father's ship when he learned of my father's navigational skills." Her face glowed with pride. "My father can draw a chart like no other man, if you should need one, Captain."

"Are you finished with your story?"

"No, the pirate took my father prisoner and allowed the passenger ship to continue onward. No one understands Mr. Gaspar's reasons for allowing the other passengers to continue."

"Gaspar loves to do the unexpected," Jack admitted.

"Naturally, the kidnapping distressed Mr. Ramfus. At the first opportunity, he transferred from his vessel and returned."

"McNeal wrote, I mean, you wrote that you could give me the exact position of the ship at the time Gaspar boarded."

"I can," she said. "Mr. Ramfus related everything to me in great detail."

"Where were they?"

Biting her lip, Miss McNeal hesitated. "First, I need to know your intentions. Do you plan to use these facts to find Mr. Gaspar?"

"I plan to capture him and clear my name. Then I can get back to my trading business."

"Good, I'm going with you."

He stiffened in alarm. "With me where?"

"I'm joining your search for Mr. Gaspar. He has my—"

"Stop!" She was beyond senseless. "No women sail on my ship. Especially not a bookish one," he added.

Her eyes flashed with anger. "I can help. My father

taught me how to do the sea charts. He does them for the whalers as I was attempting to inform you."

"Listen, Miss Librarian, this isn't some fairy tale you've read about in a book. *Mr. Gaspar* wouldn't think twice about inviting you to dinner and then cutting off your head to use for his centerpiece. I hate to tell you, but the chances of your father surviving are little to nothing."

"You survived when Gaspar captured you," Mary McNeal said, her voice softening.

Jack surveyed her features that had paled even in the ashen light. Distress shone in her eyes. A strange feeling of tenderness rose and caught in his throat. Clearing it, he tried to focus his thoughts. He had no desire to discuss his incarceration and less desire to discuss her father's death.

"What made you write to me?"

Her arms dropped to her sides. "Mrs. Harrison brought back a newspaper on her last visit to her sister in Massachusetts. She'd wrapped some china in it. When she took the plates out, she donated the paper to the library. I read about your trial."

He studied her. In her high-necked prim dress, she seemed harmless. She had said nothing to lead him to believe she was like the others who had hurled their accusations of pirate at him. Trying to read the truth behind her speech, he asked, "Weren't you afraid to meet with a man charged with piracy?"

"The jury declared you innocent. You're a hero." Mary's voice rang with excitement. "President Madison recognized your valor during the war at the naval battle on Lake Champlain. He gave you a medal at a ceremony."

Jack shook his head in frustration. "You'd do better with the authorities."

"They've given up," she cried.

"They must know Gaspar. He's the only man I know who preys on humans for the joy of it. I can't help you." He turned, eager to escape this hopeless situation and to quell the memories of his past.

Mary grabbed his arm. Her soft green eyes peered intently into his. "Please, you're my only hope."

An overwhelming desire to take her into his arms and promise to help her swept through him. A dangerous feeling. *Hell, where had that idea come from?* He jammed his hands into his pockets and stared down at her coldly. "I've had a rough voyage. I'm tired, and I'm standing on a roof arguing with a book person."

"What's that mean?" Her hand slipped from his arm.

He shook his head in resignation. "Nothing. Where can I get something to drink?"

"The Red Dog is behind the bank that is on—"

"Thanks, I'll find it," Jack said with a sigh. The woman had more worthless information than anyone he knew.

"If you'd like a hot meal, I'm a good cook."

He smiled. "No thanks. I thought I'd find Mr. Ramfus. He can tell me what you won't." He pivoted on his heel to leave.

"He's dead," Miss McNeal said quickly.

"Dead?" Jack swiveled back toward her. "Sudden, wasn't it?"

"I'm afraid his encounter with a buccaneer put a strain on his heart."

He looked closely into her eyes and saw a shadow. She was lying.

"I'll just pay my respects then. Good evening." With a polite inclination of his head, Jack left. He expected her to run after him, but she didn't. On the street below, he didn't glance back. Whistling a tune his mother would detest, he tried to drown out his desire to slit Gaspar's gullet like a fish. Again that demon had damaged two innocent lives, Miss Mary McNeal's and Mr. Marcus McNeal's. He had to find him and destroy him before he ruined anyone else's.

On the widow's walk, Mary shifted from one foot to another while the brief encounter with Captain St. George filtered through her mind. Since reading about him, she'd imagined him so often in her mind that she had difficulty believing he'd arrived.

Still, she'd known before writing the letter that he would come. Her heart had raced when he'd bounded up those stairs, like a knight charging a dragon. Standing before her in his blue pea coat and tan breeches, he had the stance and voice of a man in charge, the type of man she needed to save her father.

Of course, the man wouldn't know the difference between *Poor Richard's Almanac* and *Romeo and Juliet*. And stubborn! He had simply refused to have her on his ship, and he hadn't given her any sensible explanation for his rejection of her proposal. He was nothing like the refined, intellectual gentlemen she preferred.

Yet, his image blotted out all thoughts of others. She recalled that his hair had been as black and silky straight as she'd imagined. His eyes, though, had been a surprise. They reminded her of the gray of a troubled sky. And he'd been thinner than she imagined. His health must have suffered during the past year of captivity. The thought conjured up the image of her father, thin and sick.

Briefly, Mary closed her eyes to end the vision. The mental picture brought back the realization that she must find her father soon. No one else would. A feeling of nausea overwhelmed her. She'd pinned all her hopes to this man, and he hadn't even listened to her. He'd been unfair. She could help him on his ship. Her navigational skills were nearly as good as her father's. She had to convince him. But how?

Use reason, her inner voice told her. Yes, she needed to explain. First, she'd leave the note for Mrs. Harrison to take her place at the library during her absence, and then she'd collect her waiting bag at home. With luck, she would arrive at the Red Dog in less than half an hour. She hoped Captain St. George would still be there.

Jack thanked his stars that he'd found a seat at the Red Dog. From his rough-hewn table, he watched the patrons. Tonight they crowded inside, filling the tables. Others were forced to stand in small clusters near the brick fireplace where a meager fire chased away the spring chill.

Most of these men had tanned arms and faces that spoke of days at sea. An unwashed odor attested to it. He wondered if Marcus McNeal had spent time here. If he was anything like his daughter, St. George doubted he did. He'd never met anyone like Miss McNeal. She was a little strange, although she was attractive enough. Hell, *beautiful* described her better.

Unfortunately, *too persistent* depicted her, too. She'd been quite insistent about his medal of honor. He wished he could clearly remember the day he'd received it. Then maybe he could recall his parents' joy. Instead, Jack remembered the pain in their eyes every time they looked at him, their only child, the branded traitor.

Tightening his hand on his drink, he forced the memory from his thoughts. Searching for another recollection, Jack mused over the image of the librarian. He recalled her full breasts and narrow waist. Jack guessed her age at twenty, five years younger than he.

But why in the name of Neptune had she been writing down the times of the sun? He groped for a reason and remembered the spyglass hanging around her neck. While he pondered the question, he caught sight of a flash of brown. Craning his neck, Jack saw Miss McNeal squeezing past a throng of men. He swore in surprise, and she saw him and waved. Appearing to apologize to another group of men, she ducked under a man's raised arm and scurried toward him.

Jack stared at her in a mixture of confusion and exasperation. She was like a pesky gull. Still, something about her held his attention. "Have you come to write down how many times I raise my drink?"

Mary took a step closer to him behind the table. "I realize you've had a long trip and weren't ready to hear my explanation. After you've enjoyed your refreshments, you'll listen to reason."

"Refreshments?" Jack glanced down at his dark, bitter ale in disbelief.

"What are you doing here?" a barrel-chested man asked.

Jack fixed his gaze on the burly man swaying before him. Two more men flanked the large-chested man on either side.

"He's Captain Jack St. George, and he's enjoying our hospitality," Mary said with a tilt of her head.

The burly man took a threatening step toward them. "I know who he is. A few months ago our ship docked in New Bedford, and he was all the talk. He's that sea captain that turned pirate. I saw him when they took him to the courthouse for his trial." The man balled his hands into fists. "We don't want the likes of him here."

The librarian drew a deep breath to continue her worthless lecturing, and Jack's patience snapped. He leapt to his feet and caught her arm. Since he'd become an outcast in society, he'd learned to act rather than to reason.

"Let's not argue," he said, drawing her away. Then he sprang forward and tipped the table before the threatening men.

The men jumped back.

From inside his coat, St. George whipped out a pistol and aimed it with deadly precision at the unwelcoming trio.

"Come along, Miss McNeal. It's late. Librarians should be in bed." He gripped her wrist as they edged toward the door. His pistol point never wavered from the men. Around them, everyone in the room had frozen. With gaping mouths the customers watched them slip through the entrance.

Jack barely passed through the door when a lanky man with thinning hair and spectacles blocked the way. "Mary?" he asked in a high, tight voice.

"Oliver, what are you doing here?"

"Excuse us," Jack interjected. He didn't like the familiar look that passed between them.

As Jack secured his grasp on the librarian, he heard shouts from inside. At any moment, the Red Dog patrons would burst outside, looking for him. Jack scanned the moonlit street for the quickest and safest escape route. "When I arrived, I came through town. Is there another way to the harbor?"

Mary nodded.

They stole past the tall man, and he offered no resistance.

Jack released her wrist, and she intertwined her fingers with his. The warmth of her skin seeped into his. Her action surprised him, but he had no time to question it. He silently allowed her to lead. Around the dark stores and Cape Cod style homes, she took a zigzag course, never faltering. For the first time, he noticed that she carried a burlap bag in her other hand, but he didn't ask why. Escape was all that mattered.

Finally, the town disappeared. Overhead a few stars shone on them. Frogs croaked their welcome, and a marsh rose up to greet them. The soggy ground sucked at Jack's feet and slowed their progress. Black flies attacked them, and the smell of the ocean grew stronger. Ahead, Jack spied a river. His ocean lay at the end of it, and he could taste the salty air.

Reaching the waterway, Mary led him to a dock where several small boats floated. He released her hand and rushed toward two small crafts.

"This one." She pointed toward a little skiff.

Jack didn't question her choice but knelt and untied one of the half hitches that held the small boat. Close beside him, Mary lay on her stomach untangling another line. The hint of lilac and another scent lingered about her. Glancing at her long fingers in the moonlight, he noted ink on their tips. Strands from her hair had escaped their confines and rubbed against his dark coat sleeve. Her closeness sent tremors of excitement through him, and he wanted to reach out and touch her.

The loop came free in his hand, and he turned his attention to the boat. He scrambled into it. On the dock the librarian pulled at her line, and it slid away from the mooring. He grabbed the oars resting on the seat and shoved the vessel out.

"Wait!" she cried with alarm ringing in her voice.

Her cry spurred him to row faster. Over his shoulder Jack called, "Good-bye, my little librarian."

He heard a splash. Glancing back, he saw her arms flaying about in the river. Her head rose above the water, and she gulped for air.

Damn Blackbeard's Ghost! What now? Couldn't she swim? He maneuvered the boat back to her. Reaching down, he grabbed something hard, her shoulder. The cold water numbed his fingers, but he held firm. Then her fingers encircled his wrist. He yanked.

Gasping, Mary emerged. Jack pulled her to the side of the boat. She coughed and held onto it. He reached down and caught her by the waist. With her soaking clothes, she was as heavy as an anchor. He gave one last yank. She tumbled into the boat, fell backwards, sputtered and coughed.

Jack had no time to question her. He wanted his ship. Pulling fiercely on the oars, he waited until the shoreline disappeared before he noticed her again. She lay in the small boat, her breasts rising and falling in rhythm to the sound of the oars dipping into the water. Her dress had bunched up above her knees, revealing slender calves. With interest he followed the lines of her leg till it disappeared beneath her clinging garment. His gaze traveled up her slender waist to her breasts.

Mary sat up and disapprovingly frowned at him. Her silent reprimand triggered his anger.

"You can't swim?"

She folded her arms protectively across her chest, blocking his view. "It never seemed necessary until now, and I've lost my bag."

"You nearly lost your life. Don't you have any common sense?"

"Your *abrupt* departure overruled my good judgment."

"I suppose your good friends at the Red Dog lost their

good sense, too. What was the name of the man who threatened us?"

"I don't know," she said, wringing out part of her skirt.

"You haven't helped him pick out any books lately?"

"Given his inebriated condition, I doubt that gentleman could read his name." She ran her fingers through her hair, apparently searching for pins. "If you treat all ladies as you have me, I can understand why you're alone in life."

"I'm alone because I choose to be." He glanced at her dripping hair. "You look like a wet mop."

"Thank you, Captain." She shook her head, spraying him with cold water from her tresses. Jack's protest died on his lips, and to his delight, more hair fell over her face. Complaining loudly, she pushed it from her eyes and provided him another view of her wet bodice. A need rose within him, and he shoved it away. Once he cleared his name, he'd find a woman that really suited him, not one that stood on a rooftop and preached about dead Greeks.

Ahead, he saw his ship come into view. Pride filled him as her familiar sturdy hull rose proudly in the water. "My ship," he whispered. "The *Goodspeed*."

"She's not what I expected." Mary tipped her head back, studying the vessel.

"Sorry she's not up to your standards," Jack said in an acid tone. "She's old, but she's seaworthy. The *Goodspeed* keeps pace with the best of the newer ships. She's seven hundred tons in weight and one hundred and seven feet from stern to bow."

"On the contrary, your vessel is more beautiful than I ever expected." Her eyes glowed with amazement while she whispered, "Lovelier than a poem by Byron."

Jack stopped rowing to contemplate this woman. How

could he and Miss Poetry share the same feelings about his vessel?

From aboard the *Goodspeed*, the watch called out to them. Returning his mind to their situation, Jack declared their identity and steered close to the black, scarred hull. From above, a rope ladder descended.

"Ladies first." He swept his hand before her.

She barely had placed a black, ankle-booted foot on the ladder when he added, "In the morning, one of my men will escort you home."

The librarian opened her mouth to protest, but she appeared to think better of it and resumed her climbing. Below, Jack glimpsed a flash of her white stocking. Smiling, he followed her. He marveled at how fragile she appeared, and at how slowly she climbed. He'd seen faster turtles.

Finally, they reached the deck. Several of his men congregated around them, gaping at their temporary guest like she was the first woman they'd ever seen.

"Stand aside," Jack bellowed. They greeted his command with silence, and he realized he'd spoken much more gruffly than usual.

"She's a librarian." He shrugged.

"Captain," the first mate, Daniel, said to Jack. "A ship is approaching off our stern."

Jack rushed to the rear and saw the outline of a vessel skimming toward them.

Joining him, Mary declared, "That ship belongs to Oliver's father!" Jack turned to her and sharpened his gaze upon her. "Whose father? I thought you didn't know those sharks inside the Red Dog."

"I didn't."

Across the lapping sound of the waves, a shot rang out and ended in a splash.

"The man firing at us," she said, "is my fiancè."

Two

"And a very loving man he must be," Jack said when another shot rang out. "How did he propose, with a firing squad?"

At the mention of firearms, the librarian whirled toward him. Her eyes shone brightly with admiration. "You were magnificent against those ruffians tonight. I knew you were the type of man I needed. A rogue who thinks like those scoundrels."

"Take care, your words will turn my head," he said wryly.

The auburn-haired first mate interrupted, "Request permission to return fire."

Jack splayed his hands on the uneven wooden rail and studied the ship closing the gap between them. His men would welcome the skirmish. He glanced at the woman. Already she'd brought trouble to his ship, and she'd been aboard less than a minute. He needed to get rid of her, yet as captain, he held responsibility for every passenger and member of his crew and that included a nuisance woman. Could he turn her over to this man shooting at them?

"Was he firing at us for any particular reason, or does he shoot at all ships in the harbor?" Jack tightened his jaw.

"We passed him outside the Red Dog," Mary said,

watching the fast-approaching vessel. "He must have overheard and followed us."

Next to him, Daniel cleared his throat, waiting for orders.

"No need to ready the men," Jack said. "We'll simply return his *fiancée.*"

At his command, Mary folded her arms across her chest. "I should have said he *was* my fiancé. We're not engaged any longer. We quarreled this morning. I told him I'd rather be illiterate than marry him." A loud boom and spray of water punctuated her sentence.

"That must have put him in his place," Jack said dryly.

"Begging your pardon, Captain, but the last shot nearly hit our starboard. Request permission to fire back." The first mate glanced at their attacker and back at Jack.

Jack began to snap in agreement when Mary stepped in front of him. All signs of her stubborn facade had vanished and had been replaced by a pleading look. "I'd rather drown than be with him."

For a moment he hesitated, swinging back and forth between his alternatives. He looked down into her green eyes that begged him to reconsider, and he knew he had lost. "Prepare to sail," he shouted.

Without warning, the librarian brushed a kiss across his cheek.

Jack's face heated like a cabin boy's, and a sudden surge of excitement raced through him. He willed it away. "You go back tomorrow." He marched away feeling the surprised stares of his men fixed upon him.

With the grace of a cat, the *Goodspeed* sprang forward in the shadowy water. Above Mary, the stars journeyed across the sky with increased speed. Dizzy, she grabbed hold of the railing and watched their pursuer shrink into the darkness. She was alone with a crew of men. Her stomach dipped although the ship held a steady course.

She swallowed her unease and reminded herself this was the first part of her dream. She sailed with Captain Jack St. George, a war hero who could outsail, outmaneuver, and outwit any man alive. Exhilaration began to tingle within her, and Mary held fast to the excitement to banish her quaking feelings. She'd imagined this moment, and now it was happening. Cold water sprayed her face. The sea wind pressed against her damp clothing, but nothing could cool her growing fever of adventure.

Smiling to herself, Mary remembered how she'd hidden her identity in her letter to him. Sailors were a superstitious lot. They believed in haunting spirits and that women on ships brought bad luck. Captain St. George must share this last belief. Obviously, he lacked an appropriate education. Well, she wouldn't sail with him for long. She'd bear his faults to save her father.

She glanced back and saw him in conversation with a young man. Mary scanned the open sea. No one followed them. Oyster Bay was nowhere in sight.

Apprehension gripped her. Alone for the moment, she reached into the pocket of her skirt and closed her hand around the small telescope. When she'd fallen into the water, she'd let go of her bag to keep the small instrument safe. With a sigh of happiness, she withdrew it and carefully wiped it as best she could with her damp skirt. To her relief, the inside lens appeared dry.

"What's that, Miss?"

Clutching her telescope tightly, Mary looked up at the thin young man Captain St. George had called Daniel. She noticed for the first time that a thin scar ran down the side of his freckled face. He wore a white shirt that would have fit a man twice his size. Remembering her manners, she smiled. "This is my telescope. My father gave it to me on my birthday. Care for a look?"

When he didn't answer, she pressed the scope into his hands, giving lengthy, detailed instructions on finding the North Star.

The young mate bobbed his auburn head up and down and swallowed when Mary finished her directions. With encouragement, her new pupil put the glass to his hazel eye and stared straight up at the sky.

The lad didn't quite have the knack of it. Leaning over his arm, she tried to detect the direction of his star gazing.

"Daniel!" Jack bellowed. "Get to your post."

The first mate stiffened. With a glance of apology, he handed the telescope back to her.

"We'll try again later," Mary whispered and strung the cord around her throat.

"Miss McNeal, I'll see you below in my quarters." Jack dismissed her with a nod.

Raising her skirt and tilting her chin in the air, Mary swept past him. Her exit ended when she realized she had no idea where to go. Whirling around, she saw the captain speaking to his men.

Above, the sails snapped as the winds picked up. The deck rocked and creaked beneath her feet. She glanced up only to observe the light of the stars and moon dim and disappear. Storm clouds gathered in the night sky.

On the deck, Jack stood before her, frowning. Then he gestured for Mary to follow. He led the way to the higher deck by the wheel and grabbed a small lantern. Together, they descended through a narrow, dim passageway. *Did the crew retire to their quarters here? Would she have her own cabin?* Her breath came in short gasps as the stale damp air, and her anxiety, threatened to smother her.

Ahead, the captain stopped before a thick wooden door. Mary hurried to catch up to him. With great curiosity, she entered the cabin and noted a high narrow bed built into the wall. An old, black trunk sat at the end of the bunk. On the other side, she saw a wall iron-cabinet, and beside it, a pine desk and chair. Against the outside wall, a square table with a chair sat under the small porthole.

Captain St. George gestured for her to sit. Once Mary did, he paced the room, rubbing his chin. Several times, he paused as if he were about to speak, then suddenly strode back and forth again.

Watching him, she admired his energy and felt drawn to him like a sailor to the polestar. Her own alarm disappeared as she recognized his agitated state. "May I make a suggestion, Captain?"

He stopped and raised a brow in irritation. "No."

She frowned and folded her hands in her lap. Someone had to speak. "I know my presence distresses you, but you've no cause to worry. You won't even know I'm aboard."

"No, I won't, because you're going home tomorrow."

Panic filled her. She had to find her father. "Why? I won't cause any trouble. You haven't given this sufficient consideration."

"Miss McNeal, you don't want me to repeat my thoughts, sufficient or not. Tonight, you'll sleep in my cabin. Tomorrow night, I'll return you to your Oyster River friends. After my last greeting, I prefer a more clandestine arrival."

"Haste makes waste, and the people at the Red Dog weren't my friends."

He loomed over her. Worry creases appeared between his eyes. Their gazes locked, and her heart took a perilous leap.

His jaw tightened. "No, you prefer people who shoot at us."

"Oliver's upset. He didn't take the end of our engagement well," she said with a sigh of resignation.

"Did you quarrel?"

She bit her lip, debating how much to reveal. "My father plans to build an observatory in our house. Afterwards, I'll be quite busy helping him chart the stars. Oliver objected to that and to other plans I have. Since then, I've realized marriage is not for me."

"I'll drink to that." From his pocket, Jack withdrew a key and unlocked the top section of the cabinet. She spied a stack of papers and boxes before he removed a brown bottle and shut the cabinet door. Cradling it beneath his arm, he gathered two glasses and returned to her. The captain filled a glass with amber liquid and gave it to her.

Mary took the tumbler, warmed from his grasp, and stared down into the sweet-smelling drink. Looking up, she found him sitting on a footstool at her feet, his knees only inches from her own. At his nearness, she swallowed tightly.

The scent of canvas surrounded him, and his gray eyes looked more clouded than when they'd first met. With a flick of his wrist, he downed the contents of the glass.

Giving him a nod of encouragement, she held out the other full glass. He took the drink and rested it on his knee.

"Won't your mother worry about you?"

"My mother died when I was very young. Unfortunately, I have few memories of her. My father was both parents, a difficult task he handled magnificently. I still remember the day he set Galileo's theories before me and said, 'Mary, today you learn to read.' " She sighed, then seemed aware of his presence. "What about you, Captain?"

"Never mind me, my mother, or Galileo. Now, about Gaspar."

"I'll tell you everything once you agree to let me stay."

"You'd trust my word to take you?" He leaned closer and peered into her eyes.

Under the intensity of his gaze, Mary had difficulty gathering her thoughts. Staring down at her hands, she strove to keep her mind focused on the conversation. "President Madison decorated you for valor during the war. I can put faith in such a man."

"Two years later I was arrested and tried because of my involvement with pirates."

"You were innocent."

"You saw tonight how people value that judgment." He lifted his glass and frowned at it as if he saw something displeasing inside. "I'm not the man to help you."

"You're precisely the man. Gaspar held you captive like he holds my father. After a year on his ship, you know more about that pirate than anyone."

"Miss McNeal, are you always so opinionated?"

"I'm not opinionated. I'm right."

He gulped the second drink. Without warning, he scooted his stool forward until their knees pressed together. He took a stray strand of her damp hair and wound it around his finger, drawing her face closer to his.

Caught, Mary couldn't draw away. Alarm shot through her, but other powerful emotions of intrigue and fascination overpowered her. Staring into the darkness within his eyes, she was lost in strange new sensations. A deep, restless urgency rose within her. Biting her lip, she tried to gain control.

"Most women would be nervous to find themselves alone on a ship of men, Mary." His voice, deep and seductive, sent another ripple of awareness through her.

Mary's mouth grew dry. She didn't want to confess she had reservations earlier, but the strange feelings bubbling inside of her blocked all her doubts. He continued to hold her prisoner with a thin strand of hair and with his suggestive tone.

His gray gaze roved over her and fastened upon her mouth.

A confusion of emotions surged through her. She longed for him to kiss her. She wanted him to release her. Then from deep inside, her common sense roused. She sat back. Her hair snapped free with a twinge of pain. "How ridiculous. I've nothing to fear with you here, Captain. This is your ship. You can control those hooligans."

He sighed in surrender. "My crew are not hooligans, and whether you do or don't tell me about Gaspar, you can't stay on my ship. I'll not have an unattached female wandering aboard."

Rising, he knocked his stool over. He shoved the glass on the top of the desk and added, "Sleep well."

The door closed, and Mary heard the click of the bolt. Captain St. George had locked her inside.

For a few seconds, Mary sat lost in the strange feelings the captain had aroused. Then her anger rose. How dare he lock her inside. No doubt, the man only associated with women who couldn't be trusted. What would she do now? She couldn't go home, and what would she do inside this cabin? The ship rocked, and she braced her feet upon the floor to keep her seat. The thud of the glass hit the wooden-planked floor and tore her from her musing. Reaching to retrieve the tumbler, she noticed the built-in writing table. Tentatively, Mary grasped the brass drawer

handle, and it slid easily toward her. Inside lay papers
and a black, leather-bound book.

"The ship's log," she whispered. She opened to the
first page. Numbers and phrases stared up at her. She
glanced at the locked door. It couldn't hurt to take a peek.

Jack shouted commands above the wind's moaning. For
nearly an hour, they'd fought to stay on course and on
their two feet. Finally, the wind's bite had lessened to a
snarl. His wet clothes weighed upon him like a suit of
armor. With effort, he trudged on leaden feet toward his
cabin to change his garments.

Reaching the door, Jack remembered his room already
had an occupant. He'd been too busy to consider his
guest. Wearily, he rested his forehead against the old oak
door. The librarian was on the other side. Her soft, pleading look when she'd asked him not to send her back swept
into his mind. *How had she handled the storm? It must
have frightened her. No doubt, she'd never experienced
such fierce tossing. She might even be sick.* Without hesitation, he fished the key out of his pocket and unlocked
the door.

For a moment, he searched in the dim light of the whale
oil lantern. Then he saw her. She sat at his desk, her hair
streaming down her back, her eyes wide like someone
just awakened. She was beautiful, and she was alone in
his cabin. He strode forward to offer words of reassurance.

His gaze fell on the desk. Personal letters lay scattered
across the top, and the open log rested on her lap. Anger
stirred inside him like a whirlpool.

Mary glanced at him. "I read your log, It was quite
fascinating."

He cursed, and she jumped up from the chair.

"I know we're on a ship, but you don't need to use profanity like a common sailor."

He glared.

"While I'm here, I could keep your log," she offered.

He advanced.

She retreated.

"I helped my father keep . . ." She bumped against the bunk, ending her backward withdrawal.

Jack towered in front of her, blocking any escape, holding her prisoner. "Do you know what the word *personal* means?"

"The dictionary says—"

"I know what it means," Jack snapped. "While on my ship, you will respect my properties and cease your snooping immediately. Understood?"

Mary didn't answer.

"Well?"

"I thought it was like the last question, and you didn't want an answer. Certainly, I will respect your belongings. I have a deep appreciation for your navigational skills. My father is—"

"Miss McNeal, I'm not here to discuss my sailing habits or your *all-knowing* father."

"You needn't be sarcastic." She raised her chin in the air defiantly. "Why are you here? Are we in danger from the storm?"

"The rain is nearly done." He had no intention of confessing that he had foolishly thought she might be frightened. Running his hand through his hair, he grasped for another reason.

"I supposed you might have changed your mind about giving me information." He drew away to replace his log.

When he looked at her again, she stood with her arms folded across her chest.

"Promise I can stay on the ship, and I'll tell you everything."

"Have you read much about Gaspar?"

"Read?" Mary asked, blinking in bewilderment.

"That's what most librarians do, isn't it?"

"Well not entirely, but I know a little about Mr. Gaspar."

"Do you know what he does with his booty?"

"His treasure?" Mary tilted her head to the side. "Doesn't he bury it somewhere?"

"Gaspar asks for a volunteer to dig the hole for him. Of course, the newest recruit usually obliges. Later he can slip away and remove the treasure. Wealth will be his. Imagine!"

Her lips parted. Her eyes sparkled. Jack knew he had all of her attention.

"A more eager volunteer you couldn't find. Working from dawn to nightfall, he digs a hole for the riches. Then—" He leaned closer.

"Yes?"

"Gaspar slits his throat." He drew an imaginary knife across his throat.

She gasped, and her hand clutched her throat. "Wh . . . Why?"

"Pirates believe that a ghost buried with the treasure will protect it. At least the volunteer has his riches."

"The poor man dug his own grave," Mary whispered. "We must rescue my father."

Jack stepped back. He pushed down the stab of remorse caused by the pain in her voice. "Miss McNeal, Gaspar is not a man you ever want to meet. Go home and make amends with your future husband. What was his name again?"

"His name is Oliver Wendell Page. He's a banker."

A banker and a librarian, a match made in dullness. He could imagine them in the evening discussing words and numbers.

She lowered her voice. "I'll never go back to him."

Interested in this piece of information, Jack dropped his wet coat on his bunk. Straightening the stool, he sat at her feet. "No?"

She raised a brow in disapproval at his tone. Her lips tightened into a straight line. Obviously, she had no intention of discussing the banker further. Curious, he pressed. "Bankers have always seemed . . ." he grasped for the word.

"Stuffy?" she asked.

"Is that how you'd describe him? How boring was this Ollie?"

"Oliver, and he wasn't a bore, although he was a little upset with you."

"Me? We've never met."

"No, I told him about the letter I'd written to you. I also mentioned how you could save my father because you were a naval hero, and how Gaspar held you prisoner, but you escaped." She paused to catch her breath. "He didn't like the idea that you are the *perfect* man. To rescue my father," she added rapidly.

His jaw dropped open, and he gave her a sidelong glance of utter disbelief. In all his life, no one had described him as flawless.

Warming to the discussion, she smiled at him, and he recognized more than admiration in her green eyes. She was a young woman in love with a dream. "Listen, Miss McNeal. I am not the man you think I am." He held up a hand to signal the end of the discussion when she started to protest.

"Let's discuss this banker." Used to speaking bluntly to his men, Jack searched for an appropriate phrase. If he offended her, he'd never learn anything about this near-union. "I don't suppose he'd ever think about anything daring?"

"What do you mean?"

"Oh, like kissing his future wife in public."

"Captain St. George, you've asked a most personal question," Mary said with reproach.

He gave her a knowing smile.

"Oliver was affectionate, yet proper."

"Sounds like a real button-down. You must have caught up on your sleep when he was around."

"He wasn't boring." She smiled confidently. "Once, we danced together at the church social until our feet hurt."

"He liked feet, did he?" He sent her a regretful look. "He wasn't much of a man."

Irritation flared in her gaze. "You're making little sense. Oliver was quite a daring man. Why once, he kissed me in front of my father."

A picture of the librarian in that owlish man's arms flashed through his mind. An unexplained anger surged through him. "Did he?" He stepped closer until his chest pressed against her. His voice was low and threatening. "How did you feel about this kiss?"

"Why I—" She flushed and opened her mouth, but no words came out.

Without thinking, he swept her into his arms. She gave a small cry of surprise as he crushed his lips to hers. The fragrance of lilacs filled his senses. Her mouth was sweet and warm like a soft sailing breeze. Jack thought he heard her sigh and forgot that he'd been angry. He knew only that he wanted her.

Her hands gripped his shoulders, and an unexplained hunger erupted inside of him. Again and again he kissed her. His hands roamed everywhere, hot and possessive, and he knew that he wanted more, much more.

The realization shook him. Jack's legs buckled, and he released her. He ran his hand through his hair and stared down at Mary. Her face was flushed, and her eyes glimmered with emotions of shock.

Sanity took hold. Hell, he'd kissed a librarian! Had he become that desperate for a woman? "I'd better leave," he muttered.

"Now? I don't think . . . I mean, I don't know." She took a deep breath. "Well, yes, leave if you want."

With a shake of his head, he moved to the door. During his captivity, Jack had watched Gaspar murder men, throw them overboard to the sharks, and torture them. He had hardened his heart to stay alive. Now however, from some hidden crevice, passion swirled. An unpredictable and risky emotion. He had to leave before he did something else foolish like spouting words of affection and sounding like a damn poet. He'd rather be shark bait.

Forcing himself not to glance at her, he left. Not until he reached the deck did he realize he'd never changed his clothes.

Mary watched as the door shut quietly without the telltale click of the lock. What had happened? She could still feel his lips pressed against her own. His mouth had tasted dark and something else. Something that made her hands shake and her mind whirl.

Thank heavens he'd left. Her heart was beating too fast

to allow her to think, much less speak to him. *Think. Yes. Think.* For some reason, she had trouble keeping her thoughts in order whenever he was near. She mustn't allow her emotions or that primitive man to carry her away. She was simply overwrought by her father's disappearance. No need to fret over the man or her actions.

Still trembling, she collapsed on the bunk. *Forget everything that just happened,* she told herself. She must turn her mind to more practical matters like staying on board to rescue her father. Musing over this problem, her gaze fell on the captain's coat resting on the end of the bunk. For the first time, Mary noted a small hole in the elbow and that the fabric shone from too much wear.

Too bad she couldn't offer her services as a seamstress. Then he might allow her to stay on his ship, and she wouldn't have time for these strange feelings. But where would she get the supplies? Surely, the captain needed something else. He had a navigator.

Perhaps a member of the crew could refer her to another seaman willing to help. Her head ached from thinking. It must be past midnight. Removing her telescope, she wedged it between the trunk and the bunk. With her instrument safe, Mary fell into a dead sleep.

When she woke, the grayness of morning glazed through the one porthole in the cabin. The lantern had died sometime during the night. Blinking, she stumbled across the cool room and out into the passage. Finding the stairs, she made her way above. Stillness greeted her. She breathed a sigh of relief that no ruffians confronted her.

The ship sat silently, surrounded by a thick fog and an acid smell. Mary wondered how Captain St. George would greet her after their kiss. Her pulse raced with the thought.

"Good morning, Miss."

She spun about to face the first mate, Daniel. He was dressed in the same large shirt. "Is it?" She peered into the white mist.

The young man nodded with a cheerful smile. "Soon as the weather clears, we'll set sail for Oyster Bay. The storm has blown us near Maine. But we don't like to land in this part; too many smugglers left from the war. In a little while we'll be back on course, and you'll be back in your library."

Maine? They were no longer in the United States. Mary peered closer at the short young man. "Where's your home, Daniel?"

"Mine? Right here."

"You live on a ship? Don't you have any family?"

He smiled. "Of course. My dad's at home in Salem, Massachusetts, but I'm a grown man. I can't live with him."

"I've always lived with my father," Mary said quietly. "I miss him."

"I guess it's different for men," he said rapidly.

"Have you always lived on a vessel?"

"I've lived on one since I turned sixteen and joined the navy. That's how I met the captain. After the war I got my discharge, and thought I'd get work, only I couldn't. There weren't any jobs. If the captain hadn't offered me a post here, I don't know what I'd have done. I might have turned to piracy, like some others."

"You must know many sailors, Daniel. Do you know of any that would help me find my father?"

"He's not in Oyster River?" the first mate asked.

Apparently, the captain hadn't discussed her situation with the crew. Uncertain, she hesitated. "He's been kidnapped."

The first mate's eyes grew round with astonishment. "You must be anxious to get home and search for him."

"Not precisely. Gaspar took him."

"Gaspar!"

"Yes, I believe the president is most anxious to be rid of this fellow and might offer a handsome reward. So would you kindly recommend one of your friends who might be willing to assist me?"

Daniel shook his head. "Does the captain know?"

"He does," Mary answered.

"The captain can help you. He's sailed with that devil and survived. That's why Gaspar hates him. The captain beat him and lived."

A shiver of fear and pride crept up her spine. "The captain doesn't like women on his ship."

"He's not used to dealing with women, being in the war and all."

"Surely you must know someone else who wouldn't mind looking for the pirate."

"Mind? Miss, most people would flee in the opposite direction if they heard Gaspar sailed in the same waters."

"Gaspar can't intimidate everyone."

"I'd help if I could. Gaspar killed my brother, and he didn't die easy. I'd like to run the devil through as much as the next person. That's another reason I signed on with this ship. The captain wants the pirate as much as I do."

"I'm sorry, Daniel," she said, reading the pain in his eyes.

"It's no matter," he answered in a muffled tone.

"When the weather clears, I'll show you how to use my telescope," she offered.

The first mate bobbed his head up and down. "Thanks. You must be hungry. You'll want food from the galley, and you'll find the head next to it." He blushed. "You'd best hurry. Cook doesn't make extra food because of the rats."

Mary swallowed. "How appetizing." With directions from the first mate she set off to take care of all the necessities. The head was a tiny dark room with a rotting stench. She used it quickly. Next, she discovered the cook.

A short bald man, Cook squinted at her as she entered the galley. This room proved to be a small kitchen with cabinets, a table, stools, and a wood stove. Begrudgingly, he gave her a stale, flat lump of hard dough and something to drink. Cook was a man who'd never have to worry about smile creases, she suspected. Telling herself she needed to stay healthy, she forced a bite down her throat. The drink tasted like weak tea.

A lanky newcomer appeared in the doorway. "Captain's awake, and the fog's cleared. He wants the librarian on deck."

A rush of excitement coursed through her when she thought of meeting with St. George. Mary pushed her cup into Cook's hands. "Thank you. It was . . . lovely."

Bursting through to the upper deck, she collided with Captain St. George. His expression of shock cleared as his glance skimmed her features, seeming to measure every detail of her.

Her heart beat wildly, and she warmed, remembering their kiss. Dimly, she noted that the fog had evaporated.

He smiled, but showed none of the emotions she'd witnessed in his eyes the previous night. "Good morning, Miss McNeal. Remember an overdue book?"

"Captain, I—"

"Ship off the stern!" called a man from the crow's nest.

Captain St. George's smile slipped away. "With my luck, it's probably your banker."

"Oliver?" She trailed after him to the rail. With surprise, she followed Captain St. George's gaze and saw the fast-approaching ship.

Three

Sailing out of the last of the fog, Mary spied a most unusual brig. Smaller than the *Goodspeed*, what this new ship lacked in size, it had in style. The starboard side was gaily decorated in stripes of blues, reds, and greens. Mary knew Oliver would never navigate such a ship, nor would Gaspar.

"Who is it?" she asked curiously.

Captain St. George ignored her and shouted orders for his own ship to allow the new visitor to approach. Obviously, this vessel offered no threat.

"Is the captain a friend of yours?" Mary leaned across the railing, attempting to get a better view. Now that the ship cruised closer, a herringbone pattern of colors on the port side was discernible.

"Miss McNeal, please contain yourself. You look eager to leave."

"Can I meet the commander of that ship?" She stared in awe.

"I'll do better than that. You'll meet the owner, Thomas T. Beckett." Unexpectedly, his hand grazed her cheek. Then he spun away.

Gazing out at the unique vessel, Mary touched the tingling spot his fingertips had skimmed. Her hand brushed over her hair, and her heart turned over. Her tresses hung loose like an unrespectable woman. She'd need to pin her hair before anyone else saw her.

Rushing below to the captain's quarters, she swept her locks up into the chignon, smoothed her skirt, and wished she hadn't lost her clothes. At least if she went home, she'd have some dresses and be in the company of people who wore proper attire. Mary sighed and spied her scope beside the bunk. Carefully, she carried it to the trunk and shut it inside with a man's shirt and breeches.

At the sound of footsteps passing outside the door, she wondered if the owner of the smaller ship had boarded. Hastening atop, she quickly took in the scene. Captain St. George stood near the wheel. All other crew members had gathered at the stern and were loudly shouting remarks about the brightly decorated vessel.

"It makes a good target for a cannonball," shouted a *Goodspeed* sailor.

Mary took her place next to St. George, conscious of every move he made. The man hadn't mentioned their kiss. It must have meant nothing to him. She was no fool. It meant nothing to her either. She turned away from him and focused on the sea.

In the clearing light, Mary made out the bobbing figures of men standing on the visiting ship. Dressed in white uniforms, they seemed a perfect contrast to the colorful brig.

"What kind of boat is that?" Mary asked, standing on tiptoes to observe more of the vessel.

"A yacht named for Helen of Troy. At least Beckett calls it by that name. My men have a different name for it."

"What?"

"Uh?" St. George glanced at her as if he just realized

what she'd asked. He cleared his throat uncomfortably. "Never mind."

He cupped his hands to his mouth. "Beckett," he shouted. "Stop hiding before I get seasick looking at your sorry vessel."

"Jack, you'll sink before you recognize true art."

Mary searched for the man who'd yelled. Then she saw a sandy-haired, slim man.

"Come aboard, and I'll show you a real ship," the newcomer said as the smaller vessel pulled up beside them.

Mary gazed down at the speaker and recognized the surprise in his eyes as their gazes met. He was fair and very handsome.

"Jack, bring the young lady with you. We'll have dinner in my quarters in an hour." Gazing at her, he gave a salute.

Mary smiled in delight while the captain muttered something unintelligible. "Did you say something, Captain?"

He ignored her and shouted, "Let's hope your cook knows more about food than you know about painting your craft."

The other man waved, and his ship sailed a short distance away from them.

"Well, Miss McNeal, I'll expect you ready in an hour."

Mary stepped into his path. "Who is Mr. Beckett?"

"He's an old friend from the war. A wealthy friend. His father's money built his ship. Some have questioned how his family made their wealth. I've been trying for a few years to interest him in financing my pursuit of Gaspar, but he has other interests."

A man with money. A man who can sail. Mary bit her lip. Perhaps she could convince Mr. Beckett to assist in her search.

"Captain," she said, running after him. "Tell me one more thing about your friend."

St. George continued speaking with a scraggly-haired man. Mary waited, pulling on the cuff of her dress till the captain gave her his attention.

"Miss McNeal, since you're not part of my crew, call me Jack."

"Oh. Well, I suppose you may call me Mary."

"I hope I will be worthy," he said with a grimace. "Now, Mary, unless you wish to be assigned a duty, please stay confined to quarters."

"About Mr. Beckett," she reminded him.

He sighed in resignation. "What's the question?"

"Was he on your ship during the war?"

"Yes."

She'd found another man with naval war skills. Beckett may be the answer. She could leave the *Goodspeed* and continue her search. Why did she feel a sudden sadness? Maybe the sea air had affected her mind. She'd have to research the topic of salt air when she returned home.

Once in the cabin, she realized she had nothing to occupy her time. Longingly, she touched the drawer that contained the log, and with difficulty she drew away. Now she wished she had a duty, whatever that might be.

Unbidden, the memory of Jack's kiss popped into her thoughts. Mary shoved it firmly aside. Busy hands would cure her idle mind.

She began experimenting with her hair. Loosely, she looped it over her ears and braided it down her back. Done with this, she glanced about the cabin. Why hadn't she thought of this earlier? She'd find a mop or broom and would clean the room.

Where to look? She headed for the galley and found one of the men who'd watched her eat. When she requested her cleaning utensils, he scratched his head and then disappeared for several minutes. Mary glanced around the galley only to meet the suspicious squinting eyes of Cook. Thankfully, her messenger returned with a mop and pail.

Delighted, Mary hurried back to begin her task. The time passed quickly. Before she'd finished, she rearranged the captain's trunk and neatly folded his clothes, another white shirt and tan breeches, inside the chest. Her scope lay inside.

Finished, she lugged the dirty water to the door and swung it open. Mary found at least five men clustered before the cabin, staring at her.

Then they scrambled away. In their haste, two men crashed and fell on the floor. One regained his feet and hurried away.

A scraggly, dark-haired man rose and dusted off his blue pantaloons with holes in the knees. His feet were bare.

Didn't any of these men know how to dress? He appeared harmless. "Sir?"

He looked up at her. "Huh?"

"Would you kindly empty this pail?"

For a moment, he blinked his brown eyes like a man deciphering a foreign language. Finally, he rose and reached for the bucket and the mop.

From the corners of the dimly lit passage came catcalls, reminding her of young adolescents waiting outside the school room.

"Thank you Mr. . . . What is your name?"

"Finn, miss." He gave her a salute that ended with the mop handle hitting his nose sharply.

"Mr. Finn, you have my sincere appreciation. Are you hurt?"

His face reddened. "No. Please, don't thank me."

Mary shook her head and closed the door. Men continued to mystify her. Hadn't she complimented the seaman?

She barely had time to collect her thoughts before Jack barged through the door.

"Mary McNeal, what have you done to my men, and what has happened to my cabin?" His jaw dropped open in amazement.

"I don't know anything about your men, but I've given your room a good cleaning."

He glared at the floor while apprehension tinged his voice. "Did you use the bucket I saw with Finn?"

"Why, yes. He kindly took it from me."

"Miss McNeal, that was Cook's—" He appeared to be searching for the word. "Slop pail."

"Oh, dear. I do apologize."

He closed his eyes in exasperation. "Never mind. Come with me where I can keep an eye on you."

He frowned and walked to his trunk that she'd pushed near the porthole and table. "What was wrong with where it was before? I liked it just fine."

"Well, in the morning when you get your clothes, you can look out the window and see what kind of day to expect."

"I'm sorry I asked you. Are you ready?"

"What?"

"Are you ready to meet Beckett?"

"Yes, yes, I am. But what about the room?"

"Don't worry." He guided her toward the door. "Once you're off the ship, I'll fix it."

Seated in the spacious, white cabin decorated with landscape paintings, Jack was not enjoying his dinner. It wasn't the duck cooked to tenderness, nor the wine that pleased each of his senses. No, it was the blasted librarian.

Observing her sitting on the red velvet seat at the shiny cherry table, his irritation rose. While Beckett recited the same old, tired battle story, Mary stared at him in apparent fascination. "Beckett," Jack interrupted. "You're boring Miss McNeal."

"Oh, no, I love hearing how we beat England and France," Mary protested. "Perhaps your names will appear in one of our history books in the library."

"I'm sure if anyone is desperate enough, they could put my friend in a book titled *The Biggest War Yarns.*"

With a shake of his head, Beckett replied, "Excuse Jack. The war left him a cynic. Your stay on the *Goodspeed* is not too trying, I hope."

"She's not staying with me," Jack said firmly. "I've explained that she followed and was forced to escape with me."

Mary glanced at him, frowning her disapproval. "The captain has made it abundantly clear that I will be returning at his earliest convenience."

He scowled. "You'll be back home tomorrow."

Beckett stood abruptly. "Then let's take advantage of the time we have together. Jack, I'll show Miss McNeal around the ship before dessert."

Instantly, two men dressed in white appeared and carried away the empty platters.

"I'd appreciate your opinion on my latest contract." Beckett withdrew a sheaf of papers from his inside coat pocket. "Jack has a sharp mind for trade. Whenever I can, I have him look over my agreements."

"You're a businessman, then, sir?" Mary asked, surprised at the announcement.

"You might say he's worth his salt and pepper," Jack interjected.

"Salt and pepper?" Mary prompted.

"My friend has a strange sense of humor," Beckett explained. "One of the goods my ships transport is pepper." Beckett linked his arm through her own. "I'll explain everything on our tour."

Jack watched their retreating backs and shook his head in disgust. Unfolding the sheafs of the contract, he stared at the writing. Reading halfway down the page, Jack stopped. He remembered nothing of what he'd read. Instead, he remembered how the librarian had fussed over the pastel paintings on the wall, and how she'd drunk in every exaggeration his friend had fed her. Then Jack's mind summoned up Beckett's fondness for women. His old friend had many females.

What did he care? Mary McNeal had wanted to come. She'd nearly fallen overboard with delight when he'd offered to introduce her to the ship's owner. For some reason, Jack had expected her to be smarter than other women he'd known, and he'd had his fair share.

Hell, Jack thought she'd see through Beckett. But he wasn't her keeper. Then the memory of their kiss sailed into his mind. He recalled the softness of her body, and the small gasp of surprise when he'd first held her. *Enough.* Gritting his teeth in determination, Jack plowed back into reading.

Seated on a soft, red-velvet settee, Mary feared that her companion might hear her heart beating. To further add to her concern, the tour had quickly ended in his cabin. Beneath her feet a plush beige carpet cushioned the vibrations from the engine, but they were nothing compared to the warnings that quivered through her.

Her gaze fell on the gilt mirror above the mahogany dresser. The glass reflected the gold coverlet on the bed that seemed to fill the room. How long would Jack need to study Beckett's financial document?

Mr. Beckett pressed a crystal glass into her hand, bringing her attention to him. "All of my wines come from France."

"Do your ships import it?"

"Yes, I'm very fond of the country. Since the war, however, the area is in poor shape."

"Do you speak French?" Mary asked, wondering when she could mention her father.

"My grandmother was French, but the war was very hard on her family."

"How interesting." Ordinarily, Mary would have loved to discuss another country's culture, but time grew short. She needed to discuss Gaspar.

Beckett rose. "I'd like to show you an item. I'll fetch it."

Tapping her foot, she waited for his return. The need to control the conversation grew with her impatience.

He returned and held out his hand.

Her gaze fell upon a tortoiseshell snuff box sitting in his palm. A raised letter M decorated the lid.

A smile lit his eyes. "It belonged to my grandmother, a gift from Napoleon when he was free. Hold it."

Feeling her chances slip away, she took the box. "Beautiful. Mr. Beckett, have you ever seen Gaspar?"

"Gaspar? Did you think I took the box from a pirate?"

She hadn't done well introducing the subject. "No."

He took the small snuff box from her and rested it on the table. Leaning against the soft velvet cushion, he

draped his warm arm across the back of her shoulder.
"Shall we have another drink?"

An alarm rang in the back of Mary's mind. "Can we
discuss Gaspar, too?"

"What caused the fascination with this pirate?" he
asked, blinking in surprise. "Was it Jack?"

"My father." Relief surged through her. At last, she
could talk about the topic dearest to her.

Beckett filled her glass with more wine and unbuttoned
his white starched collar. "This sounds like a serious discussion."

"Saving my father is a duty I can't ignore, not even in
the presence of Napoleon's snuff box."

He handed the brimming glass to her and scooted
closer until the space between them disappeared. He
smelled like limes. "In times like these, it helps to con-
fide in a friend," he coaxed. "Tell me everything, my
lady."

The warning within Mary screamed as his leg pressed
against her. She searched her mind for a way to control
the situation. "I'd love to have your support, Mr. Beckett.
But I'm quite distressed."

"Thomas." His arm tightened around her shoulder. In
a coaxing voice he added, "Now tell me about your father."

Jack stared at the nearly full bottle of wine. At least
Beckett could have brought him some decent whiskey.
How had a person like his friend made it through the
war? Beckett had confided once that he'd joined the navy
after an argument with his father.

Now Beckett sailed around the world in this oddly
shaped vessel. If only Jack had the same money at his

disposal. He'd buy a beauty of a ship and capture Gaspar. The pirate would probably die of old age before Jack caught up with him.

The thought brought a bitter taste to his mouth. And what about the little librarian? He pushed his chair back from the table and fixed his attention on the porthole, trying to judge the time and how long they'd been gone. He'd read enough of the contract to know it was the usual business deal. His friend knew it too, Jack decided.

Pushing the papers aside, he decided to find Miss McNeal and return to his own ship. In only a few moments, he'd located a crew member and had directions to the owner's quarters. "Tour of the ship," he muttered. Only Mary McNeal believed that nonsense. No doubt, Beckett hadn't changed at all. He could never resist charming anything with a skirt. He jammed his fists into his pockets.

The closed door rose in front of him. What were Beckett and Mary doing in there? Unsummoned, a vivid picture of Mary in his old friend's arms appeared in his mind.

He raised his fist to pound on the door and stopped. Without hesitation, he yanked on the knob while throwing his weight against the entrance.

The door swung open, and Jack flew into the room. Regaining his balance, he stared at the couple in an embrace.

The twosome turned wide eyes and gaping mouths at him. Mary broke away from Beckett. "What's wrong?"

"Wrong?" Jack asked, taking in the bed. "I thought you had more morals than to bed with the first, er, second man you met."

"Captain St. George!" Mary gasped, covering her mouth.

"That's enough, Jack. Miss McNeal became over-wrought while explaining her father's absence. I offered her some comfort."

"I bet you did."

"Captain St. George," the librarian scolded, "you've no right to burst in here without knocking. Certainly, you've also no cause to accuse Thomas, your friend, of ungentlemanly conduct."

"Thomas? I didn't know you were so friendly." He scanned the room again. "Can't you recognize a trap when you see one? You don't think he brought you in here to discuss your family? He didn't even know you had one."

Anger snapped in her eyes. She stood toe to toe with him. "Everyone has a family, Captain, even Gaspar."

Jack opened and closed his fists. *This is a ridiculous argument,* he thought. Yet, his anger washed over his reason. "Is that right? You know Gaspar's parents now?"

A knock at the door interrupted their tête-à-tête, and a crew member asked to speak with Beckett privately.

"I guess I can leave you two alone," the fair-haired man said. "There are no pistols in the room." With a wink, he disappeared.

Mary stepped back and cleared her throat. "At least Mr. Beckett wanted to hear my story."

"Did you grow up in a library?" Jack roared. "Any woman with any sense would know what he wanted."

"What do you think he wanted?" She folded her arms across her chest.

He shook his head in disbelief. "Do I have to explain it? Wine, only the two of you, a bed . . ."

"Are you accusing your friend of improper advances?"

"You said it, and if this is what you want, I'll be happy to leave you two alone. It's time to get back to my ship."

"You'd leave me here?" Her arms dropped to her side, and her eyes widened in disbelief.

"Do you want to stay?"

"Ah, still chatting?" Beckett asked, returning.

"Thanks for the food," Jack said. "I'm returning to my ship."

Beckett stepped in front of him. "My apologies, Jack, but you won't be going anywhere."

Jack glanced out the porthole. "We're sailing. What in the name of Neptune is happening here?"

"I thought you might enjoy a cruise after dinner."

"Save the explanations, Beckett. Either you're keeping us prisoners or—" Without finishing, he strode up onto the deck with his friend's protesting behind him. Across the calm clear waters, he saw his ship waiting, and in the distance he also saw another ship, growing larger and deadlier.

"A French frigate." Jack gave a low whistle of disbelief. "Looks like you've been fishing for a few enemies."

"What is it?" Mary McNeal asked with dread in her voice.

"Perhaps *Thomas* can give us an explanation. Why are we running from a country when we're at peace with them?"

Beckett smiled limply. "It is all a misunderstanding. I paid a visit to Bonaparte for my grandmother."

"For your grandmother?" Disbelief raised in Jack's voice.

"She's French," Mary interrupted.

"I don't care if she's Marie Antoinette. We're in danger, or we wouldn't be sailing. Give us an answer, or I'll have to demonstrate what I've learned during my buccaneer days."

"Don't talk nonsense, Captain," Mary McNeal said,

stepping between the two men. "We all know you wouldn't harm us. Thomas, tell us the truth. Our patience is at an end."

Beckett shrugged his shoulders and smiled falsely. "For some odd reason, they think I'm plotting to rescue Napoleon from St. Helena."

"Great Blackbeard's Ghost," Jack gasped. "The French will kill us."

Four

Mary's stomach rolled a few times as she watched the power bear down on them. "I hope we have plenty of fuel."

Jack scanned their surroundings. "We're small, and Maine has rocky shorelines. If we pull out in front, we can hide in an inlet."

"Always a true leader," Beckett said, slapping Jack on the back. "I'll speak with my navigator. Excuse me, Mary."

Hypnotized by the larger vessel, Mary felt her arms break out in goose bumps, and excitement mixed with fear rushed through her. She stepped beside Jack and rested her hands on the rail. She could feel the heat from his body. She cleared her throat, pretending not to be affected. "Is this how one feels when confronted by the enemy?"

He shrugged. "Not exactly. We're a little outgunned here. This bucket of Beckett's may have speed, but if they're inclined to turn their cannon on us, you'll get that wish to sail to your stars."

"You're not offering much encouragement." Mary tried to smile, but her mouth was too stiff.

"Beckett's a good sailor. He's given many a ship a slip." Unexpectedly, he reached out and covered her hand with his.

Beneath the warmth and strength of his larger palm, her pulse skittered. A delightful shiver ran through her, and she wished he'd take her in his arms.

What a ridiculous thought. Mary suddenly realized how foolish and weak she must appear. With the first sign of danger, she'd acted like a swooning female. She'd never convince anyone to allow her to sail with them if she continued in this manner. *Think affirmatively.* With a seaman like Jack, they would escape.

Straightening her shoulders, she took a deep breath. "I have every confidence that between Mr. Beckett and yourself we are safe." This time, her lips slid into a smile.

"We are? Ah, yes." Appearing startled, Jack removed his hand.

Without his reassuring pressure, a chill swept through her. Fighting to stay collected, she studied his profile of power, absorbing it like a good book.

"I've spoken with my navigator," Thomas interrupted. "Ahead we'll find a small cove and take refuge there. What about your ship, Jack? Will they follow?"

"I ordered them to stay anchored. They won't disobey."

"I'm glad to hear loyalty lives," Beckett said. "May I suggest that we adjourn to lower quarters. The sea may be rough, and we'll be safer below. We can discuss that contract. Miss McNeal, after you."

Mary paused to sneak a last look at the French ship. As the small ship cruised forward with increased speed, the wind reached out and pulled at her hair. The loosened wisps curled about her face, and her skirt billowed out behind her like a sail. On the sea, the French ship kept pace with them.

Below, she settled again in the cushioned chair at the table and observed the two men discussing Beckett's latest business venture. She marveled at their collectedness.

Had both men been born with mental strength similar to Atlas's?

Beneath her feet, the ship hummed. How closely did their enemy follow, and how long till they reached the cove? Even then, she knew they weren't guaranteed safety. Absently, she reached to toy with the cord of her scope and remembered she'd left it in Jack's trunk.

From the floor, the yacht's vibrations sputtered, ceased, and began again. The men's conversation halted, and they all sat in silence listening to the craft struggle to regain strength. Finally, a hush descended. Without a word, Beckett leapt to his feet and raced away.

Mary glanced at Jack. He'd pushed his chair back from the table and appeared to still contemplate the contract. His serene self-control kept her composed. No need to panic. With his experience, he'd know how to deal with this situation.

"Do you speak French, Mary?"

A flicker of dread coursed through her. "You don't think we'll make it to an inlet?"

"I've had many unusual occurrences in my life. They've taught me never to rely on one option."

She leaned forward. "Do you think the French mean to harm us?"

Jack shrugged. "They're a long way from home, and they don't seem to believe that our friend was being neighborly when he called on their ex-ruler."

His words made sense. "Why would Mr. Beckett want Napoleon free?" she asked.

"Wealth, trade, power." He shook his head. "I've always believed lots of money destroys men's morals and their judgment."

"You think riches have harmed Mr. Beckett's power of thought?"

"Would you cruise around in a boat like this?"

"I know this is a bad time to mention it," she said with reproachful ringing in her voice, "but we're both sailing in it."

The cabin door banged open. Beckett ran into the cabin, his eyes wide.

"The engine has failed. Too bad Robert Fulton isn't here. I'd have plenty to say to him."

"If you used sails and oars like normal vessels," Jack countered, "we'd not be in this predicament. Why do you have to try every new invention? A steam-powered ship!"

Beckett fixed his attention on his friend. "Jack, how far do you think those tales of your trial reached?"

"What do you mean?" Mary asked with unease.

"He means," Jack answered, "that he'd prefer not to have a pirate on board when the other ship overtakes us."

"You're not a pirate!" Mary protested.

Jack rose slowly from his chair and stood in front of Beckett. "She goes with me." He jerked a thumb at Mary.

Beckett's gaze darted from his friend to Mary. "I'm not sure that's best."

Jack folded his arms. "We came together. We leave together."

"Perhaps we should let the lady decide," Beckett offered.

Caught between the two men, Mary froze. Her gaze swung to Beckett in his impeccable white attire, and then she glanced at Jack in his rough linen shirt. Fierce determination glittered in his eyes.

"Well?" Jack pressed.

She met his intense gaze and made her decision. "Captain St. George is correct. I should leave with my escort."

"Mary, this is not a time to be polite," Beckett warned. "Your life is at stake."

"She's a lady," Jack said. "She can be as polite as she damn well pleases." He grabbed Mary's hand and pulled her to his side.

"Sorry to leave so abruptly," Mary said, trying to gather her senses while pressed against Jack's firm side.

"That's right," he said. "Thanks. Have our boat readied."

With brow raised, Beckett hesitated, nodded, and left.

"How's that for polite, Miss Librarian?" Jack asked with confidence lacing his voice. "I bet your fiancè, Ollie, couldn't have said it better."

"Ex-fiancè, and his name is Oliver. But I don't really think now is the time for lessons in manners, although after this episode is finished we may discuss your propensity for profanity."

"Forget I asked." He stepped away. "You think too much. We're getting out of here, aren't we?"

Mary twisted the cuff of her sleeve. "Won't the crew of the other ship see us?"

"Are you changing your mind?"

Mary shook her head, wishing he'd take her hand again and ease the doubts spreading through her.

They ascended to the top deck in silence. Bright sunshine promised a beautiful spring afternoon while the craft drifted along in the calm, glassy sea. The stillness of the air offered little hope of a current sweeping them out of their predator's path.

Holding her breath, she glanced at the sea and hoped their pursuer had given up. Instead, she could distinguish each of the three masts on the approaching vessel.

Her confidence shaken, she saw Jack motioning her forward. A small boat was being lowered over the side.

"Wait!" Beckett ran to Mary and pulled her away till they stood with their backs to the others. In his hand, she

saw a small square form wrapped in a white handkerchief.

Bending, he whispered in her ear. "My grandmother's
snuff box is inside here. Keep it safe. I don't know what
will happen once the French board. I suspect that our
valuables will disappear."

He gave her no time to protest, but pressed it into her
hands. A few feet away, Jack grumbled for her to hurry.

"Your grandmother's box will remain safe," she whispered.

"Enough, woman!" Jack yelled. "Any longer and we
can step aboard the frigate. Let's go."

Stuffing the snuff box inside her dress pocket, Mary
gave a nod of reassurance to Beckett and hurried to the
ship's side. Jack frowned at her in annoyance. Swiftly, he
slipped onto the rope ladder. He moved with the agility
of a man born at sea. Once in the small sloop, he waved
for her to follow.

She gripped the railing, but a hand reached out,
grasped her shoulder, and turned her around. Before she
had time to gasp, Beckett laid a wet kiss upon her mouth.

"Travel well," he said. "We'll meet again, upon the
Goodspeed."

Stunned by his action, Mary climbed down into the
small craft without a thought to the waves slapping
against the sides of the yacht. Her cheeks heated when
she saw Jack's narrow, reprimanding gaze. In silence, he
rowed for the distant coast, stopping only once to roll up
his sleeves. With each oar stroke, Mary watched the muscles in his tan arms tighten and loosen. A strange sensation curled in the bottom of her stomach. She swallowed
and looked back at the *Helen of Troy*. No one watched
them. While from behind, the French frigate's brown hull

grew in size. She now could recognize shapes wandering upon its deck.

"Won't they come after us?"

"They've bigger fish to catch."

He studied her, and his gaze fastened upon her mouth.

Her face heated further. She guessed he was thinking of the kiss Beckett had given her. Staring at her skirt, she said, "I hope nothing happens to Thomas because of his visit to his grandmother."

A sound like a snort came from Jack.

"What does that rude sound mean?" Mary frowned in disapproval.

"Oh, only that you must be the most gullible woman I've ever met. Until today, Beckett has never mentioned a French grandmother."

"He probably knew you didn't care about her," Mary said, searching for possibilities. "He could have told the truth. People don't always reveal everything about themselves."

"Listen, I know the name of the first woman that Beckett . . ." He raised an eyebrow and added, "kissed. When you're in a life-and-death situation with a friend, you don't hold back."

Mary leaned forward with excitement racing through her. "During the war? What happened? Were you hurt?"

"Never mind." Jack sighed. "Why'd you choose to stay with me?"

"It was a difficult decision. Thomas has great naval skills and—"

"Why me?"

She clasped her hands in her lap. "I've determined that you possess a quality that will save my father. Although you threatened to leave me, I knew you never would. You possess a fierce loyalty to those under your charge. I saw it in your eyes."

Shock swept through him at her confession. "Me? Sorry, you've made a mistake." He gave a disgusted sigh and pulled on the oars. Then paused. "And stop looking into my eyes."

At his angry dismissal, tears of worry choked in her throat. She couldn't be wrong. She needed him. Her hand wandered into her pocket and closed over the handkerchief.

"Once our visitors have left the area, we'll head back to my ship. I don't want to lead them back to the *Goodspeed*."

She inhaled deeply to clear her throat. "Where shall we stay?"

"The Maine coast offers lots of hiding places. It's a favorite with many pirates. During the war, it proved a popular spot for smuggling." He eyed her. "Your father might be around here with Gaspar. Is this the last place he was seen?"

For a moment, Mary debated the wisdom of giving him the information. Suddenly, she saw no point in withholding this news.

"My father's ship was about four degrees north of Portland, Maine when they were overtaken." Mary smoothed the wrinkles from her skirt before daring to look at him.

Jack had ceased rowing and appeared to be studying her. The sound of water dripping from the oars was the only reply to her statement. Then he resumed paddling with a smile upon his face. "Cove ahead."

Unsettled, Mary gladly twisted around and saw the rocky coastline reaching out for them. Soon the brown rocks covered with green seaweed surrounded them like welcoming arms. Ahead lay a wall of stone decorated with splotches of green. Resting on the narrow banks of the cove, a few gulls sunned themselves and ruffled their feathers at their approach. Mary spied something brown slink into the water.

Within a few moments they reached the inlet, and Jack allowed the boat to float closer to the rocks.

"We'll wade ashore." He pointed at a sloping boulder and steered toward their destination.

Mary looked down into the water, past her reflection, past a school of small yellow fish swimming by, and saw only blackness. Where was that brown creature she'd seen? Unease filled her. "Is it deep?" she asked, hoping her anxiety didn't show.

The bottom of the boat scraped across an unseen surface, and Jack jumped into the ocean. Waist-deep in the water, he held onto the side and pushed the dory in the direction of the shore. After several feet, he stopped. "We can't get any closer. Stand up." His voice rose with impatience.

Startled and unsure, Mary stood. "No need to shout. I hear—"

His tan arms reached out and picked her up with ease, her feet suspended only inches from the water.

"What are you doing?" She tried to hold her feet higher.

"Quiet," Jack said, securing his grip on her. "You'll attract the sharks." He pressed his mouth against her ear. "I'll drop you."

She froze. A tingle ran down her spine, but she didn't know if it was from his warm breath or her fear of the water.

"Hold tight," he ordered.

Mary searched the water for movement, her hand creeping about his neck. Instinctively she leaned into his arms. He still bore the fragrances of roasted duck and wine from Beckett's yacht, yet beneath these odors, she smelled distinct fresh scents of canvas and ropes.

Reaching solid ground, he stopped, and his arms tightened about her. Beneath her hand, she felt the coarseness of his coat. The gentle lapping of the water whispered reassurances. Mary glanced up, and her heart lurched madly as a strange expression flitted across his face. All her doubts and fears drained from her, and there was the familiar tingling in the pit of her stomach.

Slowly, Jack lowered her. His gaze deliberately moved over her body. She fought the overwhelming need to return to his arms. Under her feet the hard, rocky surface grounded her. Averting her face, she hastened to the top of the craggy mound, hoping to regain her poise. Behind her, she knew Jack had scrambled back for the boat. Turning, she watched him haul it up onto the dry ground.

Mary cleared her throat, pretending to be unaffected by him. "There's probably not a shark for miles," she said, folding her arms. "I don't believe they swim this close to shore. Our library offers an excellent number of resources on their natural habitat." When he didn't answer, she tried another subject. "Do you think Mr. Beckett's visitors accepted his hospitality?"

"Stay here." He ambled past her.

"Captain, er, Jack, you should remember that we are no longer on your ship." When he didn't pause, she raised her voice. "I no longer need your orders to maneuver on land."

He stopped and pivoted back to her. "May I remind you that we are in a strange place that may or may not be safe? Unless you want to announce our arrival, I *suggest* you wait here quietly for me."

Mary glanced up the jagged coastline, remembering

his words about pirates and hiding places. Anxiety knotted in her stomach. "Certainly. You only had to say so."

With a disgruntled mutter, he left. Mary watched him disappear behind a large mass of boulders, and she sighed. As much as she wanted to find her father, she hoped that Gaspar wasn't here. She had imagined facing the buccaneer with cannons, and a navy led by Jack.

Jamming her hand into her dress pocket, Mary clutched at the snuff box. Reminded of its presence, she pulled it out. Holding it in her palm, she saw the sun reflect off the blue cover, and she lightly traced the design with her thumb. Curious, Mary held her breath and removed the lid. The empty box stared up at her.

Releasing her breath, she started to rewrap the snuff box.

"Missing Beckett?"

"What?" Mary swiveled toward Jack. She hid the box behind her.

He didn't answer, but with lifted brows he nodded toward her back.

With a sheepish smile, she produced the box. "Thomas wanted me to keep this while the French were on his ship. It belongs to his grandmother."

When he didn't respond, she continued. "How long do you think they'll detain him?"

"That depends if he has any other presents from his grandmother aboard." He edged closer for a better look.

His arm brushed hers and her pulse hummed.

"My guess," Jack said, "is that you're holding one of Beckett's so-called art treasures. He must have thought the French would take it."

"Then I'm glad he gave it to me. I shall protect it." Snatching the box away from his scrutiny, Mary gently placed it back into her pocket. She left a corner of the handkerchief peeking out as a reminder of the need to be careful.

Jack's gray eyes looked doubtful, but he pointed over her head. "I found some bushes up above. We'll hide the boat there. Come along, Mary. You've work to do."

"Was that another command?" she asked, wearily following. "You certainly enjoy being a captain."

"Be careful. My enjoyment hasn't even begun yet."

Mary paused for a few moments, then decided that he needed her assistance too much to delay. Picking up her end of the small craft, she found it extraordinarily heavy. She trudged up the slope following Jack's lead. Her arms ached. How did most people take their boats out of the water? Surely there was a simpler way. If not, her father could invent one.

Straining beneath her load, Mary staggered. Her right foot caught in the hem of her dress, and she heard the sound of material ripping. For an instant, she teetered like a drunken sailor before regaining her balance. "I have to put this down for a few moments."

Jack easily lowered his end.

With a sigh, she deposited her burden and stared at the front hem dragging on the ground. "Look at my dress! Now what shall I do? I'll trip whenever I walk."

"Allow me," he said at her elbow.

Before she guessed his intentions, she heard further tearing. In disbelief, she noted a good four inches from the end of her gown and petticoat missing. A cool breeze fluttered about her exposed, white-stockinged legs.

"Much better," Jack said with satisfaction in his voice. "Don't waste time, Mary. We need to move this boat further into those shrubs."

What an insensitive man. "You've destroyed my dress!"

He straightened, and his gaze took in her form from her ankles to her bodice. "If you ask me, it's an improvement." His gaze flitted up to hers, and a gleam of admiration sparkled in his steel-colored eyes.

Mary bit her lip and strove to settle the flutter in the pit of her stomach. *The man is worse than a chronically overdue borrower,* she reminded herself. "You may be unaware of this since you've spent most of your time on a boat, but—"

"Ship," he corrected.

"What? Oh. Even *you* should know that proper women do not go about half-dressed in public. In particular, they never reveal their limbs."

"Are you going to stand there showing off your legs all day, or are you going to carry this skiff?" He scanned the area while he rubbed the back of his neck.

"Showing off my legs! Your manners are sorely in need of a lesson. I shall ignore your comment since we are in a precarious situation, but in the future kindly keep your distance. You'll probably rip the rest of my dress."

He mumbled something that sounded like "my pleasure," but she chose to ignore him. Seizing hold of the craft, they carried it deeper into the wild raspberry bushes. The bushes clawed at her stockings and scratched her legs. Quickly, Mary deposited her end of the dinghy and moved away to examine the snags in her hosiery and the stings in her legs.

"We can't hide it better without carrying it away from here," Jack said, dusting off his hands. "At least, it won't be easily seen from any ship on the water. We'll head up the beach, if that's fine with you?"

"Thank you. I'm ready." Mary lifted her chin and surveyed the jagged rocky tops. They clustered together like small islands surrounded by the ocean. Carefully, she picked her way across the uneven surfaces. Beyond, smaller rocks poked their heads out of the sea. In the distance, she caught sight of a narrow strip of white sand before it disappeared into the pine woods.

Warm sand! Mary imagined her bare feet sinking into the soft grains, heated by the sun. She could feel the tiny pebbles sifting through her toes. She could hardly wait.

Taking a deep breath of salt air, Mary darted toward her destination. She felt her heel slip on a piece of sea-weed, and she skidded across the slick surface. With a scream, Mary slid into the tidal pool. Water flowed over her head. Quickly, she pushed for the surface. Spurting out salt water, she sat up in the shallow basin.

"No time for a bath, Mary." Jack stood on the rocks above her. He held out a hand and then dropped it. His attention shifted. Bending, he picked up a small, snail-shaped shell resting on the edge of the rock.

"What is it?" Mary asked, struggling toward him. Her waterlogged shoes were as heavy as bookends. Reaching him, she glanced down at the small sea creature in his hand.

"Can you hum?"

"Perhaps I should write my biography. Then I could answer all these questions that seem to pop into your head at odd times. I'm standing here, my feet and gown soaked, and you ask—"

His baritone voice rose over her complaints.

Her eyes widened as she recognized the strains of a child's lullaby. The deep, rich tone of his voice felt like a caress and lulled away her protests. Somewhere from within her floated a memory of a mother dressed in white, humming the same song. But the image faded from her grasp, and she focused on the small tan shell. A small white head poked out from it.

"She likes to be serenaded," Jack murmured in a tender voice.

Mary stared in awe at this man whose strong voice could command a crew yet could gently woo a woman. "With your voice, you could sing to any female."

His gray eyes locked with hers, and there was a spark of some indefinable emotion in his eyes. Tongue-tied, she shifted her attention to the shell, but his hand had closed around it.

Suddenly, Jack grasped her wrists and pulled her to him. For a second, she stood pressed against his wide chest. Her skin prickled from the heat of his body against her wet dress, and Mary felt as though she couldn't breathe.

Slowly, Jack released her. "We'd better get off these rocks. The French can easily see us." His gaze went to her breasts.

Following his stare, heat rushed to her face, and Mary mused that *he* had no trouble seeing. Folding her arms over the front of her, she followed behind him. She took only a few steps when a small shell caught her attention. Bowing, Mary poked it with her finger. When she saw no response, she swept it up into her hand.

Softly, Mary hummed a few strains. Nothing happened. She raised the shell closer for inspection and hummed louder. A small white head appeared, opened its tiny mouth, and spit in her eye. She cried in surprise and pain. The offensive urchin fell from her hand.

Her vision blurred. With one hand over her burning eye, and the other hand extended in front to ward off any large obstacles, Mary stumbled over the uneven stone surfaces. She yearned for firm ground and clear vision. Mary had only gone a few paces when Jack reached her.

"What is it?" he asked, his arm wrapping about her shoulder.

"I'm having trouble seeing. That sea creature spit something at me." To her frustration, tears blurred her vision and Jack's shape.

Twisting away from him, she rubbed her eyelids.

"Hold still. I'll get it out. It's probably a grain of sand."

Before she could protest, he yanked Beckett's handkerchief from her pocket.

The snuff box flew out and landed with a crack.

"Oh, no, Thomas's snuff box!" Pressing one hand over one side of her face, Mary dropped to her knees and gingerly picked up the fragile object. From her one good eye, she saw that a thin fracture line ran around the bottom, confirming her worst fear.

"Now I'm half-blind, half-dressed, and have a broken snuff box," she moaned, wiping away the bothersome tears. "How shall I ever replace it? Thomas entrusted me with his grandmother's gift, and I've ruined it."

Jack's large hands removed the box from hers. One arm came around her back, and he steered her through the rocks.

"I'll never explain it," she continued. "A gift from Napoleon destroyed. Damaged. Ruined. How can anyone put their snuff inside?"

"I'm sure Beckett's grandmother can sniff fine without it. Now, let me look at you."

"I'm not hurt. Only my life is ruined. I've always been so responsible. When Mrs. Harrison visited her sister, I took care of her pigs. Then when old Mr. Beanpot's gout bothered him and he was confined to bed, I brought him books to read and always reminded him when they were due. He never had to pay a fine!"

"You've lived an admirable life, Miss Librarian."

Mary pushed back the wet strands of hair clinging to her face. "You're laughing at me."

Creases formed above his dark brows, and the hint of a smile ghosted his lips. "No, no I'm not." He placed his hand over his heart. "I swear on Beckett's grandmother's life, I'm not."

"Now I know you are." Annoyed, she closed her hand over the fractured box and swept it from his hand.

His fingers wrapped around the brown fabric of her sleeve. "I'm not laughing. If I owned something of value, I'd trust you with it."

Her gaze traveled over his face and searched his eyes. Mary recognized tenderness and another emotion that she couldn't name, but it sent a tingling through her. "Thank you."

Lightly, he fingered a loose tendril of hair on her cheek and wiped away a tear. "Your poor fiancè never had a chance."

"What do you mean?" she asked, her heart hammering.

But he didn't answer. Jack pulled her closer till she couldn't tell if it was her heart pounding, or his. Propriety told her she should draw away, but she didn't listen. She was in a dream. A dream where Captain Jack St. George kissed her passionately. Slowly he bent his head, and she lifted her face to meet his lips.

Closing her eyes, Mary moved closer, but instead of his warm mouth upon hers, he brushed a gentle kiss across her forehead.

Disappointment swirled within her. Mary blinked at

him standing in front of her. She wanted him to continue, yet how forward could she be?

He took command of the situation. Taking her hand, he led her past the narrow beach toward the tall pines. "We have only a few more hours of light. I'll scavenge around and find a safe place for the night. You keep the lookout on the ocean." When she didn't answer, he added, "If you'd be so kind."

Unable to trust her voice, Mary nodded. Standing above the beach, she studied the ocean to avoid looking at him. Unexpectedly, his coat came about her shoulders. She glanced up to mumble her thanks, but Jack had already strode away.

Mary sat in the shade of the forest wondering why she felt so alone. Jack's scent emanated from his dark blue coat, offering her comfort. She didn't want to think about him, Mary thought, hugging his coat closer. Instead, she stared hard at the sea. Countless wave after wave rolled onto the beach, each identical to the last.

Her eyes grew tired from the constant watch. Weary, Mary lay on her side and propped her head on her arm. From this position, she could view the empty ocean. The voices of the rolling waves mesmerized her, whispering Jack's name to the rhythm of the rising and the falling of the waves.

Her eyelids slipped closed, and she dreamed Jack was kissing her. Only this time, he didn't kiss her like a sister. She sighed and gave way to the dream.

Mary stirred. Slowly she became aware that the ground had grown cool, and the sun had disappeared. The taste of salt lingered on her lips. She heard the familiar roll of the ocean and the creeping and croaking of the nocturnal creatures. A mosquito buzzed around her head. In the state halfway between sleep and wakefulness, she tried to uncurl her body.

A hand clamped over her mouth.

Five

A shiver of panic ran through her. Then her senses stirred and Mary detected Jack's familiar scent. She smiled, remembering her dream. In the moonless night, he signaled for her to be quiet.

Jack crawled toward the edge of the pines and peered below.

Still wearing his coat, Mary paused and wrapped it around herself for protection. Hesitating only a few moments, she squirmed her way through the dirt and pine needles to join him. The soil rubbed against her legs and clung to the damp portions of her dress. The sweet, pungent scent of pitch stuck to her hands and permeated the air. Within seconds, she covered the remaining feet to him.

Mary lay beside him with excitement and questions streaking through her. A strange sensation tingled in the pit of her stomach and she had to fight the urge to press against him. He seemed oblivious to her. She scanned the waterfront. Through the blackness came the flicker of a light and the creaks of a ship.

"What is it?" she whispered. "The French?"

"Mooncussers," he answered, not bothering to explain.

She frowned in thought. "Jack, I vow to look up the definition of this word when I return to Oyster River, but—"

"Men who come out on moonless nights," he said without glancing at her. "They try to wreck ships on the reefs. The spoils belong to whoever gets to the vessel first."

A chill ran down her spine. "Could it be Gaspar?"

Abruptly, he faced her. One dark brow quirked upward in humor. "Then our prayers are answered. Stay here. I'm moving closer."

"I'll go with you. Gaspar has my father."

"No. You stay here. If I don't return soon, my crew will search for me. You can tell them who took me."

"But I won't know who captured you," she protested.

Jack reached out and squeezed her hand. His touch sent a current racing through her. Unbalanced, she strove to comprehend his words.

"Wait. Once I know how many there are, I'll come back for you."

His command focused her attention. "Not another order."

He clenched his jaw and seemed to consider an answer. "Miss McNeal, you're now a crew member."

"I am?"

"Yes, and you must act like one."

In the darkness, she made a grimace, but he'd disappeared. He'd only made her a crew member so he'd have authority to issue commands. He was a tyrant like Napoleon. Why had she felt any attraction for him? At least he hadn't ordered how she should wait. She crawled between two towering pines.

She frowned in thought. What kind of a match would they be for Jack? Were they on foot? Were more men waiting? Surely, one man couldn't take all of a wreck's cargo.

Craning her neck, she searched the beach and the edge

of the forest for other human forms. She grasped at her throat for her scope's cord. No telescope. No Jack. Impatience and uneasiness filled her. She decided to move closer.

Cautiously, she crept only a few inches at a time. The earth scraped and found its way into her stockings and the pocket of Jack's coat. The snuff box pressed against her. This method was too ineffective. She'd run. Yes, that was the answer.

Hard metal pressed against her back. Mary froze.

"Stand up slow, and raise yer hands."

Mary stood to face her attacker. In the dimness she could make out two figures, one tall and lean, the other short and stocky. The taller man pointed a shotgun at her.

"Who are you?" she asked.

"What's your name?" demanded the tall, red-bearded man.

She gestured at their weapon. "I'm not dangerous. I'm a librarian."

"Luke, she says she's a librarian!" The short man's hairy brows melded together in a straight questioning line.

"No, she ain't, Morley." Tall Luke looked up and down her form.

Mary fought the urge to cower in front of him.

Luke waved his shotgun for her to move. "I know how to prove it."

Forced to follow, she walked to the end of a rocky trail where the bluff rose up to block her path. Standing before the mound, she noticed that it was formed of solid granite.

Luke signaled Morley forward, and the short man jostled a large rock aside. A small black hole appeared in the hill. "After you." Luke smiled, revealing brown, stained teeth.

"I-I can't see," Mary said, hanging back from the cave entrance.

With a mutter, Luke grabbed the lantern and led them forward. The icy coldness of the walls and the odor of damp earth reached out and clung to her sodden clothes. The narrowness of the passage squeezed the breath from her body.

Confused, she knew only that the path spiraled downward.

Finally the walls opened, and they stood in a small room on an uneven stone floor. Morley settled the light on the ground with a clang.

Staring about her, Mary recognized ashes from a fire in the center of the cave while wooden barrels and chests of all shapes lined the walls of the cave.

In the shadows, Luke rummaged through a coffer. Then with a grunt, he darted to her. "Read this." He stuffed a yellowed, musty piece of paper below her nose and stood back.

Taking it, Mary focused her attention on the writing. "One pair of black leather boots, two pairs of socks . . ."

Morley grabbed the paper from her grasp. "Aw, that don't prove nothing. Besides, how do we know what's writ on there?"

Mary's head snapped up. "You think I have a propensity for prevaricating about a clothing inventory?"

Morley scratched his head. "You understand that, Luke? Was that English?"

"Don't matter." Luke wrapped his fingers around her wrist and yanked her closer to the lantern light.

"Please," Mary said, trying to peer into the man's yellow eyes for a hint of reason. "Can't we discuss this? I assure you that I am a harmless librarian."

Luke jabbed at her torn skirt with his rifle. "No librarian dresses like this. We've got ourselves a woman." He leered at Mary.

Fighting the urge to cringe, she searched her mind. Proof of her identity seemed so important. Surely, these men wouldn't have evil designs on a woman who worked with books. "I could recite Macbeth."

"Who's he?" Morley asked.

"It's a play." She drew a deep breath and recited, "By the pricking of my thumbs, something wicked this way comes."

"Huh?" Luke stared at her.

Mary opened her mouth, but the distant echo of a gunshot blew away her idea of an explanation. "Captain St. George!"

"St. George!" shouted the men, stepping away in unison.

"You know him?" Mary asked, startled by their reaction.

"Do you mean Johnny St. George who sailed with Gaspar?" Luke asked in a quivering voice.

"Yes! We were together, until you so unkindly kidnapped me. He may be hurt. We have to find him."

Morley scratched his head. "I thought Gaspar sailed north."

Luke's eyes took on a bright gleam. "So you're St. George's woman. What do you say we do with her, Morley?"

"Shoot her and throw her in the ocean," Morley offered.

"That's quite unnecessary." Mary's throat tightened at the suggestion. "I can disappear without any assistance." She edged toward the opening. "No need for you to go out of your way, I'll just leave. Not that it hasn't been delightful."

"We don't have to worry about St. George. He won't see us," Luke said. "Hope Henry didn't take off in the dinghy for the *New Moon.*"

Mary thought a more appropriate name for the mooncussers' boat would be No Moon.

"Jack will shoot you," Mary warned. "He's a very dangerous man. Why, he knows all those pirate tricks. There's not a man alive he can't outsmart." A gag came over her mouth. She continued talking, but only muffled protests sounded from the rancid-smelling cloth.

Luke wiped his brow. "That woman makes my head hurt."

"Can we throw her off the cliff now?" Morley asked.

Can't the man think of anything else? Mary wondered.

"Wait!" Luke grabbed the short man's arm. "I've got a better idea. St. George will come looking for her. Let's sell her back to him."

"What if he don't want to pay for her?" Morley wrinkled his forehead and cast a doubtful look at Mary.

She squealed in protest.

"She makes a lot of noise, even when she can't talk," Morley said.

Luke put his arm around his companion's shoulders. "First, we'll have some fun with her, and then, if St. George don't want her, we'll get rid of her."

Somehow Mary doubted that she'd enjoy their fun. Goose bumps broke out on her arms. In her mind, she saw the dark tunnel and herself fleeing through it. She just needed the right moment.

"I have what she needs." Luke winked. "We won't need to tie her."

He removed the gag, and Mary squared her shoulders and tilted her chin. She would not give them the satisfaction of seeing her cower. "Do your worst, gentlemen."

She closed her eyes and held her breath. Something heavy and grimy was pushed into her hands.

Opening her eyes, Mary gazed down at the black, scorched bottom of a frying pan. "What's this?"

"It's for cooking," Luke explained. "I'm hungry." Morley scratched his crotch. "Good idea. We'll eat first. Then we'll have fun."

Standing on either side of her, the men each grabbed an arm and led her to the fire. One of them threw a lifeless fish into the pan. The dead eye stared at Mary.

Fear rippled through her, and she strove to control it. At least she'd received a reprieve. Anytime, Jack would come. But how would he find her? Mary frowned over the question and slid a glance at the men sitting on the side passing a jug. With a shudder, she speculated that they were probably preparing for the after-dinner entertainment.

Staring at the fire, she watched the smoke spiral toward the top of the cave and then float out the passage. A new idea sparked in Mary's mind. She'd send Jack a smoke signal. True, it was dark, but he'd get suspicious when he smelled all the smoke. Surely, he'd follow it.

All she needed was a big fire. Beside a chest, Mary spotted odd pieces of wood. She grabbed a couple and threw them into the fire. The flame flickered and threatened to die. Hurriedly, she blew on it.

"Hey, how's the food?" Luke asked.

"I have to build the fire up a bit." She added the rest of the fuel. With the front of her skirt she rapidly fanned it, keeping her back to the men. Suddenly, the fire roared. It burned her eyes and drove her back. Dark smoke filled the room.

"Are you crazy?" The men's hands wrenched her backward.

She stumbled against a barrel. Glancing down at the keg that reached to her knees, she read the label, POWDER.

In the center of the cave, the two men jumped around the fire. But the smoke grew with their efforts to control it.

Mary's fingers tightened around the powder keg. Grabbing it, she raised it above her head.

"Now, gentlemen," she yelled.

Their eyes widened in recognition. "No, not that one!" they shouted in unison. Morley threw up his arms before his face.

Mary scanned the cave for the quickest escape. "I want you outside now." Her arms trembled under the weight of the barrel.

Morley stepped away from the fire.

"Wait," Luke yelled. "She can't scare us. Morley, go to her right, and I'll go left."

They circled round her like sharks smelling blood.

Icy fear twisted around her heart. "I'll throw it in the fire if you come any closer." Mary heard the tremor in her own voice and raised the keg higher to emphasize her threat.

Delight glinted in Luke's gaze. "It's two to one, little Missy. Who do you think will win?"

A shot rang out in the air.

Startled, Mary and the mooncussers froze. The sound of metal against metal, which signaled reloading, greeted their ears.

"I'd say that's not a fair fight." Out of the smoky cloud stepped Captain Jack St. George. In his hand he held a pistol, still blazing from the shot he'd fired. A fierce, deadly expression burned in his eyes, daring anyone to cross him.

Mary's breath caught in her throat. He looked like a

hero who'd sprung to life from one of her books, and he'd come to rescue her.

"Mary, are you hurt?"

"No," she managed to answer.

"We didn't mean no harm, Johnny," Luke said, wiping his perspiring face. "Just wanted the lady here to help us with the cooking. She nearly killed us all with this smoke."

"Stand still." Jack raised his weapon. "I might accidentally shoot you while you enjoy your last meal." He nodded to Mary. "Miss McNeal, it's time to leave. Don't bother saying good-bye. Bring that barrel with you."

Mary picked her way around the fire till she reached him. "Are you hurt?" he asked, without taking his gaze from his targets.

"No. I knew you'd come."

His hand wavered, and she saw the surprise in his gaze as he glanced at her. "Get behind me." He nodded at Morley. "Take off your belt and tie up your friend."

"What you goin' to do?" Morley asked.

Jack ignored him. "Mary, put down the keg and leave."

"You need me."

His gaze flickered to her and back to his prisoners. "Never question the captain of your ship. Go."

Knowing how stubborn he was, Mary knew it was useless to argue. She rested the powder keg at his feet. When she hesitated, he raised a questioning dark brow.

"I'm leaving."

"Take the lantern." He gestured to one on the side. "I followed the smoke inside, but you'll need a light to help you find your way outside."

Mary fled through the narrow passage. She didn't like leaving Jack with those unscrupulous men, but for once, she'd follow orders. Smoke lingered in the passage and caused her eyes to well with tears. Plunging deeper into the cave's spiral corridor, she squinted and buried her nose in Jack's coat to help her breathe.

Finally outside in the cold night air, Mary wiped her eyes and peered into the cave for St. George. She leaned further inside at the sound of footsteps. "Jack?"

"Stand back," he shouted. Jack's large frame came into focus, and he squeezed through the opening. In his hands he held the keg from which he poured a fine black powder.

"What are you doing?" she asked, stepping out of his way.

"Blocking the cave, unless you'd like those men to join us."

"I'd—"

"Run," Jack ordered.

She didn't question him. Mary sprinted down the worn path in the rocks and stopped only once to judge if she had strayed from the trail. Then she remembered that she'd left the lantern behind her. Oh well, Jack would need it.

Onward she raced. Her breath burned in her throat, and pain shot through her knee. A sound like a distant cannon rang out into the night. Jack! Mary circled back and collided with him on the path.

He grabbed her arm and pulled her along. She attempted to keep pace with him, until she felt his arm around her back nearly lifting her off the ground as they dashed into the darkness. By the time they reached the cove, breathing was Mary's major concern. While she dragged in gasps of moist night air, her heart pounded in her head. Gradually the need subsided, and she became aware that Jack had hauled their shore boat to the top of the rocks.

In one swift movement, he swung it up over his head and carried it to the water. "Get in."

Mary barely took a step when he reached her side and swept her off her feet. The feel of his strong arms about her set off new sparks of excitement. She could only sputter, "What . . . what?"

"No questions, Miss McNeal." He easily settled her into the boat.

"Where are we going?" Mary asked, her stomach clenching.

"I feel safer in the water."

In the darkness, a wave reached up and pulled them into the dark sea. She grasped the sides of the small boat as it rose and fell.

"They didn't harm you?" Jack asked.

"I'm a little shaken. By tomorrow I shall be fine. I could carry ten books up and down the stairs without need for a rest."

Jack went perfectly still, and in the darkness she could feel him staring at her.

"Mary, I don't suppose it will do any good to remind you that I told you to stay in the woods?"

"I did." She raised her chin in protest. "Those men forced me to accompany them. Then you appeared like a hero out of the smoke."

He sat silent for a moment as though her words stunned him. Then he gave a short laugh. "I'm glad your father doesn't know they let you out of the library."

"I was hardly chained there."

"Chains. Now there's a thought."

Something in his tone cut off her retort. Mary leaned closer in the dark night, trying to discern his features for a clue to his meaning. But she could read only determination as he poured his energy into the rowing. He had taken charge with an air of efficiency that fascinated her.

Absently, she clutched at her neck for her telescope and then realized it was not there. Sighing, Mary pushed her hand deep into her pocket and closed her fingers around the broken snuff box. How would she explain how she'd destroyed Thomas's one-of-a-kind Napoleonic treasure?

Six

In the early morning light, Jack rowed and watched Mary sleep curled in the bottom of the boat. He glanced down at her exposed legs. An urge to caress them seized him.

Mentally, he shook himself. What was wrong with him? This woman belonged in a world of polite discussions and disagreements. A world that would not accept him. Resentment rose and stuck in his throat. Jack pushed it away. Mary had a knack for getting into trouble and taking him with her. He couldn't become involved with her. He had enough problems locating Gaspar.

At the thought of the pirate, the hair on the nape of his neck prickled. Why did he have this uncomfortable feeling of being watched? The sooner he reached the ship, the safer he'd feel. A speck in the distance caught his attention, the *Goodspeed*. She waited like a child for her parent's return.

With renewed energy, he headed for his destination. Mary stirred and mumbled a word that sounded like Beckett. Hesitating in his rowing, Jack bent closer to hear her more clearly, but she remained silent. *Beckett. She can't forget him even in her dreams.* Scowling, he studied the area for any sign of a French ship or a yacht. Nothing.

Paddling closer to his ship, he heard the familiar voice of the man on watch, and Jack answered. In the bottom of the boat, Mary woke and stretched, providing Jack a full view of her rounded breasts. He gripped the oar tightly.

"It's morning. Are we near the ship?" she asked lazily.

"Ahead." Jack waved toward it and avoided staring at her.

"Already? You didn't wake me for my turn at the oars."

"We rode the current most of the way. Besides, you needed to rest. I'll not have my crew looking like washed-up seaweed."

"I'm glad you find my appearance so appealing." She stretched, exposing her bare legs from under her short-ened skirt.

Jack clenched his jaw, trying to throttle the lust racing through him. He could show her how appealing he found her.

She straightened the remains of her hem and asked innocently, "Do you think we'll learn how Mr. Beckett fared?"

Beckett. She has been dreaming of him. "Don't worry about him. He is like the fish that never gets caught. No matter how many nets, Beckett always swims away. Now prepare to board."

At his words, Mary smoothed the hair from her face and loosened her braid. She shook her head, and then nimbly reworked the strands. No hint of ink stained her fingertips, and she smelled of last night's wood smoke. Jack watched, unable to tear his gaze from her strong, slim fingers threading through her tresses. He could re-member how soft her hair felt. And her hands. He could imagine them stroking him. *Hell.* Jack pulled fiercely on his oars.

Mary paused in her grooming. "You're full of energy."

He grunted.

"I hope the crew hasn't worried about you," she said.

"What?" he asked, refocusing his attention on her question.

"I know you're the captain, but they must have been upset when you didn't return from the yacht." She shot him a reproachful look. "You didn't send them any word of your delay."

"Miss McNeal, I'm not their father." Her father would have Jack locked away for his thoughts.

"No, of course you're not. I'm speaking about how individuals feel about others with whom they associate. Each individual deve—"

"Stop!" What had he ever found appealing about such a mouthy, female creature? "We're at sea, not at some tea party."

"You mean courtesy rules on a ship are different from on land?"

"Yes," he said, satisfied that he'd avoided her one-sided discussion.

"I'll have to give it some thought."

He wanted to yell that she had nothing to consider. Instead, he poured his frustrations into reaching his ship quickly.

"We covered the distance to your vessel in incredible time," Mary said, preparing to board the *Goodspeed*.

Aboard, his crew gathered to welcome him back. The librarian smiled politely and gave him a knowing glance.

Not wanting to get involved in another useless conversation about his crew's feelings, he ordered Finn to escort the librarian to the galley. He ordered Daniel to meet him in twenty minutes.

The young man saluted, but a hint of discontent dulled the sparkle in his eyes at his quick dismissal.

Jack vowed to be ready in ten minutes. Inside his cabin,

the sight of his comfortable bunk occupied his mind. How good it would feel to rest for a few moments. But he had no time. Yet, his legs worked slowly. In the privacy of his quarters, he allowed his mind to dwell on the memories of Mary curled in his boat. He imagined his hand traveling up her shapely calf and felt the smoothness of her skin and the heat from her body.

Daniel's knock at the door intruded on Jack's daydreams.

Biting his lip, the first mate stuttered his greeting.

"Tell me." Jack ordered.

"It's the French, Captain A frigate was here, and an officer wanted to speak with you."

"They came to the *Goodspeed*?" Hurriedly, Jack rubbed a towel over his chin, wiping away the soap and water. "When?"

"Yesterday. I told them you were sick, and we had orders not to disturb you." He swallowed and waited for an answer.

"Good. What did this officer say?"

Daniel's hint of a relieved smile disappeared. "He asked for Miss McNeal, Captain."

"The librarian! A Frenchman knew her name?"

"He did. I told him she wasn't on this ship. I couldn't understand why he'd be looking for her until Mr. Beckett arrived. He explained everything."

A bad premonition spun into his mind. "What did Beckett tell you?"

"He said the French thought he was one of Napoleon's supporters. I guess he convinced them he wasn't. But when they were on his yacht, all of his crew was questioned. One of them overheard your names and reported the information to the French."

"With directions to the *Goodspeed*?"

"Begging your pardon, Captain, but we were the only ship in the same waters. It's logical that Miss McNeal would be on board."

Why had they wanted Mary? What information did they think she possessed? Damn Beckett for dragging them into this.

"Have you any idea where the French or Mr. Beckett are now?"

Daniel shifted uneasily. "The frigate sailed south. Mr. Beckett's ship left early this morning to search for you."

"I'm glad my life didn't depend upon him."

"Captain?"

"Find Miss McNeal and send her to me. We'll sail immediately. With so many *friends* surrounding us, it's best to take precautions."

After the first mate left, Jack considered his options. First, he'd determine that no one followed them. Once he determined they were safe, he'd put her ashore where she could get transportation home. At least his own misery with the librarian would end soon.

He recognized her light knock on the door. Jack straightened his collar, then caught himself. *Look at the effect she has on me. I've become a dandy.* With a grunt of disapproval, he flung open the door.

Her smile of greeting faded when her gaze roved his face. "You wanted to speak to me?"

"Come in," he snapped. Best to get this over quickly. "I've decided to wait a few days before returning you home. I want to make sure it's safe."

She halted in surprise. "Thank you, Captain. I did prove I could take care of myself." A furrow of doubt creased her brow. "I did do well with those mooncussers, didn't I? I mean, not that you weren't stupendous appearing out of nowhere." She paused, and a dreamy expression flickered across her face.

He couldn't tear his gaze away from her face. A wave of desire swept through him. He took a step back and swallowed tightly.

"And Beckett?" she asked.

"What?" He blinked at her, trying to understand her question.

"Have you seen Thomas? Do you know how he is?"

"He's fine. Daniel saw him and the frigate. A member of my good friend's crew reported us to the French."

"Oh." Her brow creased in thought. "Now they think you're a Napoleon supporter. At least you're not suspected of piracy."

"One type of traitor is as good as another." Jack cleared his throat. "There's a good chance the French are shadowing us."

"Captain, from the start, I knew we'd face trying times, but you shouldn't despair at the first sign of trouble."

Jack struggled with the shock coursing within him. "First sign? I can't believe your memory is that short." He held up a hand when she attempted to interrupt. "No, I won't repeat our numerous problems since we've met. I'm your captain. I'll do what's best."

Her face clouded. "We need to have a discussion. I can't pay you to find my father. You won't refuse to help me, will you?"

Fury boiled in him at the suggestion. What type of man did she think he was? "You believe I'd risk your life for money?"

"I think it is a logical conclusion that you'd like to be paid. Most people like reimbursement for their services.

"I'm not some stud horse." He clenched his fists as anger and lust mixed together. "I have to leave."

"You shouldn't run away when you're angry."

"Run away?" He wanted to shout sense into her. Instead he lowered his voice so she'd hear every word. "If I'd run off at the first signs of trouble, I'd not be stuck with you." Tamping down his emotions, he left before he lost control.

Mary sank onto the bunk. Anger and guilt threaded all her doubts together. She should never have mentioned money. She should never have mentioned a discussion. Jack didn't like them. He was too stubborn to listen, and after she'd shown her fearlessness with those mooncussers. At least he hadn't refused to rescue her father.

She could see her father now. The shirttails of his white shirt spilled over his dark breeches while he pointed at the sky above their gray Cape Cod house. A summer breeze stirred his black hair.

The dew already had covered the grass and soaked through her matching brown shoes. Mary stretched up on her toes to her full three feet, wishing she could grasp a star and hold it in her hand.

"Your mother is up there, Mary. She's looking down upon us."

"I'd like her better here with us." An idea snapped into her mind and left her shaking with fear. "You won't go to heaven, too?"

Her father laid a hand upon her head. "We'll always be together, Mary. I promise."

"Always," Mary whispered. She twined her fingers through her father's large hand.

Gradually, the memory faded. Mary could still feel the warmth of her father's grasp and the weight of their promise to each other. They'd always be together. She had to reach him.

Queasy with worry, Mary lay on the bunk. Her throat ached with tears. One rolled down her cheek, and she brushed it away with the coarse gray blanket on the bunk. The roughness of the fabric rubbed against her cheek. She paused and studied the old woolen material. A notion shaped in her mind. Once she found a needle, she could keep her mind and hands occupied and safely away from her problems.

With the sun rising high into the sky, the *Goodspeed* sailed near the jagged coastline of Bath Harbor. Several seagulls glided on the light sea breeze above Jack, who had kept a watchful vigil for the French. He decided to moor outside the harbor for a fast retreat.

Standing on deck, Jack gazed out at the blue sea, but instead of clear waters, he saw himself meeting Mary in the Oyster River library. She would be sitting behind a large oak desk. He'd bend to speak with her, and the soft lilac fragrance would tease him. Her thick hair would be caught up behind her head in a doodad.

He'd lean closer and then—? What? Mary would never want to see him again once he returned her to her home. She'd hold him responsible for her failure to save her father's life. She'd always blame him for ruining her one chance. And what if she tried again, the little fool.

What would happen to her? With her luck, she'd end up involved in another crazy scheme. He had to protect her from herself. When Daniel appeared, Jack ordered him to see if the French had anchored nearby and to find transportation to Oyster River for the librarian.

Jack dismissed him. Now he'd speak with Mary about

her departure. He headed below. At least, he'd have his own quarters soon. He had to stoop in that small cabin off the steerage that he'd been using.

Mary opened the door immediately, and Jack swore he smelled lilacs. Silently, she stood aside while he entered.

Standing in the center of the cabin, he observed her paleness and red eyes. Still, she had a lovely face, soft and warm. It was the kind of face that could make him forget why he'd come. He stiffened his resolve. As she closed the door, he noted that the spyglass again dangled from a cord about her neck.

Tilting her chin, she asked, "Did you come for your coat? I wouldn't have taken it, but . . . " She glanced down at her dress.

A pain of regret shot through him. Daniel should have bought her a new one with the money. Of course Mary, a lady, would be embarrassed to embark in her present clothing. Quickly, he pulled out the remaining bills. "I think you can buy something suitable for yourself with this."

Mary shook her head. "I'd prefer you gave it to Mr. Beckett for his snuff box." She crossed to the desk. "Since I don't know when I'll see him again, I've taken the liberty of using your pen and paper to write him a letter of explanation. When I do return to Oyster River, I intend to have a replica made. I'm certain I can retain a craftsman in Portsmouth that's only a few miles from my home to reproduce it. I know it won't be the same." She removed the spyglass and held it out to him with the letter. "I shall leave my telescope for Mr. Beckett as collateral."

"You will not." Jack forced the words through clenched teeth. "Beckett put us in danger. We owe him nothing."

"Captain, please stop ordering me about. My evening

with those mooncussers was trying, but I never was in danger with you nearby."

"What?" Jack advanced to her. She was mad.

Mary held her ground.

"You're like a character out of a book." He fisted his hands. "You think nothing can happen to you, and that everything has a happy ending. Well, it doesn't, and it's time you get that through your head. Thank God you're going home soon."

Her eyes widened with shock, and her lip trembled. "I apologize, Captain. You can have your cabin." She attempted to dart past him, but he caught her arm.

Regret clogged his throat and made his voice unsteady. "I've . . . I've been at sea too long. I've forgotten how to behave."

"You simply told the truth." Her voice choked, and she kept her head lowered. Finally, Mary lifted her face. Her green eyes glistened with tears. Tears he had caused.

Guilt and lust mixed together. He gently pulled her to him. "Don't cry. I won't know what to do. I haven't read the book on crying," he added, hoping to make her stop with his feeble joke.

Despite his plan to stay away from her, he closed his arms about her waist. She was small and fragile, like a sea pearl. He buried his face in her hair. It smelled like the ocean breeze. Her arms tightened around him, and she clung to him. The need to have her throbbed through him. Lightly, he ran his hand up her side and rested it on the indentation of her waist and then over her beating heart. His own was pounding in his head. He'd wanted to touch her for so long.

Finally he tilted her chin so that he could look at her tears. Her eyes, the color of the sea, held him, and his breath caught. Sensations crashed over him, threatening to sink the last of his control. Lightly, he traced the soft fullness of her lips. His hunger deepened. Their last kiss had been too brief. What would it be like to taste lilac and sea breeze? How would her hair feel with his fingers wrapped in it? The questions drove him forward. His lips brushed hers. Her mouth opened beneath his.

His mind whirled. All his thoughts of mooncussers and Oyster River disappeared. He could think of nothing but wanting more. He pressed her closer and delved his fingers into her hair. She gripped his shoulders as though she'd lost her balance. She wanted him, he thought.

His senses swam with pleasure. A deep need started to uncurl within him. The need for more. His lips moved over hers with gentle persuasion until she responded. Her tongue shyly met his. He wanted to taste more of her and trailed hot kisses down her throat. She groaned softly. The cabin grayed, and he felt unsteady. Beneath his feet the ship rocked and pitched. Were they sailing? Confused, he pulled away.

"What was that?" he asked, hearing a tremble in his own voice. His ship hadn't gone anywhere.

Glancing at Mary, he saw her flushed face, and her eyes no longer gleamed with anguish, but sparkled with happiness and desire.

He shook his head and grasped for words. "What happened?"

Mary tilted her head and studied his face. "It was like two stars colliding, or two ships." She smiled tentatively.

Rubbing his chin, he struggled to make sense of the feelings coursing through him. His body reeled with the urge to continue kissing her. Searching through his mind, he sought the last of their conversation. Nothing came to him. Jack felt like a fool. He couldn't speak. At last, he mumbled, "I have to go on deck."

He saw the flash of disappointment in her eyes.

She turned quickly away from him. "I'll leave the note for Mr. Beckett. I hope he is safe."

Beckett. Always she speaks of him. A pain of irritation shot through him. "Not if we're lucky." He felt her confused gaze upon him as he marched from the room.

Shortly before noon, Daniel returned. Jack listened to the report that no French foreigners had been seen in port. The first mate also reported he'd met a friend who reported Gaspar's ship sailing north of Bath.

Jack silently figured how quickly they could set sail after the sighting.

"A ship would be leaving for Portsmouth, New Hampshire, tomorrow," Daniel said. "Do you want me to secure a place for the librarian?"

At his question, a deep sense of disappointment settled over Jack. What was wrong with him? Mary only wanted him to find her father. He should feel nothing for her. But the memory of kissing her soft mouth told him the truth. He was caught. Damn. He wanted her, but he didn't want her.

"Captain?"

"She stays aboard," Jack barked. The expression of surprise flitted across Daniel's face before Jack composed himself and left.

For the rest of the day, Mary kept to the cabin. Jack wondered how she spent the time. Maybe she read his log. He could wander below. No, he'd not go near her, not until he had better control.

To avoid her, he ate later than usual in the galley. Despite Cook's subtle complaints about men who couldn't keep schedules, he managed to swallow all of his food. Silently congratulating himself for eluding her, he'd reached the deck when he saw her.

The sun had dipped into the flat line of the horizon, turning the sky to fiery orange. She stood with her back to him. Her head tilted up to the sky, and her long thick hair trailed down her back in the familiar braid. The brisk evening wind tousled loose strands. For a second, he stood enjoying the sight of her.

Then he noticed her attention riveted on a particular spot in the heavens. Above the masts, high in the early evening sky, the first light had appeared. She stared at it.

With a sigh, Mary turned to him. A look of surprise passed over her face, only to be replaced by another expression he didn't recognize. Was it dislike, even hate?

"First star," she said in a low voice. "Make a wish."

Without another comment, she swept past him.

Jack had no time to decide if he should go after her. Daniel suddenly appeared at his side.

"Tomorrow should be a perfect day for sailing," the first mate announced, pointing at the red sky.

Jack glanced at the sky and out to sea. The last rays of sun glimmered off the water like shards of ice. As he watched, the icy azure turned into the cold blue eyes of Gaspar.

The man haunted him. Jack could still feel the cold of Gaspar's pistol against his temple as though it were happening now. Splinters from the deck had dug through the fabric into his skin while he knelt before Gaspar on his ship.

"Because I am a fair man, I will give you time to pray to God before I kill you. Say your prayers aloud." Gaspar had smiled like a man telling a pleasant joke.

Jack knew he was going to die. A cold sweat of terror broke out on his brow. He felt his hands tremble with fear. He mustn't show his horror. From deep inside he conjured up all his hate for Gaspar. It flowed through him and stemmed his fright.

Gaspar's cold eyes widened with surprise. "Beg," he shouted.

Jack hated Gaspar more than any person in his life. He had felt the loathing well inside of him as he spit in his enemy's face.

The pirate froze. His face drained of color. With a curse, he raised his hand with the weapon.

Jack silently breathed a prayer that his life would end quickly.

And Gaspar had struck him, again and again, until Jack's world darkened.

"Captain, are you sick?"

Jack drew his mind back to the present and met the concerned gaze of his first mate. Jack was safe. He was on the *Goodspeed*.

"I was thinking of Gaspar. With your friend's information, we'll face the pirate tomorrow. He's very close. Very close."

Seven

In his bunk, Jack slept poorly that night. The night faded into a clear bright morning, and he found himself standing on deck awaiting Mary. He paced until he heard a whistle from one of the men. Spinning about, he spotted the lady. She walked across the deck with the grace of a queen, and on the bottom of her dress she'd sewn a gray strip of cloth. Squinting his eyes, he stared at the familiar strip of somber material but couldn't recall where he'd seen it. He did remember her words, "A lady never shows her legs."

Even with her legs hidden, men had stopped their work to watch. Jack spotted Finn hanging on the rigging. Another man stopped swabbing the deck and saluted with his mop when she passed. Everywhere, men gawked while Mary floated across the deck.

The lady nodded and smiled bashfully at her audience.

Enough. He clenched his fist. He wasn't about to allow his crew to act like spineless jellyfish. "Get to work."

Instantly, the ship hummed with activity. Satisfied, Jack strode to his cabin for some peace. Opening the door, he spied the telescope on top of a note to Beckett. He'd be damned if he'd let Beckett have her spyglass. Picking it up, he marched to his trunk and shut it inside.

Relief surged through him. After he sent her home and captured Gaspar, he'd sail for Oyster River and visit her.

She'd have to welcome him to get her spyglass. Smiling, he opened his log.

Mary wandered to the galley, where Cook demanded to know if she wanted food. Shaking her head, Mary inquired after the first mate.

"He's gone below to gather canvas for Finn. The sailmaker keeps his supplies below."

She left and wandered below deck where she found a large open area covered with swollen mounds of white canvas, reminding her of fair weather clouds. Daniel moved from behind a large pile.

"Sorry, miss, didn't hear you. Do you need me?"

"I wondered if you might have more information on Gaspar. The captain is rather busy and hasn't had time to keep me informed."

Daniel's eyes grew wide with excitement. "I met a friend in Bath. Says Gaspar's ship *LeDefenseur* has been spotted north of here."

With this information, Mary returned to the deck. She mused over the information the first mate had given her. The *Goodspeed* was sailing. Surely, Jack had ordered them to the spot where Gaspar's ship had been spied. As she wandered across the confined space, questions and doubts buzzed in her mind.

She emerged above deck where she saw everyone at work. Men swabbed the deck, climbed the ropes, and inspected the sails. Sailors were uncouth, but at least they were industrious.

She saw Mr. Finn and darted to him. "Good day. Can you tell me where Captain St. George might be?"

Carrying a bucket of water, Finn paused and blinked

at her as if the question involved deep thought. "The
captain is in his, I mean your, uh, the cabin."

"Thank you." Picking up her skirt, Mary fled down
the damp stairs. Jack must be looking for her. She burst
into the cabin.

From his desk, he looked up in surprise.

"Excuse me." She hesitated, feeling foolish for her
abrupt entrance. "I wanted to speak to you about my stay
on the *Goodspeed.*" He glanced down at the map
stretched before him.

Mary edged closer to peer over his shoulder. Briefly,
she closed her eyes and inhaled his familiar scent.

"No need to discuss it. At the end of the forenoon
watch and at the end of the first dog watch, your meals
will be brought to you. You will not leave the cabin."

At his unintelligible words, she knew two things. Captain St. George had very broad shoulders, and he hoped
to keep her confined. She should have known. All that
talk about being a member of the crew had been a lie.

"I can't spend my life in this room." Annoyed, she folded
her arms across her chest and stared at the map. A land
form caught her eye, and she recognized the Atlantic
Ocean. "Are you calculating how far we are from *LeDefenseur*?"

He covered the chart with his large hand. "What do you
know about *LeDefenseur*?"

She stepped back at the suspicion in his tone. "I overheard someone saying we were trying to find it."

"Overheard, did you? All the more reason you'll stay
confined. The less you know, the safer you'll stay."

"Don't speak in riddles, Jack. Knowledge is the key
to wisdom, and as part of your crew, I'm entitled to know
where we're headed. In fact, I'm sure I could help."

"Miss McNeal, as I've reminded you over and over, you're to follow orders, not ask about them."

"Do you think Gaspar is near?"

A speculative light grew in Jack's gaze. "He's nearer than your stars."

He gave her a sharp and assessing look. Under his stare, Mary self-consciously pulled on the cuff of her sleeve. The memory of their last embrace sprang into her mind, and her hands grew damp.

"Did you notice anything important about that snuff box?"

"What?" She tried to focus her attention on the conversation and not on the man before her.

"Different? Outstanding?"

She forced away the memory of his strong arms about her. In her mind, she saw the sun reflecting on the blue cover. The shape of the M or W formed and a connection snapped together in her mind. "It's a M or W like—" The image of the night sky with the stars glittering flew into her mind. "—like the constellation Cassiopeia!"

"The snuff box has stars on it?" His chair creaked as he straightened in it.

"It's the same configuration as the queen of Cassiopeia." At his blank expression, Mary continued. "In Greek mythology, Cassiopeia is the wife of Cepheus, king of Ethiopia."

"Wait!" Jack held up his hand. "I'd like the short version of this tale."

"I'll try. Let me see, where was I? Oh, at her death, Cassiopeia was transformed into the constellation that bears her name. It's in the shape of a W. What do you think it means?"

He sighed and rubbed his temple. "Probably nothing. You're beginning to make as much sense as Beckett."

Her hand went to her throat. "Jack, where is my telescope?"

"I put it in my trunk. You can't trust Beckett with your scope. He could trade it for another strange trinket."

"You've trusted him." She crossed to the trunk and pulled back the lid. Her scope lay in the corner, cushioned by a man's white shirt. Jack's shirt.

Gingerly, Mary picked up the instrument and cradled it in her hands. Staring at it, she remembered the day she'd received the precious gift. Her father's face had glowed with anticipation as he watched her unwrap the small present. Inside the brown wrapping, she found the small telescope. Her heart had beat furiously as she held it in the palm of her hands, turning it over and over in admiration. She heard her father's voice, *"Soon, you can use it in our new observatory."*

"You can look at the map."

"What?" she asked, suddenly brought back to the present. She glanced over at Jack, who studied her with a curious intense expression on his face. Why did her stomach go all aquiver when he looked at her like that?

Avoiding his scrutiny, she approached.

"We're here." All business, he pointed to a spot a few leagues off the Maine coast. Lightly, his finger traced an invisible line northward. "The ship seen by Daniel's friend was last seen here." He pointed to an expanse of ocean south of the Canadian border.

Wetting her lips, she bent closer. Jack was only inches from her. Her heart thudded against her chest. *Concentrate,* she warned herself. Then a thought struck her. "When I was in the cave, the mooncussers said that Gaspar had sailed north."

"I know," he answered calmly. "I questioned them after you left. It's likely those scavengers have dealt with

Gaspar or one of his crew." He bent over the map again. With his finger, St. George retraced the route. "Daniel reported the ship had been seen here. We should reach the area in only a couple of hours."

"Do you think it was a true sighting? Maybe it's a trick. Some kind of a plot by Gaspar."

"I've considered the idea. He may have realized that I'm after him and has set a trap for us." He rolled up the map with a grim expression upon his face. "Who is the hunter here?"

His words stirred an icy fear. Out on the dark seas, Gaspar stalked them, watching their every move. She forced herself not to look out the porthole. Could Jack protect them? Mary considered the man before her. His strong hands, his broad shoulders, even the manner in which he walked, all suggested a strong, confident leader. Surely he was more than a match for Gaspar. Yet another question nagged at her mind. The mooncusser had known Jack. How?

"What is it, Mary? You have a puzzled look upon your face. Are you worried that I suffer from fits of madness?"

"Of course I don't."

"You should. I have no proof of the sighting."

"I hadn't even considered that you're wrong."

"Ah, yes, you have more literary pursuits to keep you busy." His chair scraped across the planks, and he stood before her. His nearness filled her senses. "Would you shriek in horror to learn that I've never memorized the works of Shakespeare."

Disapproval tightened Mary's throat. She struggled to speak calmly. "The Bard can be quite tedious. I don't care in the least if you've never read one word."

"No?" A hint of a smile crossed his face. "You

shouldn't lie, Mary. What would the patrons of your library say?"

"I'm sorry I attempted to enter into a serious conversation with you," Mary responded matter-of-factly, hoping to disguise her irritation that he understood her so easily.

"How serious do you wish to become?" He examined her face, searching for something.

"I don't know what you mean." Mary caught a glimmer of something dangerous in his eye, and her mouth went dry. "But it's time for my duty."

"You don't have one." He stepped closer until the buttons of his coat pressed against her ribs.

Mary stood her ground despite the strangeness in the pit of her stomach. She cleared her throat, pretending not to be affected by him. "Very well, I do have a question for you. Those men in the cave knew you. How?"

He stilled, and his eyes darkened. "Have you forgotten that I sailed with Gaspar? He forced me to accompany them on their raids and made sure that my name was heard by all. Word soon spread that I had turned pirate. Once my reputation was ruined, Gaspar thought I'd have no other alternative but to join him. It was quite a coup for him, an American hero who'd become a traitor."

" 'The man doomed to sail with the blast of the gale,' " she said. When he gave her a skeptical look, she hastily added, "It's a misconception that will change when you capture Gaspar."

"I have a question for *you*." His gaze fastened on her lips.

She wished her heart would be still.

"Do you regret not staying on Beckett's ship?"

So this was why he'd looked at her in this strange manner. He thought she wanted to leave his ship. Mary slowly shook her head. "You're the man I need."

Surprise flared in his eyes. He reached out and ran a finger lightly over her cheek and down her neck. His hand skimmed lightly across her breast to the telescope. He held the spyglass in the palm of his hand.

"A beautiful treasure," he whispered.

She nodded, although she didn't understand his meaning. Her mind was too full of the tingling sensations from his touch and voice. Dimly, she knew the boat swayed beneath her feet and that above them a crew of men worked. But all of this faded from her memory. Mary felt and inhaled Jack, the center of her world. Her wish had come true. Jack was with her.

He encircled her waist with his arms and pulled her against him.

Mary closed her eyes, waiting for him to kiss her. Her pulse beat rapidly and excitement raced through her.

He did not disappoint her. His mouth closed over hers, warm and rough. She lifted herself and slipped her arms about his neck. Pressing her lips to his, she welcomed him eagerly. The kiss deepened, leaving her breathless. Mary's world spun.

She had to lock her trembling knees to keep standing. Desperately, Mary sought control over her hold on reality.

Then he pulled away.

Confused, she blinked at him.

He shook his head as if clearing it. "I need air."

Mary followed him to the door, still gathering her thoughts. She could think of only one thing to say. "But my . . . duty."

He paused and looked as though he was trying to understand her protest. "I'll . . . later." He stopped at the door and pointed at her. "Remember, you're confined to quarters."

Mary's mind sharpened at his words. She raced toward him as the door shut in her face. She stamped her foot. The oafish man. Did he think because he'd kissed her that she'd allow him to order her about?

Mary wandered to the chair. Her fingers clasped and unclasped the wooden drawer handle of the desk while she tried to determine her next step.

She closed her eyes, anger tumbling in her mind. The man had a way of destroying all her rational thinking. She would leave the cabin whenever she wished, and she'd be useful, too. Captain Jack St. George was about to learn a lesson.

Mary looked about the cabin for anything that would help her. Should she look at the map? She knew they had sailed north and out on the wide expanse of ocean where her father sailed with Gaspar.

Her hand tightened over her telescope, hoping that the latest sighting would contain a clue to Gaspar's whereabouts. But what should she do in the meantime? She couldn't sit in this cabin all day waiting for all these forenoons and prenoons. And she couldn't sit there trying to fathom the action of a brute who believed women were useless!

First, she had to rescue her father. In the meantime, she needed to be useful again. What should she do while she waited for them to encounter Gaspar? Gradually, Mary became aware that she clutched her telescope. Releasing it, an idea grew within her. She could teach about the heavens. Yes. Pulling the drawer open, Mary searched for paper. Finding none, she opened the forbidden logbook and ripped out a page. In the back of the drawer, she found writing utensils.

With elation rising within her, Mary scribbled notes for her first lesson. She'd speak to Finn about gathering the men to listen to her. Captain Jack St. George would learn she was useful. The *Goodspeed* would have the most educated crew at sea.

Night had fallen, and Jack paced about the deck of his ship. He'd deliberately left Mary alone so he could busy himself with work. Yet she constantly plagued his thoughts. He couldn't forget how she'd pressed against him. Hellfire, he could have held her forever. Nor could he ignore how his mind pitched and tossed during their kisses. In his ship, he'd fought battles and storms with a cold reason that had made him a leader. Still, he had never felt more out of control than when he experienced these overwhelming sensations from kissing Miss Mary McNeal, the little librarian. Damn. He'd keep her out of sight in her cabin.

She was a bad obsession, like too much drink. Work would take his mind off her and that meant speaking with Beckett. The man had caught up to the *Goodspeed* and had been following them all day. Jack ordered the shore boat lowered, and he quickly embarked out on the black waters. He watched the yacht grow closer in the shadowy night light. He pictured Beckett relaxing before his long dining table, tasting some fine wine or eating an exotic dessert.

Boarding the yacht, Jack made his way to Beckett's quarters. He remembered the way well. He'd found Mary there with Beckett. Grating his teeth, he banged on the door.

* * *

At the sound of the watch bells, three men ringed about Mary, waiting in the cool night air. She'd hoped to catch Jack's attention, but Daniel reported that the captain had left for Beckett's yacht.

Mary searched her mind for a starting place. "You're all sailors. You must be familiar with the constellations."

Tilting her head, she studied the dark sky. Clouds covered parts of it. The visible stars appeared to sail across the dark heavens and disappear with remarkable speed. It made her dizzy. The sensation reminded her of the kiss with Jack and threatened to block out all memory of her talk. She must concentrate. Looking at the northern sky, Mary saw the familiar W of the constellation Cassiopeia.

"Are you ready, Miss?" Daniel asked.

Mary pulled her attention back to the sailors. "Gentlemen, Hipparchus, an astronomer, added to the theory of the sun and moon's paths."

Out of the corner of her eye, Mary saw Daniel wander to the railing. Leaning his hip against it, he seemed distracted by his view of the sea.

"Can we look through the telescope now, Miss McNeal?" Mr. Finn interrupted.

"Wouldn't you like to hear more about the history of astronomy?"

"I don't mean any disrespect about your talk, but I'm a sailmaker and don't have many other interests."

Mary tried to tamp down her disappointment. "Of course, Mr. Finn." Her fingers wrapped around the scope's leather cord.

"Ship astern," called the watch.

"Look!" Daniel pointed at the vessel gliding past them.

Mary ran with the others to the side. The other craft's resemblance made it easy to recognize. It was the *Goodspeed*'s twin."

* * *

Beckett greeted Jack with the cheerfulness of a man celebrating a party. "I knew you'd come tonight."

A fear floated through Jack. *Were his actions that predictable? Surely, Gaspar couldn't predict them, or could he?*

Beckett settled into a cushioned chair. "Sorry, I don't have any more champagne. Wine?"

"I didn't come to drink," Jack said, brushing aside Beckett's offer. "We need to understand each other."

A light of interest shone in his friend's eyes. "I'm happy to discuss any topic. But let me guess, you'd like to talk about Gaspar or Mary."

"What does the librarian have to do with this?" Irritation rubbed against Jack's patience. "She's nothing to you."

"She chose to stay with you and that makes me curious. Come, Jack, don't be bitter. You know the old saying, 'A beautiful woman is worth a thousand pieces of gold.' "

"That must be an old saying from your French grandmother." Jack flung himself into a chair. "Mary stays with me until I can safely return her to Oyster River."

"How many years will it take till you can return? Two? Three?" Beckett smiled broadly.

"What's so funny about it?" Jack asked, his aggravation rising.

"You. I've often wondered what kind of woman would capture Captain Jack St. George. Who'd have thought it'd be a librarian."

"Are you drunk?" He leaned closer to smell his friend's breath.

"I've never been more sober. But let's discuss Gaspar. I've heard he has robbed a Spanish ship of a treasure, and it's rumored he will use the money to help Napoleon."

Jack raised his brows in surprise. "All the more reason to capture him quickly."

"When we find the money, we find Gaspar."

"On the other hand, he might not have any of the funds," St. George speculated. "Gaspar likes to spread stories about himself. A story that he's now wealthy would delight him. Have you any proof of this money's existence?"

"Not the kind you mean. But I have every reason to believe it is real. You'll have to trust me, Jack. We've been through hell and back in that war. What are your plans?"

Finally, he could give his terms. "First, you need to go home. There's no way you can help."

"No." Beckett lounged back in his chair. "I'm a little bored. I thought I'd join you for a while. Besides, if you capture Gaspar, I can return the stolen money, and we'll both look like heroes."

"Listen, Beckett, you're not inconspicuous. Second, this ship isn't armed."

"If it was, the French would have put me in irons."

"Third, with you along, I'm now responsible for two crews, or whatever you call these men in white. It's too dangerous."

"This is interesting," Beckett said. "Am I supposed to sit at home? Be fair. What am I expected to do while you are sailing around searching for the pirate and enjoying Miss McNeal?"

"My search for Gaspar is personal, and my men know the dangers. Yours do not. I'll not risk their lives, and Miss McNeal only wants to find her father."

"Say you find your enemy. How do you intend to get

the money he's raised? Gaspar won't hand over a fortune to you, and we don't want it to help Napoleon."

"I never reveal my maneuvers, Beckett. Once I have him, I'll send you a message. You can be the first to interrogate him."

Beckett shook his head. "Sorry, I can't accept those terms, and you need finances to continue. I can provide them. I know you often take on cargo to make money, but we'll have no time for stops. We have to prevent Gaspar from raising another army for Napoleon." He leaned back with a smile. "If my ship is too noticeable, I'll have it painted. I wonder what color is Mary's favorite."

Jack gritted his teeth. "Even painted, you could hardly be inconspicuous. Your ship is too odd."

"And I can arm it." Excitement glowed in Beckett's eyes.

"Who'll use these weapons? Not your white-bellied men."

"You mean my crew? Give me some of your men. We'll exchange."

"Never!" Jack shot up from his chair. "Let me make this easy for you. No librarian. No exchange. No—"

The ship lurched wildly. Furniture toppled. Glasses flew through the air and shattered. Jack stumbled and tried to grab the table to right himself. The dining table disappeared from his grasp.

Eight

A heavy weight pressed on Jack's chest. It was the dining table. Beckett's men seemed to take hours to move it. On the top deck, the scent of fear floated more steadily than the yacht wobbling beneath their feet. Obviously, it was every man for himself. And Beckett thought this crew could capture Gaspar. Jack shook his head over the notion and looked out to sea for clues to their situation.

Pieces of colored wood from the yacht floated around them.

"My God!" Beckett gasped. "Your ship hit us."

"What?" Panic welled inside of Jack. He gripped the rail and searched the waters. What had happened to Mary and his crew? The librarian couldn't even swim. He squinted into the night.

Through the darkness, he made out his ship and the shore boats heading toward them. He loosened his hold. "It's not my ship, and here comes a rescue mission."

"Thank God," Beckett said.

Jack peered further into the blackness. Beyond the *Goodspeed*, he saw another ship. "Beckett, look closer. We've another vessel out there. I'd guess that ship hit us. Mine is still anchored."

Beckett followed his gaze to the offending ship. "What kind of a sailor steers into another vessel? And you think I'm a bad captain."

"Do you notice anything strange about it?" Jack asked.

Beckett strode closer to the rail. "Besides the fact that it's the size of your ship?"

"Look again." In the darkness, no lights or cries could be detected from the other craft. "That ship rammed us, yet no one aboard seems concerned. In fact, do you hear or see anything?"

Beckett shook his head.

While they stared out at sea, a woman's voice rose in song and drifted to them.

"What's that?" Beckett asked.

"It's Mary," Jack said. "She must be conducting our funeral."

Daniel climbed over the side and was followed by Finn and other crew members.

Jack shouted to Daniel to round up Beckett's men and take them to the shore boats. Jack turned back to the rail and looked across at his ship. Despite the fact that the woman could be an annoyance, tonight he needed her faith that everything would end happily ever after.

The time dragged into hours while they prepared to leave. Finally everyone had left except Beckett and Jack. They climbed into the small rescue craft. Across the dark waters, Mary's sweet voice continued to rise, and it temporarily filled Jack with a sense of hope.

Stepping over the *Goodspeed*'s side, Jack met Mary. "Glad you've learned how to stay put, Miss McNeal. What was that song you sang?"

"It's a hymn to lift one's spirits. I learned it at church."

"Don't tell me, you were the choir director." Wearily, he closed his eyes for a second.

"I've been waiting forever," Mary confided. "Are you hurt?"

His fatigue vanished at her words. He looked down at

her and saw that her chestnut hair was falling out of the tidy knot on her head, and her eyes glistened with emotion. Fear? Was that fear for him? A sudden need to touch her filled him. He stepped closer.

"Mary!" Beckett cried, joining them. "What a pleasure to be greeted by a beautiful woman on such a terrible night."

"What happened to the *Helen of Troy*?" Mary asked anxiously.

"The engines won't start. The flywheel won't fly, or whatever it does. Jack, I hope you've lots of room for us here. Mary, I shall at last have the pleasure of your company."

A feeling close to horror gripped Jack. He pictured the future in his mind. Beckett fawning over Mary, telling her his ridiculous war stories with Beckett as the hero. And on Jack's own ship!

"Thank you, Thomas." Mary turned to Jack. "Are you positive you're uninjured?"

Beckett groaned, gaining Mary's attention. "It's terrible. My ship, I mean, not my shoulder." Beckett massaged the sore area. "I twisted my arm rescuing Jack."

"You rescued Jack? Tonight? How brave! We must get you someplace to rest." Mary gently grasped his elbow.

"It was nothing," Beckett answered with mock humility.

"I agree. He watched his crew lift a table. He doesn't need any relaxation." Jack seized his friend's wrist and pulled him from the librarian's grasp. "I will assist *Thomas*. Where's Daniel?"

"Sorry, Mary," Beckett said with a shake of his head. "Despite my injuries, I must attend my crew."

"Be careful," Mary said.

"To quote a poet, 'Sweet Lady! Speak those words again.' "

"Byron," Mary breathed.

"Nothing wrong with him that a good knock on the head wouldn't fix," Jack mumbled. "Here comes Finn. He'll take you to your cabin."

"Ah, Mary, I must leave. Duty calls and all that."

"Time to do your duty toward your crew." Jack grabbed his friend's arm and propelled Beckett toward the sailmaker. With a shake of his head, Jack attempted to tamp down on his annoyance.

"Jack," Mary trailed after him.

"Can't talk now," he grumbled. "I'm looking for Daniel to learn where he's placing Beckett's men. Go back to your cabin. When we're settled, I'll come and tell you everything." He paused and bent closer. "In private."

She bit her lip and reddened at his last statement.

He chuckled over her reaction. The prospect of meeting Mary without Beckett taunted and delighted him.

However, it took two hours to settle his friend and his crew. Afterward, Jack stood by the rail, enjoying the momentary quiet. He stared across the turbid night waters at the *Helen of Troy*. Then he glanced a few yards away to the ghost ship floating, taunting them.

Jack imagined the deserted ship's fate. How many innocent lives had Gaspar destroyed? Had the pirate taken the crew with him? Which fate, death or life on Gaspar's ship, was worse?

Unwanted images from his own capture rose into his memory and held it captive. *He saw the steam rise from the ship's deck as the band of men closed around him. Like starving, wild animals, they had circled and prepared for the kill. Suddenly, a blond-haired man broke through the crowd. His sharp gaze fell upon Jack like a guillotine on a condemned man. He bowed. His voice had carried the cold edge of irony.*

"I welcome the famous Captain St. George to my ship, LeDefenseur."

Quickly, Jack shoved away the painful remembrance. From behind came the sounds of light footsteps and a whiff of fresh soap. Mary.

She joined him at the rail. "I wondered how much longer you'd be." Glancing at the sea, she asked, "Could ghosts lurk on board?"

"The ship appears abandoned. I'll know when I search it."

"Why would anyone leave such a vessel?"

"They may not have done so willingly."

"If the ship was attacked by Gaspar, my father might have been on it. I want to go with you."

"No!"

Determination filled her eyes. "I wish you'd remember I'm not helpless, and I must search for any clue related to my father."

"No one leaves the *Goodspeed* without my orders. That includes you. I'll lock you in your cabin if necessary." His hand thudded on the railing in emphasis. "Do you understand?"

"For the moment." Her lips tightened with resolve. "But if my father has been on that ship, I want to know."

His hand relaxed. He doubted that Gaspar would leave evidence of anyone's identity, unless he wanted to send a message. And Jack had no intention of delivering it. "I agree."

A small amount of tension left her. "I haven't inspected your injury." She spoke in a soft, conciliatory voice. Gently, she laid her hand over his.

Without warning, his body throbbed with desire. He

wanted her. And he needed her to chase away the haunting memories.

"What is it?" she asked softly.

He hesitated. "I don't want another man to suffer on the *LeDefenseur*, Gaspar's ship, like I did."

Mary shuddered at imagined horrors. "What did he do to you? Starve you? Beat you? Please tell me."

Jack reached out and tucked one of her stray strands of hair behind her ear.

"Will you tell me?"

"You have to understand that Gaspar is dangerous."

"I know he is."

He wanted to laugh at her naivete. "Do you know why men call Gaspar the devil?"

"Because of his actions?"

He leaned closer, his gaze intense upon her face. "He is Beelzebub. He doesn't care about a man's body. He wants his soul. He tortures each man until he is ready to trade it for anything." He stared into her puzzled face. *"Anything."*

Jack saw the glimmer of shock as she comprehended his words. No doubt she was thinking of her father. It was too late for her parent, but not for her. He reached out and covered her hand, trying to wipe away her fear. "I swear Gaspar will never touch you."

Biting her lip, she nodded.

"It's nearly midnight. We should head for our cabins. I'll walk you to yours." He held out his arm, attempting to lighten the moment.

Her face had grown white, and her eyes glimmered with fear as she linked her arm through his. He had scared her, but she needed to stop throwing caution to the wind. Gaspar was deadly.

He led her below. She was strangely silent. Once inside, she whirled upon him. "You must tell me more about Gaspar."

He sighed. "I thought you were too quiet."

She took a step toward him. Her green eyes were wide with curiosity and concern. The last emotion sent surprise shooting through him.

"Sit." He waved to the desk chair and she sank into it.

Jack began to pace. "It happened two years ago. I'd begun a trading business after the war. We were sailing off the coast of Carolina when we came across a ship moored out at sea. A small boat with a few men from the ship approached and asked for supplies. They reported that they'd been becalmed for days and many had fallen ill.

"I decided to deliver the supplies and determine what other steps I could take. When I boarded the other vessel, I found a couple of people on deck, at least for the first few seconds. Then I found myself surrounded by Gaspar and his men." Jack shrugged, trying to control the anger that boiled beneath his calm words. "You know what happened to me then. I was taken prisoner."

"How did you get away?"

"During a raid, I jumped overboard. I swam to the ship under attack. They took me aboard only to clap me in irons, thinking I'd fallen over the side. They didn't believe I'd been Gaspar's prisoner."

"I don't understand why they doubted you. You're a war hero."

He gave a short, sarcastic laugh. "People have short memories."

"But you fought for—"

He reached her in two strides and swept her into his arms. She gave a cry of surprise.

"No more about Gaspar." He smiled as astonishment glimmered in her eyes. "I have trouble remembering, too. I want to recall what it's like to kiss you."

He felt her body tense in his arms, but he didn't give her time to argue. He captured her mouth before she could utter another sound. Tightening his grip, Jack plunged his tongue into her mouth. The fire of lust flamed and spread, chasing away the chill of pain-laden memories. God, he needed her.

Blindly, he carried her to his bunk and settled her beneath him. The mattress sagged under them. Stray strands of her chestnut hair fanned out on the gray blanket, and the hint of lilac teased him.

He raised his head and met her gaze. Bewilderment and desire reflected in her eyes. The last emotion fed his hunger.

"I don't have any pretty words, Mary, but I'll speak the truth. I want you. Now. Here in my bed."

"I don't think—"

He laid a finger across her moist lips. "Don't think or talk."

He didn't give her a chance to answer. He kissed her with all the need that had been penned inside of him. His hand traveled to her legs, those shapely limbs that had driven him to distraction in the shore boat.

She trembled as his hand caressed her calf. He felt her hand creep around his shoulder, and his lust deepened.

Her throat. He wanted to kiss that next. Slowly, he trailed a path from her mouth down her neck. The softness of her skin surprised him. He'd forgotten how a woman felt and tasted. But he sampled her now. The delicateness of her skin fed his pulsating need.

A soft moan came from her throat. It sounded almost like a name. What had she said? Raising his head, he paused to look at her. Her eyes were closed, but what was in her mind? A sudden fear gripped him. Did she dream she was once again with that banker, or Beckett?

Hell, he didn't care. He took her mouth with a fierce determination. She jolted with surprise.

His fear attacked and nibbled at his desire. With a sigh of exasperation, he pulled away again. Hellfire, he didn't want one of her discussions. He tightened his grip on her. She gave a small cry.

It was no use. "Mary."

Slowly, her eyelids fluttered open. She looked at him like a woman waking from a deep sleep.

"What's my name?"

"What?" Her voice was low and throaty.

He sighed in exasperation. "Say my name."

A slight smile curled her lips. "Captain."

A loud banging sounded on the door. "Captain," Daniel shouted through the wooden barrier. "The men are arguing. We need you."

"Get Beckett." Jack shouted.

"He said to fetch you."

Jack closed his eyes and prayed for another solution. He kissed Mary quickly and rose with the speed of an old man. "I'll come back after I murder Beckett. It's likely nothing."

"I'm afraid it's a mutiny," the first mate shouted.

Nine

Mary touched her tingling cheek and watched as Jack disappeared. She sat up and stared at the door. What had happened? She felt her hair with a trembling hand. Her top knot had completely disappeared. Her skirt and petticoat were tangled around her thighs. With a cry of distress, she yanked them downward. Good heavens, she and Jack had acted like wild, uncivilized creatures. *Think*. There must be a logical explanation for her behavior. The overwhelming sensations that had taken possession of her were still fresh and vibrating within her, clamoring for more. Heaven save her.

She rose and glanced at the rumpled gray blanket. Heat rushed to her cheeks as she smoothed it. What would she do when he came back?

Her mind whirled, but it always ended with Jack kissing and touching her. Goodness, she must get control. She must distract him. *How?* Clasping and unclasping her hands, she hit upon an idea: focus on the task of saving her father.

With Daniel, Jack sprinted below to the men's quarters. Beckett met him there. In the low-ceilinged cabin, Jack stared at the scene before him. Before the hammocks, a group of three men lay twisted in a heap. In the remaining narrow space, several crew members sparred. Punches thudded against bodies, followed by cries of pain and rage. The smell of blood and sweat filled the closed area.

A man stumbled into Jack. "Captain!" His hands shook as he saluted.

"Stand aside," Jack ordered. He turned to Beckett with raised brow. "Ready to stop the fight?"

Beckett placed two fingers in his mouth and gave a high-pitched whistle. Only two white-dressed men paused in their fighting. Their gazes widened in recognition, and they slunk to the side.

Jack yelled above the din. "Where's my first mate? Daniel!"

The young man wove through the fighters.

Jack pointed to Beckett's crew members edging toward the door. "Take these two men and fill the buckets with water."

The first mate and the other men scurried away. It took them only minutes to return. Each carried two pails.

"Let me," Beckett said, relieving Daniel of his pails. "Ready."

"Now!" Jack shouted.

Beckett and his two men tossed the sea water in perfect unison. The boxers froze in shock as the chilly Atlantic water hit them. The second buckets emptied into their shocked faces. Shaking their heads, the fighters' gazes drifted to Beckett and Jack.

Beckett shook his head. "Most of these men are yours. My men deserve medals or nursing from Mary."

"Miss McNeal is not your personal maid." Jack turned to his men. "Someone had better have a good excuse for this."

Men lying on the floor scrambled to their feet and lined up beside their fellow combatants.

Daniel stepped forward. "It was the dice, Captain. The men wanted a friendly game, but there was a lot of fighting."

"It seems you men have the rules of the game confused," Jack said with a thin grip on his temper. "You're supposed to throw the die, not each other. You're a disgrace to this ship."

Men in bloodstained clothes who'd been lounging against the wall snapped ramrod straight.

"Misconduct is a serious crime, and those involved will be severely reprimanded. Daniel! I leave the punishment in your hands. Be sure it is appropriate. Tonight we'll practice your drills since you men have so much energy. You won't have to worry about sharing your hammocks since you won't be in them. Be on deck in five seconds." Jack whirled on his heel and left.

Mary spent a restless night, anticipating Jack's return. She rose at dawn to go on deck. Pulling her telescope from around her neck, she placed it to her eye and made out the shape of the ghost ship. It floated silently on the water. She scanned the vessel, but she couldn't discern any figures. Replacing her scope about her neck, she prayed the sinister ship held no threat to her father or Jack.

A gentle breeze stirred her hair. Mary lifted her face to the remaining morning star overhead. It winked at her as though enjoying a strange joke. Was Gaspar sitting nearby, laughing at her, too? An icy fear whispered that her wish to rescue her father would never come true. Blinking back tears of frustration, Mary spied Jack. For a moment, nervousness paralyzed her. Then she decided to speak first.

"Do you have your pistol?" Mary hoped she sounded casual.

Surprise flickered through his gaze before he spoke. "Are you suggesting that I can shoot spirits, Miss McNeal? You've not read enough ghost stories. A priest is what I need."

"Don't jest," she said. "It could be dangerous on that ship. You should take care of yourself."

"I'm pleased over your concern." He lowered his voice. "I'm sorry I couldn't return last night. I had to tend to the crew."

"Oh, I didn't notice. I fell asleep." She shrugged and turned to the ghost ship before he could read the truth in her face. In the light of day, her actions of the night before embarrassed her more.

"I'm glad you're rested. You'll need your strength for tonight."

She whirled about to determine the meaning of his words, but he was gazing out at the ship.

"Do you believe in superstitions?" he asked.

At least she could pretend to have a normal conversation. "I don't believe in ghosts, but when you go into an unknown situation, you should be well-armed."

"I won't ask where you read that. No one alive is on that ship, Mary. Besides, I'll be well-armed."

"How can you know who is on board?"

Jack looked down into her face, and she tried to hide the unease that ran through her. Had last night meant anything to him?

"Why do you think no one is on the ship?" she demanded, avoiding her true thoughts.

"An entire crew doesn't disappear without a reason, and life means little to Gaspar. He takes or destroys anything or anyone he wants. That's what has made him such a dangerous foe. He follows no rules or code of honor." Jack reached out and took her hand.

She couldn't keep it from trembling. "You're really talking about my father, aren't you?" She tried to pull her hand away.

He held tight. "I'm speaking of myself. Gaspar destroyed my reputation. I want to right that wrong. I want the freedom to look at my fellow countrymen without them thinking I'm a traitor, and this ship might hold a clue of where Gaspar has gone."

"I hope there's evidence on that vessel." She stared at it as if it could speak. "I won't give up until I bring my father home."

Mary looked up at him. "Promise you'll take care of yourself."

"Why Mary," he said as he released her. "Are you ordering your captain?"

"I'm only offering a caution."

"Thank you. I don't know how I've succeeded without you." He started to turn and stopped. "I remembered a custom you might find interesting." He leaned closer. "Before boarding a strange ship, a captain receives a kiss for luck. It's an old seaman's charm."

Mary flushed. "I don't recall any books with such a tale."

"It's been passed down by word of mouth by elderly seamen."

"Then you need an old seaman to kiss."

"Only one of us has to be that," he said, sliding his arm around the small of her back. "And I qualify."

His mouth brushed her lips before she could speak another protest. A tingle rippled throughout her body and triggered the memory of how irresistible his kisses could be.

He looked down into her face. "Be ready when I return."

With emotions churning inside of her, Mary watched him leave.

Jack hummed as he made his way to his cabin. Opening the door, he saw Beckett sitting at his desk. The fragments of the snuff box were spread on the top of it. Jack recognized the note in Beckett's hand as the one Mary had written, explaining the disaster with the box. Obviously, Beckett had rummaged through Jack's belongings. Didn't anyone respect his privacy? He slammed the door.

Beckett lowered the letter. "Jack, we need to discuss the arrangements for my ship."

"We've decided. We tow her back to Bath for repairs."

"What about our search?" Beckett asked, folding Mary's note and slipping it into his pocket.

Jack moved closer. "Let's discuss the stolen gold. Specifically, let's discuss your latest story."

"You doubt me? You do have a suspicious mind. I think Mary commented on it also."

"I'm not discussing Miss McNeal." Jack paced to his trunk and back. "Now, you buy a snuff box that's very valuable."

"I didn't buy it. A general on St. Helena gave it to me."

"This general gave you a valuable box. Why don't I believe it?"

Beckett shrugged. "The truth is I've no idea if the snuff box is worth anything." He jabbed a finger at a broken piece.

Jack folded his arms across his chest. "The French checked your ships for arms and left. But why would they care about Miss McNeal? Did they think a woman single-handedly carried arms?"

"Maybe they thought she'd provide information about me. She had been on my yacht, and women often are more easily persuaded. Still, she may not be safe," Beckett pointed out. "Leave her in Bath with me. Then, I'll escort her home."

"The librarian stays with me. I'll protect her."

Beckett stared at Jack for several moments, seeming to assess the situation. "What about the money? We need to arrange to meet."

"Don't tell me you want me to send a snuff box as some type of code," Jack asked with a trace of amusement.

Beckett picked up a piece. "Do you agree it was a signal?"

"It was safer than writing a letter. Who knows? I'll send you word in plain English when I discover Gaspar's whereabouts. But I need your financing now." He held out his hand. "Agreed?"

For a second, Beckett hesitated. Then he grasped his friend's palm. "Agreed. You'll have your money before you leave Bath."

Jack nodded in satisfaction. "I'm inspecting the *Goodspeed*'s twin. Care to come along, or are you entertaining a French fleet?"

Beckett leapt to his feet. "Lead on, Captain."

Jack unlocked the bottom of the cabinet and removed two muskets. "Take one," he said. Beckett complied and, armed, they headed up top.

Up on the deck, Mary appeared deep in conversation with Finn and Daniel. Spotting Jack, she attempted a smile. Their gazes locked, and a rush of blood hummed through Jack's body.

Daniel stepped forward. "Ready to go aboard, Captain."

Tearing his gaze from Mary, he refocused his thoughts. "Good. Ready to expel some ghosts?" He handed him a weapon.

"I'd like to come, Captain," Finn offered.

Jack nodded and handed him his musket and removed his pistol from inside his coat. "For the spirits." He looked at Mary.

"I wish I could go," she said in a low voice.

"I shall memorize every detail for you," Beckett promised.

Jack ignored Beckett's comment and left to direct his helmsman to sail next to the ghost ship. Once beside the other ship, the men secured the two vessels together with grappling hooks.

While the crew worked, Mary ran to the rail. A crowd of Beckett's men gathered beside her.

"Miss McNeal!" St. George yelled. "Your duty today is to keep watch while I'm on the ship."

"Delighted." She saluted. "You'll not regret assigning me."

Jack caught sight of Beckett's laughing face. "She'll do her job," he grumbled. Drawing his pistol, he signaled his men to follow.

They climbed over the side of the silent ship. Slowly, they took in the emptiness of the deserted deck. The sound of their footsteps blended with the creaking of the ship.

Jack led them toward the wheel and inspected the area. His gaze caught sight of tracks of brown. Dried blood? He inspected it. The sticky mixture clung to his fingers. Bringing it closer, he recognized the texture and grimaced. "It's the drink, switchel."

Without speaking, they followed the trail where it ended at the door leading below. As they entered the passage, Jack heard the sounds of a creature scurrying.

Daniel's finger edged to the trigger.

"Easy, lad," Jack cautioned. "We don't want to shoot each other. It's probably only the rats."

"Should we split up?" Finn asked.

"No. We search as one until we know it's safe."

Together, the men moved through the empty ship's chambers. The vessel was an empty shell. Only one of the crew's vacant hammocks confirmed that someone had once been aboard.

At last, they arrived at the captain's cabin. It was empty except for the furniture. A sweet fragrance filled the cabin.

"What shall we do with this ship?" Beckett asked. "She's worth some money, and we can't let her sail about into others."

"Drop the anchor and report her whereabouts in Bath," Jack said.

"Finn and I'll tend to it, Captain." The two men left.

Jack wandered to the bunk and placed a hand on the empty bed, imagining the man who'd slept there, a man like himself. He scanned the cabin. The chair was pushed away from the small table as though someone had just excused himself. A pack of playing cards had tumbled upon the floor.

"You can feel him, can't you?" Beckett whispered. "It's as if he stepped out for a moment and will return at any second. I think I do believe in ghosts. Let's leave."

Jack turned on his heel and spotted a small white paper in the corner. "Hold on, Beckett."

Jack scooped up the paper. He sniffed the distinctive

sweet tobacco. "I doubt this belonged to the captain of this ship."

"How do you know?"

"I recognize the fragrance. It was Gaspar's favorite."

Ten

"Our pirate's?" Beckett asked.

"It explains the sweet scent in the cabin." Jack glanced about the room again. Every object took on a sinister countenance. Had the man been sitting in the chair when Gaspar surprised him? Had his last thoughts been of his home and wife?

Jack's hatred for his nemesis burned in his throat, fanned by his imagination of the unknown man's final moments on his ship. These people had done nothing to deserve this fate. Their only mistake had been to sail in a ship similar to the *Goodspeed*. It was a mistake which cost them their lives or freedom.

"Let's leave," Beckett said in an awed voice.

From outside the cabin door came the creep of footsteps.

"He's here," Beckett whispered. His face paled.

Jack put his finger to his lips and pointed for Beckett to stand behind the door. Beckett slid beside it, tense and ready to spring. With pistol poised, Jack stepped near the door. He flung it open. Mary McNeal's shocked face greeted them.

"Miss McNeal, explain your presence," Jack ordered, pulling her inside the cabin.

"I wanted to see if I could find anything of my father's, like his shirt or coat. You wouldn't recognize it."

"Jack, could we hold this interrogation on deck?" Beckett said. "I'd feel more comfortable." Beckett's gaze flickered uneasily around the cabin.

"Good idea. You go first, Miss McNeal." Jack gestured for her to lead the way. "I'll walk behind where I can see you."

They left the cabin and silently made their way up top. Jack breathed deeply of the fresh salt air, attempting to cleanse his mind of Gaspar's lingering presence. Then he faced Mary.

"Do you know what happens to men who leave their posts?"

"They have to eat all of Cook's meals?" she asked hopefully.

"They are confined to their quarters. I order you to return to yours now."

Mary tilted up her chin. "I think I deserve a fair trial, and you're acting like a bully." She picked up her skirt to leave and paused. "Did you find anything?"

"Later, Miss McNeal."

To his surprise, she marched away.

Beckett strode in front of Jack, blocking his view of the departing librarian. "Let her come with me. She can't be safe sailing around with you, and you've seen what Gaspar has done to this ship. Why, you've lived this. If he catches you again, he'll treat you worse since you're his escaped prisoner."

Jack ran his fingers through his hair, irritated with his friend's concern for Mary. "Mary McNeal is quite aware of the risks. We've spoken of them many times."

"Talking and understanding are two different realities. Explain to her what has happened to the people on this ship. She'll leave."

"Mary can't be persuaded that easily. But because I'm

a fair man, I'll speak with her again. Where are Daniel and Finn?"

"I'll wait for them," Beckett offered.

Satisfied that he could do little else on the empty transport, Jack headed to the *Goodspeed*. He barely had one foot on his ship when Mary joined him.

"Did you find anything?" she asked.

"I thought you left too easily," he said with resignation.

"Will we give them a memorial service?" Worry glittered in her green eyes.

He shrugged. "I don't know where they've gone. The chances are good that they've been forced to join Gaspar." He saw Beckett, Finn, and Daniel approaching.

"We found a barrel of switchel, Captain," Daniel reported, climbing over the side.

"Switchel?" Mary asked.

"A drink made with molasses, ginger, and rum," Jack explained. "During the war our enemies liked to give it to us as an insult. Gaspar must have offered everyone a drink in celebration of their capture." A chill spread through him at the image of the ghost ship's crew slumped in defeat upon the deck, waiting for their final draft.

Jack blocked the picture from his thoughts. He couldn't think about them. He had the responsibility of his own ship to consider. "Men, you're dismissed. Beckett, your crew needs looking after. Miss McNeal, follow me."

Beckett gave the librarian a thoughtful look and left them. Mary hurried after Jack. "Captain, you saw something that had to do with my father, didn't you?"

"I want to speak to you in my cabin," he answered, never slowing his steps. "Although a reminder about following orders will probably be a waste of time, considering your past record of obedience."

"What about my father?" she asked, running after him.

"Does Thomas know, too? Is that why you sent him away?"

Does she have to have Thomas *present?* Stopping, he cleared his throat in annoyance. "I want to speak in private."

Frown lines crossed her forehead, and then her face reddened.

From her embarrassment, he guessed that she was remembering their evening together. For the first time that morning, he wanted to laugh. "Come along, Mary."

Reaching the cabin, she stood in the middle of the room clasping and unclasping her hands. "Was it painful?"

Jack unlocked his cabinet. "What?"

"Investigating the ship."

His grip tightened around the whiskey bottle. "Sit."

She balanced on the edge of the bunk, and he saw how the foolish gray strip on the bottom of her dress hid the front of her legs. Shapely legs, he remembered. He could barely wait to touch her again. He took a swig from the bottle and held it out to her. "Care for a drink?"

"I'd rather you gave me the bad news. Delaying only makes it worse." She wrinkled her nose in disapproval. "Besides, members of your crew don't drink."

"Remind me later." He took another gulp. "You already know the worst. Every member of that crew has disappeared. If they're alive, they'll sail with Gaspar and die as outcasts."

"And it brings back memories for you," she said softly.

"It brings me back to why I must capture Gaspar. The man ruined not only my life, but my parents'. You can't imagine how my being branded a traitor has destroyed their lives."

"I'm sorry. I never thought about the repercussions."

"It also brings me back to you. I've warned you before. The *Goodspeed* could end up like the ghost ship. It won't matter that you're a woman. Your fate will be the same or"—he took another drink—"worse."

She tightened her hands. "You want me to accept your conviction that my father has died, and go home."

"This is your last chance." He forced the next words through his tight throat. "You can leave with Beckett."

Her back stiffened at his suggestion. "No, thank you."

Jack rested the bottle on the table, his conscience cleared. Of course with Mary, he hadn't expected anything different, but the eerie scene on the *Goodspeed*'s twin had prompted him to give her a last chance to leave. He topped the bottle of whiskey with the cork, his insides still cold. The drink had done nothing to warm him.

He glanced at Mary McNeal, sitting primly on his bed. He remembered the heat they'd shared last night and knew he had to have her. Tossing away logic and caution, he strode to her. "That's settled."

"You're not going to argue with me?" She stood. Surprise flickered across her face.

Jack's hand encircled the curve of her waist and drew her to him. Already, a warming shiver traveled up his arm.

The color in Mary's cheeks deepened, but she didn't resist when he drew her closer. "Captain, uh, shouldn't we continue our discussion?"

"Indeed, I need to discuss why the ship tosses beneath my feet when I kiss you."

She quivered in his arms and tilted her head back to meet his gaze. Surprise glimmered in her eyes. "I didn't know you felt it too." Her voice was low and unsteady.

He smiled. "I think we need to have one of those experiments."

She drew a deep breath. "I'm not certain I can help."

"You can, but I'll need your full cooperation." Before she could answer, he covered her mouth. Instantly the icy chill left his lips, and he wanted more. He seared a path down her neck and across her shoulders, spreading the flame. He could hear her heart beat. His own pounded in his ears.

Her arms stole about his neck. Encouraged, he captured her mouth again. Shyly, her tongue met his. His fingers delved into the silky softness of her hair. He sought her top knot and released the confines. Strands tumbled down her back. She trembled in his arms. He paused to whisper to her. "Are we still standing?"

"I . . . I think we are." Confusion glittered in her gaze.

She started to pull away, and he tightened his grip. "We must know for certain."

He began his assault again. She pressed against him. His hand curved around her breast. He felt her surprised intake of breath as he stroked his hand over her. The lust seared through his body.

"Mary." He could think of nothing else. She consumed him. He wanted her. He wanted her to want him and be ready for him.

She tightened her grip about him, and he knew she felt the same. He tugged at the sash that held her dress. It fell free, leaving her gown loose for the taking. For a second, his hands roamed over the curves of her body. Then he swept her into his arms.

Mary could barely think. The bunk sagged as they lay upon it. He pinned her to the mattress, yet he felt weightless. She didn't feel the toss of the ship, only the climbing of the sensations within her.

His hands stroked her everywhere, especially places where she had never been touched. A small part of her cried with indignation. A decent lady never would allow a man such liberties. But the voice of reason shrank and fell silent with his kisses and caresses. Abandoning herself to instinct, she clung to him and kissed him with a fever she'd never known.

"Jack," she murmured.

"You know me?" His voice was thick and husky.

Confused by his question, she met his gaze and couldn't remember why she'd said anything. He drew his mouth down to her own. His hands roved over her form. His shirt slipped upward. Timidly, she touched his flesh. It was hot and rough.

She felt him nudge her thighs apart and touched her where no one had dared. She gasped. He seemed to rise above her, and then he was inside of her.

An uncomfortable fullness filled her. She tried to move but he held her fast. He whispered words she didn't understand. They were low and comforting. She stilled.

Gradually, he began a rhythm that she tried to follow. The tightness eased and waves of pleasure grew and grew. Her breath came in short gasps. Her heart seemed to pound faster than she could ever remember. A floating sensation built inside of her. Then he cried out and lay still.

Gradually she became aware of his weight upon her. As though he read her mind, he rolled to the side of her.

"I don't think I can move any further." He opened one eye and peered at her. "How are you feeling?"

Embarrassment streaked through her. The skirt of her gown was wound around her waist. She tried nonchalantly to pull at her dress, and she cleared her throat nervously. "Fine."

He possessively threw an arm over her and closed his eyes. They lay together for an eternity. Mary was torn between the desire to speak and the realization that, for once, she didn't know how to talk about what had happened between them. She lay alert, listening to his even breathing, remembering how she'd felt moments ago.

As the shadows began to creep into the cabin, Jack roused. He tightened his arm about the librarian, feeling a strange stirring about his chest. What was this sensation? Why did he feel different? Mary was beautiful. And he'd tried to make it perfect for her and make her want him as much as he wanted him. He'd hoped to take his time, but, his conscience reminded her, he'd gotten a little carried away. He raked a hand through his hair.

She wouldn't expect him to spout off words of love, would she? Fear rose up to spear him. No. It must seem unusual because Mary was so unusual. She was smart. She understood they didn't fit into one another's world. The realization calmed him, yet the nagging in the back of his mind wouldn't stop. He had to get a breath of fresh sea air.

He righted his clothes and threw the gray blanket over her.

"Rest," he ordered before leaving her.

Mary listened to his retreating footsteps. She rose and hugged her arms around herself, trying to stop the rush of excitement and the bewilderment that she felt. She touched her lips and remembered the dizzy, floating sensation, but then it had ended. Quickly.

Confused, her conscience asked what she she done.

She'd allowed Jack to ravish her for a moment of pleasure. She sat up. Guilt threatened to swallow her happiness and replace it with remorse.

She needed something reassuring. If only she had a book. Her fingers itched to feel the comfort of parchment. She always found the answer to everything in her tomes.

She ran her fingers through her tangled hair. What would happen now? They'd rescue her father and . . . then? Would Jack vow undying love to her? She couldn't even imagine the man uttering the word.

Doubt ate at her. Absently, she smoothed her clothes and glanced about the empty cabin. She had to be realistic. She'd always prided herself on her common sense. Jack would sail away from her without a backward glance. Now what would she do?

Fear streaked through her. She couldn't stay in the cabin all day thinking of Jack. No, in a few days, they'd have her father and be headed home. She tried to hold onto the idea of seeing her father.

But Jack's face flashed through her mind. A pain stabbed her. She must keep busy and forget him. Searching for ideas, the names of authors and titles ran through her mind. None of them offered a solution or comfort. A terrible emptiness seized her.

The rap upon the door interrupted her worries. Opening it, she found the first mate. He shyly smiled at her.

"The captain's not here," she said, trying to hide her feelings of distress.

"I came to speak with you, Miss." He stepped inside and immediately held up his elbow, displaying a long slit in the gray-white arm sleeve.

"I ripped it hauling the anchor. I don't do a very good job with sewing. Can you mend it?"

Mary peered closely at the tear. "Of course I can. I'll

need a needle and some thread. Finn will let me borrow everything. Can you leave the shirt?"

He licked his lips nervously. "I haven't another. I'll take this off down below and send it up."

Daniel began to walk backwards to the door. "Thanks, Miss. I appreciate it." He stumbled and recovered his balance. "I know you're busy." He opened the door and tripped through the opening. Mary saw him right himself before he disappeared from view.

At least she'd found something to occupy her time. She sighed. Perhaps she could sew for all the crew. She could make them matching caps. Wasn't that what sailors usually wore?

She'd not have time to think of Jack, or feel the ache in her heart. The idea gave her a small measure of peace. She knew one thing for certain. She and Jack must never be together like last night.

On deck, Jack saw that Daniel was shirtless under an old brown coat. The unusually warm spring day didn't warrant such clothing. The lad certainly had become modest. Had Mary's presence brought about his first mate's self-consciousness. What was she doing now?

Jack hadn't seen her since their time together in the cabin. He had stayed away from her for a few hours, but images from their lovemaking had flashed repeatedly through his mind. Once again, he felt the quiver of her body, the soft curves of her breast. Hell, he wanted the woman now.

Yet he knew the truth. Once she accepted that her father was dead, she'd leave him quicker than a fish jumps a net with a hole.

For the present, he wouldn't mind continuing with their

experiment, although common sense told him that he had set upon a dangerous course with the little librarian. Yet he pushed the caution from his mind. He'd have her again.

After he spoke with Daniel, he'd go below and find her. The idea more than pleased him. He pictured her sitting on his bunk in that brown dress with the gray stripe. He stopped in his tracks. Why hadn't he thought of it before? Mary needed a dress. He'd have Daniel get her one when they docked outside Bath.

Jack spotted his first mate by the wheel. Quickly, he ordered the first mate to try to learn more about Gaspar's location when Daniel sailed into Bath again.

"I will, Captain." The young man saluted.

"And Daniel," he glanced around the deck uneasily, "buy a bolt of cloth for Miss McNeal while you're in Bath."

"What?" Daniel cocked his head to the side.

Jack stepped closer to the young man. "She lost her bag with her clothes. I want you to get material for her to sew a new dress."

"But . . . but—"

"You can't expect a refined lady like Miss McNeal to wear the same dress. Remember, she's a librarian."

"What should I buy her?" Daniel asked.

Scratching his head, the image of Mary McNeal in her soaking wet clothes sailed into his mind. Every curve of her luscious body was revealed by the clinging garment.

"Captain?"

The image vanished from his sight. Instead, he saw Daniel's puzzled face. "Buy her something bookish."

Daniel nodded and fidgeted with his belt. "Captain, about the men. I haven't taken care of the, um, punishment. I thought a stern talking to might do it."

"Talking? You sound like the librarian. Daniel, those

men turned on each other over the roll of the dice. How can I trust these men to fight for me if they fight each other?"

"I . . . don't know."

Jack shook his head. "Neither do I." He clamped a hand on Daniel's shoulder. "I leave it to you. Deal out their punishment." He dropped his voice to a low, confidential tone. "It won't be easy."

The young man swallowed audibly and nodded.

"Of course, a leader has to make tough decisions, and you're a leader, Daniel."

"I am?"

"You are. No better way to learn than by taking charge. You understand what you must do?"

The first mate chewed on his lip, and slowly nodded his head.

"I'm glad we had this talk, Daniel. You're probably one of the few men aboard who understand me."

"If you say so, Captain." With sagging shoulders, the first mate left.

The young man would learn. Someday he'd have a ship of his own. Jack inhaled the fresh salt air and directed his thoughts to sailing the *Goodspeed*. By afternoon, the day would be warm and, judging by the breeze and the sea, they'd make good time. He couldn't wait to get back on course. They'd wasted much time traveling to and from Bath like a mother bird to her young. Now to see Mary.

Pleasure hummed in every part of his body as he opened the door of his cabin and found her. He advanced two steps.

She sprang from her seat. Folds of sailcloth spilled from her lap onto the floor. In her hand, she grasped a needle.

"Sewing for Finn?" he asked, raising a brow.

"I'm doing some mending." She dipped her gaze and inhaled deeply. "Jack, we must talk."

"I like how we talked last night," he said, reaching for her.

She danced away from his grasp. "It's about last night."

"We share the same thoughts." Lust lunged through him. He couldn't wait to take her to his bed. He wanted her naked this time.

She eyed him warily. "I don't think so. Last night can't happen again."

He froze. "What?"

She swallowed, and her face reddened. "It was all quite pleasant and—"

Pleasant?" Was that how she felt about him? "You'd describe us together as pleasant?"

"Why, yes." She took a deep breath. "What word would you use?"

"I don't need any words," he roared.

She drew herself up stiffly. "No, you wouldn't. You'd rather not think at all."

"I don't need to think."

"You've made my point."

"What was it?" he asked with frustration wearing on him.

She met his gaze, and he saw determination in her eyes. "We are two different people brought together by circumstance. We've enjoyed each other's . . . company, but now it's time to realize that we need to focus on the problem and not each other."

"Is this your way of saying you don't want to share your bed with me, a man who can't think?"

"I didn't mean to insult you."

"Fine, Miss Librarian. You stay in your cabin and think

all day. I'm not about to force a woman." He slammed
the door.

By mid-morning, many of Beckett's crew and several
of the *Goodspeed*'s men had filled the small crafts for
Bath. More men waited for an opportunity to go on
ashore. They'd need several trips to get them all landed.

While Jack watched the progress of his crew and
fumed over Mary, he saw Beckett approaching.

"I've come to thank you, Jack." Beckett extended his
hand and revealed a pouch. "Here's the money I promised
to finance your pursuit."

"Thanks," Jack muttered, scooping up the small bag
and placing it inside his coat pocket.

"You're charming today."

Jack grunted again.

"Once the *Helen of Troy* is repaired and you send your
location, I can join you. I'll enjoy meeting your pirate."

Jack scanned the sea. "Gaspar's close. I can feel it."
A cold wind blew out of the north, blowing his last words
out to sea.

"I hope you capture him tonight," Beckett said. He
turned on his heel to leave and then paused. "Take care
of Mary."

"No need to lecture me on how to take care of my
ship and crew," Jack answered, trying to push down the
anger Mary's name triggered.

His friend shook his head. "Don't be pigheaded and
throw her away. Because if you do, I'll be there to catch
her."

Beckett paused by the side. "Remember to send me
word, or I'll come searching for you."

Disappointment and annoyance surged through Jack

while his friend disappeared over the side. Beckett had
an unbelievable ego. He thought every woman should be
his. He even named his ship for one. What a fool. Women.
Jack hated them all.

The day was long and tiring. Finally at the beginning
of the first dog watch, Daniel returned. Peering over the
side, Jack observed something very peculiar. With the
exception of his first mate, the other men in the boats
wore white uniforms. Beckett's men.

"Daniel, where are my men?" He glanced up at the
sinking sun. "We don't have time for another trip to
shore."

The first mate wet his lips nervously. "They're gone.
Dismissed."

Eleven

With a raised brow of disbelief, Jack asked, "I told you to let our crew go? Was I drunk? Mad? And why are Beckett's men here?"

The first mate swallowed audibly. "You left the disciplining to me. When I discussed it with Mr. Beckett, he offered his own crew members as replacements."

Staring at the slender, tan men lounging upon the deck, Jack's spirits sank. "Discharging the men was a tad overboard."

Daniel's ears reddened. "Mr. Beckett thought it was acceptable."

Jack inhaled deeply, summoning his patience.

"Did Thomas return?" Mary McNeal asked, joining them. She sent a searching glance through the flock of white uniforms.

"These men are my men now." Jack heard the resignation in his own voice. "Dismiss the men, Daniel, although I don't think they're aware that they're at attention."

The ten men sauntered away, and Jack sighed with regret.

"I didn't know we needed more crew," Mary said.

With her attention on the departing men, he studied her. She stood several feet away from him. Her stiff stature and her cool voice told him she hadn't changed her mind.

"My men might not have had the finest clothes, but they could fight. These men will drop at the sight of blood."

She drew her lips together in disapproval. Something flashed through her eyes. He didn't have time to determine the emotion.

"Excuse me," she said in an aloof voice. "I've work to finish."

Jack watched the sway of her hips while she marched away, and he felt the urge to follow her. He heard his first mate clear his throat. Looking at Daniel, a new idea formed in Jack's mind. "Daniel, did you buy the cloth for Miss McNeal?"

With a confirmation, the first mate retrieved a burlap sack and offered it to Jack.

The weight surprised him. "How much cloth did you buy?"

"Mr. Beckett also bought cloth for Miss McNeal."

"You and Beckett have become quite close. I'm surprised you didn't return wearing one of his uniforms." He opened the sack, and a bright pink color greeted him. He dropped the bag at his feet and pulled out the soft weave. "This is the color you chose?"

"Mr. Beckett picked that out for Miss McNeal. I chose the cloth at the bottom of the sack."

Jack stared at the vivid pink and fought the inclination to feed it to the fish. He pushed the fabric into Daniel's arms. "What color did you buy?"

"Dark."

Jack slung the bag over his shoulder. "I'll deliver it."

Outside the cabin door, he paused to straighten his navy coat. He knocked gently on the door. At the soft sounds of her footsteps, he bit back a smile of anticipation. Once she saw the present, she'd forget all the angry words exchanged between them. She'd want to thank him with words, but he'd show her how to show thanks without them. He smiled in expectation.

Swinging the door open, Mary blocked his entrance. "Good day." She used her sternest voice that she reserved for noisy patrons.

She stepped aside to allow him to enter. He must have come to apologize. She watched while he deposited a large sack on the bunk. For a moment, her hopes soared. Had he bought her books? Then Mary eyed the size and shape. More mending, she decided.

He whirled toward her. "I realized that since you are here—"

"Only until we locate my father," she declared.

"Of course." He gestured to the bag. "You might want this when we find him."

Mary couldn't squash the curiosity or excitement rising inside her. Jack had brought her a present. Her heart thudded. "What is it?"

"Look," he said with a smile.

Her fingers closed around the rough burlap eagerly. Opening the top, she peered inside and saw something dark.

"Take it out," he encouraged.

Mary held her breath while drawing out the heavy cloth. Black.

"I had Daniel buy it while in Bath."

Why had he given her this?

"Is there enough?"

"Enough?"

"To make a dress.

Finally, she understood. He wanted her to have an appropriate gown when she accepted that Gaspar had killed her father. "How many dresses am I to make?"

He shrugged and moved closer. "I'm not a good judge of amounts."

Mary pictured herself immersed in the itchy blackness, standing beside her father's coffin. Jack stood beside her, dangling a handkerchief from his fingertips with an I-told-you-so expression.

"Do you like it?"

She shoved the gift at him. The bolt unfolded and stretched down to the floor. "I can't accept it or the message."

"What message?"

"My father is dead." She began to push the cloth into his arms. Where did the material end? How large did he think she was?

"You can make yourself a fine coat and probably a black patch too," she said, trying to keep the folds from unraveling back onto the wooden planks.

"What the devil is wrong with you?"

She gave up and moved back. Cloth overflowed his arms and rippled down to a large black puddle of material by his feet. A puzzled frown flitted across his face.

"You thought I needed funeral clothes, didn't you? I'm sorry, but until I have proof of my father's death, I'll not wear black!"

Jack shook his head in disbelief. "Why'd I try to give you anything?" He shoved the coarse weave inside. "You don't act like an intelligent woman."

Insufferable illiterate. "What? Well, I know things you wished you knew." She put her hands on her hips and waited for his answer.

"Do you? Care to give me an example?"

"Certainly. I once found out for a patron how many toes a monkey has. And do you know how many stripes a zebra has?"

"The question has kept me awake many a night." He leaned closer. "Listen, Miss McNeal. Despite what you believe, I gave you this present to make a dress, and not a mourning gown. And I don't know how many stripes or crisscrosses any animal has." His voice rose in anger. "All I want to know is, where is Gaspar?" He leaned closer till their noses were only a sneeze apart. "Find that in your books, Miss Librarian."

He threw the bag over his shoulder and stormed from the cabin.

Mary watched him disappear. Had she been wrong in her assumption? A streak of guilt pierced her conscience. She had no other clothing. And why had she asked him those stupid questions? Her mind didn't work well under pressure. Clearly, she needed to make amends for her temper. The image of Jack sweeping her into his arms flew into her mind. Quickly, she squashed the memory.

Find Gaspar, her conscience told her. With determination, she stalked to the desk and took out the map. A good librarian knew how to use her resources. True, she didn't have many out here in the sea.

Mary pushed at loose strands of hair and ran her finger over the chart until she found their position. With exactness, she made tight circles around the invisible *Goodspeed*. Bending closer, she peered at the map until her eyes burned. Somewhere on this paper was the answer. Gaspar couldn't be that smart.

An ache nagged at her back, yet she continued with her paper search. An oblong shape caught her attention. Mary held the map and read the label, Queen's Island.

The name reminded her of Queen Cassiopeia . . . the constellation on the snuff box. Excitement shot through her until her hands shook. The name of the island matched the W on the snuff box. She had discovered Gaspar's hiding place.

Jack spied Daniel checking the rigging. With the cloth tucked under his arm, he marched up to his first mate. "Black?"

The young man blinked, his eyes in confusion. "What?"

"You bought Miss McNeal black cloth for her dress."

Relief flooded his features. "I did. Thought you'd approve. You said buy something bookish, and most book covers are black."

Jack lifted a brow in question. "Are they?"

Daniel smiled. "Mr. Beckett brought a color we'd never see on a book. He said it reminded him of the sky at sunset. He said it was right for Miss McNeal. I knew you'd disagree."

"Yes, our cloth is like the sky during a storm." He tapped a finger above his lip. "Here's the black. Bring me Beckett's."

The first mate sped away and returned in a few minutes with the glaring pink material.

He tucked the bolt under his arm and prepared for another encounter with his librarian. Surely, Mary could not complain about this being appropriate for mourning. He paused outside the cabin door and smoothed his black hair. Then he rapped loudly on the wooden door.

He heard her light footsteps running toward him. She swept the door wide. Her eyes glistened, and she burst into a smile.

"Miss McNeal?" He paused, trying to make sense of her warm greeting. A few minutes ago she'd eyed him like a customs inspector.

She reached out and took his arm. "Come in."

Deciding to take advantage of her short memory, he held up the bolt. "I think you'll like this much better."

"Oh?" Her smile disappeared, and she gazed at the new present with suspicion. "Another gift? Are you thinking of starting a new career in dressmaking, Captain?"

"You can make a suitable dress to greet your father."

Mary laid the cloth on the bunk and held the soft weave in her hands. "Pink!"

He searched his mind for Beckett's comment. "Ah, it's like the sky in the evening."

"You're rather poetic, and I thought only your friend Thomas had a way with words."

Jack shifted uncomfortably.

Mary ran her hand over the cloth lying on the bed. "I wish to apologize. I overreacted when I saw the black." She looked up at him with a soft longing for forgiveness in her gaze.

A need to be closer to her stirred within him. "If I'd known this material would have made you this happy, I'd have given it to you earlier." He closed the distance between them.

She laughed, and her eyes sparkled.

He made an important decision. He would kiss her. Jack started to reach for her.

Mary darted away to the desk. "I have a surprise for you, too. Come and look at the map. I've found the answer to our problems." She held up the paper. "Now if I understand our present position, we can reach the island by sundown tomorrow. How many knots are we doing?"

"Mary, what in the name of Neptune are you carrying

on about? Does this have something to do with your research on monkey toes and animal stripes?"

"Look! The island. Queen's Island." She pointed at a small oblong shape."

He peered closely at the drawing. "Let me understand. You propose that I sail to this spot because it's called Queen's Island."

She smiled. "It's the connection we've sought. The M or the W on the snuff box is the shape of the constellation of Queen Cassiopeia." She threw her free hand triumphantly into the air. "Queen's Island."

He hadn't thought she was this desperate. He placed his hands on her shoulders and gently pushed her into the chair. "Mary, when I command a ship, I plot my course and—"

"But we've no course.

"Our course is north to Canada. The mooncussers said Gaspar sailed north.

"The island is located northeast. We only have to change our path by a few degrees." The map rattled with her excitement as her hands shook. She popped out of her seat. "Don't you understand? My father will be there. Gaspar will be there with his pirate treasure."

Her warm breath brushed against his face. The sweet fragrance of lavender encircled them.

"You think your father and Gaspar wait for us there?" He removed the chart from her hands and placed it on the desk. Bending over it, he brushed her arm and felt the energy tensed in her body.

"It's logical. This is the next step."

Jack didn't like the calmness in her voice. "Mary, I've learned several things about you in our short time together. One is that you rarely listen to common sense. A more reasonable woman would have remained at home and allowed others to pursue Gaspar."

"I told you everyone had given up. My father has no one else to save him. You don't understand what it is to be alone in the world."

He understood more than he wanted to tell her.

"I know you think this is a strange request, but you do know how awful my father's life in captivity must be. You can save him, only you. We have to go to Queen's Island."

Memories of pain and darkness from his days as a prisoner filled his mind. Wanting to shake them off, he glanced at the librarian. In her eyes he saw hope and something else. Mary McNeal believed in him. It made him regret failing her. "I can't promise to rescue your father."

"But you'll try.

He peered down at the yellowed map while trying to still his own confusion of emotions. "We can look," he said grudgingly.

She threw her arms about him and kissed his cheek. He raised his arms to capture her, but she'd already bounded away to the bunk.

Mary unrolled the vibrant pink material. "Whoever sold you this cloth gave you enough for two dresses.

"Make them," he said, wondering if he could talk her into shortening the hemline and then into his bed.

She turned to him. Her eyes still glowed with enthusiasm. "If you don't mind, I'll use the black to make a coat for my father." She toyed with the cuff of her sleeve. "Have you given it away?"

He shook his head.

"I'll start now so that it will be ready when he comes aboard."

The guilt that had lurked within him broke free and pierced his conscience. What had he done? He'd allowed his feelings for her to take command of his ship, and he'd given her a false hope. "You do realize that the island most likely will be deserted?"

"I know you think so," she answered, refolding the pink material. "But you'll learn the truth."

Jack rubbed his chin and pondered how much further to take the conversation. Would she listen? He already knew the answer. Beckett might have been correct when he said she needed to see to believe. Once she saw no signs of her father, they'd travel to Canada where he'd find a safe port to leave her. No harm done and he would have to comfort her on the trip. He smiled over his idea.

Yet, he couldn't shake the feeling that something was wrong. He actually wished that Beckett had stayed aboard. At least she might have listened to him. He'd check his course with his navigator. He left her measuring out the cloth.

Upon deck, he heard the bells ring, announcing the dinner hour. A commotion came from the galley. Jack turned his footsteps in that direction. Several men had lined up with empty plates and watched Cook shake a spoon at one of Beckett's former crew members.

Gritting his teeth, he debated interfering. The man probably complained that the meal wasn't good enough. Jack moved between the two and spoke to Cook. "What's happening here?"

"This man insulted me. I've refused to serve him."

"Was only a comment on his cap," the tall tan man protested. He fixed his gaze on the small, white, bowl-shaped hat on Cook's head. Where had the man gotten that ridiculous piece of clothing?

"Well?" Cook asked with anger in his voice.

Jack cleared his throat while he composed his expression into a poker face. "While aboard my ship, you'll treat each man with respect." He glanced at Cook and back to the crewman. "Or starve."

"Didn't mean no harm," the new man said, shuffling his feet.

Satisfied that he couldn't offer a stiffer penalty, Jack headed for the door. His first mate stepped aside to allow him to exit.

"Daniel, I need to check our course. Send the navigator to my cabin."

"Ah, sorry, Captain, there's a problem. I'm afraid . . . I'm afraid he's gone."

"Where?"

"I dismissed him. He was one of the men fighting, and I replaced him with a man from the *Helen of Troy*."

"Was his replacement also a navigator?"

"I don't know." Daniel dropped his gaze to his feet.

"Send me Beckett's men on the quarterdeck."

During his wait Jack paced, wondering what other misfortune would happen. In a matter of minutes, the white-dressed men appeared, with Daniel lagging behind. One look at his first mate's face and Jack knew he had no one to chart the *Goodspeed*'s new course.

Mary hummed as she sketched the coat she planned for her father. Since the material had been plentiful, she'd make two coats. One would be for Jack. How else could she thank him? Her face burned as her conscience told her she knew another.

And she'd meet Gaspar. Her hand stilled. Would there be a battle? Perhaps they'd arrive at night and take the pirate by sunrise.

The firm knock on the door alerted her to Jack's presence at her cabin. Now she'd learn his plan. A thrill ran through her at the thought of being included in his confidence.

"Jack, I'm glad you've come back. I have a few questions."

He entered and held out his arms, which contained the bolt of black fabric. "I hope you're not about to ask me to model anything."

"Certainly not. I know my father's sizes better than he does." She took the cloth from his arms. How should she begin?

The desk chair scuffed the floor as Jack dragged it back and straddled it. "I'm waiting, Mary."

"Yes, well, when I learned my father had been kidnapped, I read a book about a pirate who had abducted a young woman."

"Miss McNeal, this isn't story time. Do you have a reason for sharing this book?"

"I'm reaching my point. Bear with me. The hero had a lot of guns on his ship and blew this buccaneer out of the waters."

He quirked a brow. "Didn't the explosion kill the woman?"

"Oh, I must have skipped a few pages." She waved away his query. "Anyway, my question is, do you plan to fire on Gaspar's ship in the same manner?" She spoke rapidly, hoping he didn't hear the fear in her voice.

He rubbed his chin as though considering her question. "When we encounter Gaspar, we must be prepared for battle."

She heard something in his voice that she didn't understand. "No. I wanted to prepare for our encounter with the pirate."

Mary moved closer to him. "Exactly how do you propose to scout the area?"

"Miss McNeal, I haven't survived a war without learning the importance of secrecy. But I have a few questions of my own." He opened the desk drawer and removed the map. "Where is your star located in the sky?"

"The Queen of Cassiopeia?" She closed her eyes and recalled the night sky. In her mind's eyes, she saw the constellation's glittering W formation directly ahead of them.

"We sail toward her."

"That's your direction?"

"North by northeast."

He looked down at the map. "I believe I've found your duty."

"I don't have to climb the rigging, do I? I didn't wish to confess this to anyone, but I have a fear of heights. When I first observed stars on the rooftop, I had this dizzy feeling. Of course, I grew used to it. My father—"

"No, you won't have to climb a step. I want you to make one of your star charts."

She relaxed. "You do? Do you need it now?" She glanced at the black material. "I wanted to begin my father's coat."

"I expected more enthusiasm after all your demands for a duty," he answered while he unlocked the cabinet. He removed two velvet cases and placed them on his desk. Opening them, he revealed a brass sextant and a compass.

"My father gave these to me when I bought the *Goodspeed*. They haven't gotten much use.

Mary gasped. Tentatively, she reached out and lightly touched the sextant.

"You'll need to read the log. I'll answer any questions, and we'll have to confer frequently."

She slanted a look at the sextant. "What does this mean?"

"It means you're my new navigator." He stood back, an expectant look upon his face.

"Thank you." Mary held the instrument to her heart. "I'm honored that you trust me. No one has ever given me such responsibility before." She glanced at him. "You won't regret it."

Seeing all the attention she lavished on the sextant instead of on him, Jack already regretted it.

Later in the evening, Jack stood on the quarterdeck. Below, Mary stood with three of his men. He couldn't take his gaze from her. He'd tried to win his way back into her good graces with the gifts, but clearly he needed another plan.

Now she stood with a gray blanket wrapped around her against the night chill. Her hand arched gracefully against the clear starry night. He didn't need a telescope to know she was showing them Cassiopeia. He shook his head at a thought. Captain St. George, the once great naval captain, had hung his future on a star for a woman.

Twelve

In the gray light of morning, the choppy waves thudded against the hull. The smell of rain hung in the air. Placing her elbows on the rail, Mary stood on her toes and craned her neck for a better view. Cold, salty spray rose up in her face, but ahead she saw trees and rock.

"Your island, Miss McNeal."

She whirled around and discovered Jack beside her. She evaded his gaze and mumbled, "I can't see much."

"Keep leaning over the side, and you'll soon see sharks."

She schooled her expression into nonchalance and met his amused gaze. "I'm a little anxious." Her hand went to her throat. "I forgot my telescope. Have you spotted anything?"

His eyes widened with interest. "I've spied a good many pleasing things, but if you mean on land, no. And you don't need your scope. I'm sending Daniel and a few men to the island."

"But I have to go. I—"

"Stop!" He held up his hand. "You'll have your chance to explore ashore. First, I want to know that we can safely search there." The lines between his brows softened. "Besides, if I stopped you, I have this feeling you'd jump in the water and drown trying to float ashore."

"Captain, you're an excellent judge of character."

"Funny, the judge at my trial didn't think so. Now, excuse me."

"I understand. It's time for your ordering business." She meant to smile in encouragement, but a grin didn't seem to convey the gratitude she felt for taking her to the island. Impulsively, she kissed his cheek.

He stared at her in surprise.

Her own shock was worse than his. Had she lost all control near this man? She mustn't encourage him. Her face grew hot, and a jumble of confusion tossed within her. Desperate, her mind groped for an excuse for her actions. Her mind fell back on his own words. "A kiss for luck. It's an old seaman's charm."

His expression of astonishment melted. "Tonight, I'll teach you more charms."

He left before she could answer. Good heavens, they couldn't be together the way he meant. It was wrong. Turning around, she stared at the small blot of land. She hugged her arms about herself, trying to contain the sensations of anxiety coursing through her. In the distance, Queen's Island grew closer.

Unable to stand still any longer, she ran below and strung her telescope about her neck. Above again, she saw the island looming in front of them. The *Goodspeed* had slowed to a crawl. She recognized the splash of the anchor hitting the water. They had moored. Already, the men worked on the shore boat. She spotted Jack with Daniel.

She wished he'd return and speak with her. She wished she didn't want to see him. Confused, Mary turned back and focused her telescope on the land. Her lens scanned rock. In the center grew a shallow grove of trees.

Could this small, desolate piece of ground hide her father? She clutched the scope. Had Gaspar concealed himself here? Did he have a buried treasure too? Perhaps he was peering at her at this very moment. *He'll cut off your head and use it for a centerpiece.*

"See anything?"

Mary started and dropped the scope to her breast. "Jack!"

He laid a hand upon her arm. "Calm yourself, Mary."

What was wrong with her? She was acting like a child caught reading a forbidden book. "I'm fine. I simply can't believe how small the island appears. How long will it take to scout it?"

"They'll come back when they've looked under every rock."

"The whole island looks like a big boulder with a few trees on top. I wonder where Mr. Gaspar has hidden." Mary picked up her scope and skimmed across the water back to the land to avoid Jack.

"Gaspar likes unlikely spots. He treasures the element of surprise. When you return to Oyster River, you'll have quite a story to tell. Mr. Money Bags will be jealous."

"If you're speaking of my former fiancè, he doesn't have much interest in exploring. If Oliver were Magellan, we'd still believe the world is flat."

"Strange, I'd have thought you'd have picked a man with a spirit of adventure."

His low voice made her look up in surprise. "I have." Instantly, regret seared through her mind. "To search for my father," she added hastily.

He stepped closer as though to embrace her for a kiss. Her breath faltered in her throat, and her body warmed to the stirring memory of their last time in the cabin.

"Captain," a bearded young man called, running to them. "Cook's threatening a new crew member with his knife."

"I'll come." Disappointment glittered in his eyes as he stepped away from her. "Sorry, Mary, it's most likely that cap business again." With a nod, he was gone.

Mary stood breathless at the rail. *What had happened?* Sorting through her tumbling thoughts, a new realization dawned upon her. She wanted Jack, but he didn't want her the way a true gentleman desired a lady. And he had made it clear on numerous occasions that he wanted to sail away without her. Mary had more problems than Napoleon.

Glancing at the shore boat headed for the island, Mary knew she had to think of a solution. She decided to keep busy until the men returned, and she thought out her problem with Jack.

Wandering by the galley, she saw him listening while Beckett's crew member pointed at Cook's cap. How strange! What was wrong with the hat she'd made for Cook? Then it struck her. The man wanted one and was jealous.

The idea pleased her and inspired her. She'd make one for everyone. This would keep her occupied. In the meantime, she'd finish her father's coat and begin Jack's.

Below in her cabin, the minutes dragged into hours. She heard the bells for the noon meal and kept sewing. Over and over in her mind, she saw her father's astonished face when they would meet. Then Jack's face would intrude upon her dream. Heavens, the man was everywhere.

At the sound of heavy footsteps coming to her door, Mary sprang from her seat. She opened the door to see Jack's hand hovering in the air, prepared to knock.

"Have the men returned?"

A glimmer of sympathy shot through his gray eyes, and she knew the answer. They hadn't found her parent.

"He could be hiding," Mary reasoned, stepping away

from the door to allow him entrance. "Maybe he's in a cave like the mooncussers. You have to let me go ashore. When my father spots me, he'll come out. He's afraid."

"Mary, I have every intention of letting you search every pebble on that island. I plan to personally escort you. Ready?"

"Of course. I'll put away my sewing." She gathered up her father's coat and set it inside the trunk. During her preparations, she felt his gaze upon her. She didn't want to meet it. She'd see too many accusations in his eyes. Mary McNeal had taken them off course. Mary McNeal had failed to lead them to Gaspar's hideaway. Mary McNeal had warmed his bed and now wanted nothing to do with him.

"The weather has held, but I expect fog to set in early," Jack said while he waited for her.

She glanced at the porthole and for the first time noticed how black the sky had grown. Mary tilted her chin upward in false courage and swept from the room.

Without waiting for him, she hurried up the stairs and crossed the deck to the rope ladder. Mr. Finn stood to the side holding a musket.

She rested her hand on his canvas sleeve for a moment. "I can see you're accompanying us. Thank you."

"Daniel will take charge while I'm ashore," Jack said, joining them.

"Are you expecting more ghosts, Captain?" She pointed at Mr. Finn's weapon.

"I'm prepared for anything, Miss McNeal. Ladies first." He gestured to the rope ladder.

Without further discussion, she climbed down to the shore boat. Jack and Finn followed and quickly had the small vessel under way. A damp sea breeze blew the promise of rain into their faces. They made the crossing in silence. Only the oars hitting the water broke the quiet. Her stomach clenched as each stroke brought them closer.

Reaching shore, they tugged the boat onto the rocky edge rising out of the sea.

"Finn, you stay here and keep watch. Mary, follow me." Jack drew his pistol.

Together, they scoured the edge of the island. They worked in silence, but fearful images of Gaspar springing out at them began to build in Mary's mind. Her mind teetered between fear and hope.

They headed into the copse of trees. The hemlocks and pines that blocked the gray light seemed to turn the late day into early evening. In the wet air, the odor of pine hindered her from recognizing any other scents. An uneasy feeling filled her. Someone could follow and surprise them from behind. She heard the noise of a branch breaking and spun around. Nothing.

A hand touched her shoulder. She gasped.

"Mary?"

Her cheeks warmed. "I thought I heard something behind us."

"Imagination. Want to rest?" Without waiting for an answer, Jack put his hand around her shoulder and guided her to a large pine. He leaned against the tree. "Have a seat."

Hesitantly, she joined him. She folded her hands in a pose of tranquillity on her wet lap while small quivers of fear attacked her. Leaning her head back, she dared to glance at him. His gray eyes were clouded. He was worried. She had sent them here. Was it only a wild chase? "I'm sorry," she blurted, "for everything."

He raised a questioning brow. "I thought Adam and Eve had the credit."

She stared at him, trying to make sense of his words. Then it struck her. He was joking. "Now is not the time for confessions."

"Not unless you've confused me with a priest. And despite my apparent failure to impress you with my wit, I hope you'll listen when I ask you to stay here. I want to see how much further till we're out of these woods."

She didn't want him to go even for a few seconds. And she had to know the truth. "Jack, when this is over, you'll come to Oyster River, won't you?"

"A delightful invitation, but I can hardly plan tomorrow. I never expected to be on an island with a librarian."

Yes, what was wrong with her? She was a librarian, and he was a man that couldn't even recognize a pentameter verse. Why had she thought that sharing her bed with him would change him?

He stood abruptly. "Stay here."

"I don't mind accompanying you." She bounded to her feet.

"I can move faster without you. We need to use our time wisely if we're to finish before dark. Here." He pressed his pistol between her hands. "Don't shoot at anything until—"

"You see the whites of their eyes?" she suggested.

"Sometimes your knowledge of the facts is useful. Remember those words. I wouldn't want you to shoot me when I return."

Mary watched him disappear. Why had she asked him to visit her? She was making matters worse. She sighed and sat again. The pistol handle was still warm from his grasp, and it comforted her. She drew up her legs and rested the muzzle on her knee.

Where would a pirate hide? She glanced about the scraggly trees. Had her father been here? The sound of breaking branches broke through her thoughts. "It's only my imagination." Her hand tightened on the handle. The sound grew louder. She recognized it. Running. It was an animal.

Mary scrambled to her feet. What kind of creatures lived on an island? A librarian should know. Where was the information listed? Tightening her grip, she held the pistol out before her. Any second and she'd see it. Her hand shook and the pistol wavered. Mary's finger lingered on the trigger. "Wait. Wait."

Dark hair and kneeless trousers flashed into view. Mary recognized her animal. "Mr. Finn! Over here!"

The sailmaker stopped and blinked.

"Here, it's me, Mary." She raised her skirt and hurried to him. "What is it? Did you find my father?"

He shook his head. "Where's the captain? A ship is coming."

"I'm waiting for him. He wanted to see how much longer we'd have to travel through these woods. What kind of ship is it?"

"It's a frigate and coming fast."

"Do you think the French are chasing us?"

He shrugged. "I've got to talk to the captain. Which way did he go?"

"This way." She started to lead him.

He didn't follow. "You'd best stay. The captain won't be happy if you leave when he's told you to stay."

Mary shook her head. "I'm not a dog, Mr. Finn, and you know where he went. We can look for him together. Let's go." Before he could object, she trudged in the direction Jack had taken.

"I heard you don't listen well," Mr. Finn said, lagging behind her.

"Don't worry, Mr. Finn. Captain will be too busy ordering us back to the *Goodspeed* before the French arrive. He'll have no time to think about me."

A whistle pierced the air. Mr. Finn halted Mary with a firm hand on her arm.

"Is it the captain?"

Mr. Finn put his hands to his mouth and returned the call. Silence answered. The sailmaker raised the barrel of his weapon and studied the area.

Mary held the pistol out in front of her, her knuckles white on the butt of the weapon.

"Trouble?"

Mary whirled around and was caught in Jack's gaze. His eyes widened at the pistol aimed at his heart.

"Captain, today you've made a habit of surprising me." Mary dropped the weapon to her side.

"I'm sorry, I can't say the same about you. It seems you aren't following my orders again."

"A frigate is coming," Mr. Finn said, stepping forward.

Worry shimmered in Jack's eyes. "How close is she?"

"I can't make out her flag, but I don't think it's the same ship that came looking for Mr. Beckett."

"Let's pray they're friendly, Finn. Miss McNeal, try to follow us to our boat without getting lost."

They moved swiftly through the woods. Jack shadowed Mary. By the time she reached the shore boat, the approaching ship's blood red hull could be seen rising and falling on the water.

"Miss McNeal, your scope." Jack held out his hand.

Unable to take her gaze from the ship closing on them, Mary handed him her telescope. "Is it the French? Do you see their flag?"

He glanced through the telescope and then at Mary. "Too late."

"What do you mean?" Mary squinted, trying to make out the flag. "Are they dangerous?"

Jack's hand with the telescope dropped to his side. "Mary, we've found Gaspar."

Thirteen

Jack saw disbelief streak through her eyes. Mary stepped closer to the ocean, never taking her gaze from the ship.

He ran a hand through his hair, measuring the distance between the *Goodspeed,* Gaspar, and the island. "Damn."

"My father *is* here," Mary said in an awed voice. "Queen's Island is Gaspar's hiding place."

"Are you crazy?" Jack asked. "No one can hide on this forsaken place. He's trapped us."

"But the search? We spent all this time here."

"So you could accept the fact that your father isn't on this island. It's time you accepted the fact that your father is dead. And Gaspar plans to kill us next."

She looked as though he'd struck her in the face. "No!"

Pain shot through Jack at the emotion vibrating in her voice. "It's my fault. I know him better than anyone. Why didn't I expect this?" He stared hard at the pirate's ship. He imagined Gaspar on the deck watching, smiling, waiting to pull the invisible noose tighter around their necks.

"We can make a run for it, Captain," Finn offered.

"First, we have to get off this beach and into the cover of the trees. We'll take the boat."

Mary stood motionless. Her face had paled, and pain shone in her eyes.

Jack crossed to her. From her smooth hand he removed

his pistol. The coldness from her fingers chilled him. "Mary," he said in a low and urgent voice. "Please help us. I need you."

She looked blankly at him before she nodded. Stepping up to the shore boat, Mary grabbed hold.

The three carried the small craft to the copse while Jack silently cursed his own stupidity in blurting out the truth. He should have held his tongue. Now he couldn't forget the misery on the librarian's face. He gripped the craft tighter. After they laid it on its side, he tried to catch her gaze. Mary averted her face.

"Captain, what do we do next?" Finn asked.

Mary looked up with interest. "Will they fire on our ship?" Her voice sounded hoarse. But Jack took comfort in the fact that she had spoken to him.

"Gaspar is like a cat torturing his prey. He'll wait and pounce when we make a run for it." He didn't add his thoughts that their chances of making it to the *Goodspeed* were poor at best.

"A boat is coming," Finn said, peering out at the ocean.

From the safety of the trees, they gathered in a small knot and watched the small pinpoint bobbing steadily toward them.

"It's not one of ours, is it, Captain?" Finn asked.

"No. We're about to have a visitor from our unwanted host. He's waving a white flag."

"Then I'll wait till you order me to shoot him," Finn said, training his musket on the newcomer.

"We might let him say hello. We want to be polite." Jack slanted a glance at Mary, but she gave no indication of hearing him. "Miss McNeal, may I borrow your scope again?"

She unstrung the instrument and silently handed it to him.

The small vessel grew larger through the glass, and Jack saw something red.

"Is it Gaspar?" Mary asked anxiously.

"Have a look." He passed her the instrument. While she placed the scope to her eye, he added, "Miss McNeal, when the craft lands, you're to stay here. Do you understand?"

"Perfectly." She aimed the lens at the approaching figure.

"Finn, keep your weapon on our visitor while I speak to him."

"I should speak with him," Mary said, stringing her instrument around her neck. "I'll be safer. Gaspar wants you."

"Mary, you take one step on that beach, and I'll tie you to the nearest tree." He ran his hand through his hair and shoved down the stirrings of panic triggered by her offer. "I need your cooperation. You'll cover me too." He folded her fingers around his pistol.

The lingering pain disappeared from her eyes, replaced by astonishment. "You trust me?"

"With my life." He fought the urge to take her in his arms and wipe away all the hurt that he'd caused. Why did she always stir these feelings? Later, he'd think about it.

He headed for the edge of the tree line. Squinting, he watched Gaspar's man draw closer. Jack made out a patch of red hair and a beard. He couldn't believe it. It was the mooncusser from the cave. A white scrap tied to the man's arm flapped in the slight breeze as a false symbol of peace.

Near the rocky island edge, the tall man hopped from the boat and waded ashore. Jack heard him swear as the tide tugged the craft back into the water. Tired of waiting, Jack strode toward the mooncusser.

Mary shouted his name in warning, but Jack didn't stop.

The lanky man dragged his boat onto the rocky ground. Then he looked up and saw Jack. His face broke into a grin, revealing his brown-stained teeth. "Good day, Johnny. Gaspar sends his hello."

Jack paused a few feet from the man. Instinctively, his hand crept toward his empty inside pocket where he kept his pistol. "Luke, isn't it? Funny, you couldn't tell me much about Gaspar the last time we met in Maine. Now it looks like you're one of the crew."

Luke fingered his beard and moved closer. "After we got out of that darned cave, we ran into him. He offered to take us on his ship. He was most persuasive."

"I know a lot about his forcefulness."

"He had much to say about you, Johnny. He's a little upset with the way you up and left him. I didn't have much good to say about you myself."

"Captain!" Mary McNeal ran toward him. She grasped his pistol in front of her. Behind her, Finn followed.

"Stay back, Mary." Jack quickly scanned Luke for signs of a weapon.

The tall man stood with his mouth open, staring at the librarian. His attention swiveled to Jack. "I'm to invite you back to the ship. But I can see where you might want to stay." His eyes gleamed as he looked Mary up and down. "Has she grown any quieter?"

"She's not any more obedient either," Jack mumbled, sending Mary a look of annoyance, which she avoided.

"You're not in a position to criticize me, Mr. Luke," Mary said. "Threatening to toss a person off a cliff is not very cordial."

"I can show you some right good friendliness. Come a little closer." His eyes gleamed with feral intent.

Mary backed away a few steps, and Luke cackled.

The man's laughter caused a new coldness in the pit of Jack's stomach. He stepped in front of the mooncusser, blocking the man's view of the librarian. "Enough of this. What does Gaspar want?"

"Begging your pardon, but he only wants your company. He didn't like it much that you slipped away without so much as a good-bye." The man grinned maliciously.

"Should I search him, Captain?" Finn asked, pointing to the mooncusser with his weapon.

"Go ahead."

The sailmaker handed his musket to Jack and ran his hands over the bearded man's clothes. "Nothing."

"Take off your boots, Luke." Jack nodded to the scuffed shoes.

"Might not be proper to undress in front of the lady." Luke's eyes gleamed with a predator's anticipation. "What was your name, little lady?"

"I'm—"

"Enough." Jack sent Mary a warning glance. "Off with your boots."

Grumbling, the redheaded man unsteadily balanced on one foot and pulled off the toeless boot. It thudded on the ground.

"The other one," Jack ordered.

"Now, Johnny, how can I walk with anything stuffed inside?"

"Hurry. I want to get out of sight."

Spouting words of disbelief, Luke pulled off his other boot.

Jack grabbed it and shook it upside down. A blade clattered onto the rock, and he swept it up into his hand.

"Finn, hold this. We'll take his boat with us into the woods. If Luke decides he wants to leave, shoot him."

"Captain, he might know about my father," Mary said, drawing close.

"Father?" Luke asked. "Is he a sailor?"

"Not now, Miss McNeal." Jack gestured to Luke's craft. "We have to get out of here." He sent her a look that always silenced his crew.

She tilted her chin up in defiance. "You promise I can speak to him once we're safe?"

"Miss McNeal, you can speak to him all day and night, and I'll never ask you to stop. Come along."

"Luke, grab hold." With the boat, they trudged back into the scant protection offered by the grove. When they reached the *Goodspeed*'s shore boat, Jack signaled for them to rest their load.

"We'll have our talk here. How long have you been following us?"

Luke scratched his head. "I've given up counting days. They all seem the same when you never stop sailing. Maybe the miss here could teach me something. She says she can read."

The click of Jack's pistol answered. He leveled it at the man. "Does this help your memory?"

"Maybe he can't remember," Mary said, worry marring her brows.

"Not very friendly, is he? I reckon he wasn't so proud after a few days on Gaspar's ship. Close to begging, I hear he was."

Jack raised his pistol. "I'll count to ten. I think you know how it begins. One."

"I only came to bring you back. It's where you belong, Johnny. We all know no one's been friendly to you since you left. Come back with me. Gaspar wants to offer you a position on the ship."

"I wager it's one where I hang by the neck. Sorry, I have to decline. Two."

Luke fingered his beard. "We've been following ye ever since Maine, and I don't see where ye have a choice. Ye won't be getting back to yer vessel."

"What do we do, Captain?" Finn lowered his musket to his side. "That pirate can fire on the *Goodspeed*."

"He won't. He wants to draw us out of here. The *Goodspeed* is the bait."

"Mary, we'll need material from your dress to muffle the oars."

"Like George Washington crossing the Delaware," she said, looking down at the gray strip sewn onto her ginger gown. "I suppose it's fair to return part of your blanket. I'll need your knife."

Finn handed her Luke's blade. She cringed as he placed it in her hand, but she set to work. The soft tearing of the material filled the empty silence. Soon, Mary's shapely legs were visible.

With open mouth, Luke's gaze stayed fastened on her limbs.

Jack took the cloth from her and stuffed it into Luke's hands. "Wrap the oars and do a good job. Your life depends upon it. Miss McNeal, put on my coat." He didn't wait for her answer but wrapped his coat around her shoulders.

"You can't get away, Johnny, not in this fist-sized boat. Come with me. You can bring the little lady with you. She'll be welcome." He smiled his toothless grin.

"You'll come with us, Luke. If we don't make it safely, neither will you."

"Finn, watch him. Miss McNeal, I want to speak with

you over here." He paced a few steps away from the others. Satisfied that they could speak without being overheard, Jack waited for the librarian to join him.

With a worried expression she approached. "Can I speak with him about my father now?"

"When we're back on the *Goodspeed*, we'll question him together. You're never to speak to him without me present. He knows more than he's telling. Until then, stay away from him. I don't trust him."

"How will we get back?"

"When it's dark enough, you'll go in the boat with Finn. I'll go with our prisoner." He nodded to dismiss her.

She laid a hand on his sleeve. It trembled slightly. "Jack, I won't believe my father is dead without proof."

Her touch upset his balance, and he strove to clear his thoughts. Looking into her green eyes, he saw a faint glimmer of trust. He wanted to grasp hold of that thread of hope and wrap it around them. He raised his hand to her face, and, for a second, he cradled her cheek until he saw all the fears and doubts disappear from the shadows in her eyes. Dropping his hand, Jack chose his words with care.

"Gaspar doesn't leave evidence of his dealings with people. Luke, I suspect, has as many versions of the truth as you have stars in your heavens." He covered her hand with his own. "But we shall try to get the facts from him. If he refuses to cooperate, we'll give him one of Cook's biscuits."

The beginning of a smile tipped the corners of her mouth. "Thank you. What can I do?"

His hand fell away from hers. "This is the hardest. Nothing. We must wait for dark."

"I shall be a model of patience." Squaring her shoulders, Mary settled herself against the side of the *Good-speed*'s shore boat.

During the following hours, she spoke little, seeming lost in her thoughts. Unable to stop himself, Jack's gaze fastened on her face. She looked small and vulnerable. His heart filled with guilt. She should not be in this godforsaken place, but in a cozy parlor.

He should be thinking only of escape from their hopeless situation. Instead, he couldn't stop thinking about her. He paced. Every time he thought he'd banished her from his mind, his rebellious thoughts returned to the librarian and forced him to glance at her. Dimly, he heard Luke's barbs which frequently caused the taciturn Finn to grip his musket tightly.

Finally darkness crept upon them, but it brought another companion: fog so thick a smuggler would have been in heaven. Jack glanced at Mary. She leaned against the boat with her eyes closed. Their captive sat sullenly silent. Finn looked at Jack in expectation.

Jack nodded and the sailmaker sprang to his feet. His actions caused Mary to stir.

"Is it time?" she asked in a sleepy voice.

Jack rested a hand on her shoulder. Beneath his palm, she tensed. "Once we're out of the woods, we need to move in silence. Follow any order that I or Finn give you, no matter what you think. This is important. Do you have any questions?"

Mary shook her head. Her hand stole out of the darkness and clasped his for a brief instant. Her reassuring grip brought a sudden surge of peace to him. Then she swept past him.

Her touch of encouragement lingered on his mind, and he clenched his fist. They must make it to the *Goodspeed*.

"Finn, we're ready," he announced. "Keep your bow

headed straight into the waves, and you'll steer straight to the *Goodspeed*."

He saw Mary beside her shore boat, ready to lift it. Jack turned his attention to the mooncusser. "Luke, you and I will take your boat. Remember, any attention you draw to me puts you in danger. Unless you desire a cannonball on your head, you'll keep quiet."

"Yer not a friendly sort, Johnny. All those opportunities ye had to join Gaspar and run off, ye did."

"Stop your mouth from running off and help heave this craft of yours to the water."

With mumbles of protest, the tall man complied. Resting his end of the boat, Jack hurried to help Mary and Finn carry their load. At the water line, he held out his hand to her. "Get in."

She gripped his hand with an icy touch.

"Only a few more minutes, Mary, and we'll be safe." Forcing a smile, he wondered if she could see through the mist and into his heart filled with fears. He hoped not. He had to be satisfied with the fact that she settled into the stern without protests.

With Finn, he shoved the boat a short distance into the night. He held out his hand, barring Finn from hopping into the boat. Jack lowered his voice. "Take care of her and don't worry about me. Swear to me."

The sailmaker reached out and gripped Jack's hand in understanding. Then he jumped aboard and grabbed the oars. The soft sound of parting water proclaimed their departure. Through the darkness, he tried to discern Mary, but the night and fog had already claimed them.

The uncomfortable feeling of danger stirred louder within him. He had no choice. By morning light, Gaspar would either come ashore with his men to take them or destroy them with his cannons.

"If I was about to die, I'd like to be with the lady," Luke said.

"Hold your tongue or you'll be the first to meet your maker. Shove the boat."

Shaking his head in disgust, the mooncusser scrambled to push the shore boat out into the water. Once they'd pushed it waist deep, Jack signaled for Luke to jump inside.

Jack quickly leaped inside and sat facing his reluctant companion. He aimed his pistol at his prisoner. Luke picked up the oars, and the boat glided forward.

Around him, Jack could see nothing. Only the feel of his bow breaking straight through the waves told him that they stayed on course. What if they sailed past the *Goodspeed*? They'd be easy targets on the open sea. A chill of alarm spread through him. His hand clenched on his weapon.

"Don't shoot me, Johnny. I'll join yer crew."

"Be quiet."

"When ye tire of the little lady, I'll have a turn."

Gripping his pistol, Jack contemplated how quickly he could strike the man unconscious. The man was baiting him, but worse, his voice could travel through the night air to Gaspar's ship.

Jack squinted into the darkness, trying to discern Finn and Mary. Nothing. He wished Mary was in his boat. He'd feel better about her. What was she thinking at this moment? She probably wondered why she ever put her trust in him. Had she realized he was not the heroic man of her paper tales and fables?

"Why did the lady think I knew her father?" Luke asked, interrupting Jack's thoughts.

"What?"

"The little lady asked if I knew her father. Is he one of Gaspar's men?"

"Keep rowing."

"I can row to hell and back, and we'll never know. This is crazy. We're lost in this fog."

"Quiet."

"No one will ever find us. We'll be lost at sea. It'll take days to die. Surrounded by water, yet not a drop fit to drink. A man's tongue turns black with that kind of death."

"I'll not warn you again. I'm—"

A flash shot out in the thickness of the night. Jack heard the hum of a cannonball hurtling through the air. It ended with a nearby splash. A wave rose up and grabbed the small boat. It tipped and threatened to capsize.

Luke shrieked.

Jack fell backward. The pistol flew from his hand and disappeared into the waters. He pushed himself up onto his elbows. He saw Luke's small gleaming eyes hovering over him. The oar was posed over the man's shoulders to strike him.

Jack attempted to scramble to defend himself. Too late. The oar's blow stunned him. Pain shot through his head. Blindly, he reached out to ward off another swing. Too late. Jack recognized Luke's twisted look of hate before he sank into darkness.

Mary clutched the boat's sides and listened for whatever danger the blackness concealed. She could hear nothing more than her heart thumping. She shoved away the fear seeping through her that Jack had been hit. Mr. Finn stared out into the blackness and shook his head.

She twisted round in her seat, wondering how long till they reached the *Goodspeed*. If only she could see Jack. She felt safe with him. His power and confident air always spilled over onto her.

Suddenly, she heard it again. The hurtling noise that meant someone was firing on them. Suddenly, their boat jerked from side to side. Her world tilted out of focus. A dark wave crashed onto her, filling her eyes and mouth with salt. Unable to see, she held on for her life as the huge wave threw the small craft from one crest to another.

She was going to drown.

Mary felt Mr. Finn's hand grasp hold of her arm and steady her. A queasiness spread through her. Mary thought she might be sick. She forced an eye open. The salt stung her lids. Through the blur, she recognized the sailmaker. The rocking slowed to a wobble, and her stomach calmed.

She sat upright and swallowed past the lump in her throat. "What was that?"

"I think someone is firing at us, too." Mr. Finn's voice shook.

Cleansing tears filled Mary's eyes and streamed down her face. She rubbed them away. "Gaspar?"

Another flash of light with a red center flared in the night. Mary's skin prickled with fear, and she squeezed the boat sides tightly, holding on for her life. A cannon ball whizzed through the night.

This time, the ball landed far from them. Mary breathed a sigh of relief. "How far to the *Goodspeed*?" She bent forward, peering hopelessly into the darkness. The acid smell of powder cut through the damp sea air. She swiveled about and tried to see behind her. "Can you see the captain?"

The sailmaker shook his head and poured all his

strength into his rowing. "We don't have time to stop and look."

"How do we know he's safe?"

"He'd want us to head straight for the ship."

She pointed over Mr. Finn's right shoulder. "Gaspar's ship was over there, I think. So the *Goodspeed* must be directly—"

"Too far. Let's hope she's not sunk by the time we reach her."

Fear spread through her and cut off her answer. She was afraid that if she closed her eyes the boat would slip from beneath her, and she'd drown in the darkness. One hand grasped the side of the boat until it hurt. Her other hand clutched her telescope. She swallowed the salty taste of panic. Calm. She'd remain in control of her reason and say something helpful.

Finally, an idea struck her. "Mr. Finn, can't you whistle like on the island and have the captain answer? I don't think he's behind us. I could hear voices before."

The light with the red center flashed again. "Oh, please, not again," Mary cried. Then in the flare, she recognized the little vessel bouncing over the waves to her right. "It's the captain! He's over there. We must help him."

Mr. Finn's oar missed a beat in the water. His head snapped up in shock. "The captain said I'm to get you to safety no matter what happened to him."

"We can't leave him." At the hiss of the cannonball, Mary held her breath. The black ball fell near Jack's craft. "What are they doing? They're going the wrong way. Gaspar will kill them."

Without a word, Mr. Finn changed his course. A panic like she'd never known before welled in her throat. They rowed straight for Jack and Gaspar's ship.

Fourteen

The small boat crashed through the waves. Mary leaned forward, straining to see Jack. Without the flare from the cannon, she could only hope they headed in the right direction.

Mr. Finn paused in his rowing to listen. His body tensed before he pulled fiercely back on the oars.

Mary clutched hold as the boat leapt forward. How could Jack have lost his way? The mooncusser must have steered them off course.

Suddenly, Mary saw movement through a break in the mist. "I see them! Luke is waving his oar at us. Can't I row, too?"

"Only two oars," the sailmaker spouted through clenched teeth.

A white flash streaked through the night. "Gaspar's ship must be less than a league away," Mary gasped.

Luke's shriek pierced the night.

"I think they've hit the captain." Mary clung to the side and leaned over the water, searching. "Captain!"

"Here!" Luke yelled. "Over here!"

Mr. Finn maneuvered the boat toward the shouts.

Beyond them, the small craft with Luke visible bobbed up and down. Mary cupped her hands around her mouth. "Are you hurt? What's happened? Where's the captain?"

"Lost my oar. Can't row."

"Hold on, we're coming." Mary scanned the boat. On the bottom of the small craft, she saw Jack's dark blue coat. "Mr. Finn, something has happened to the captain."

"Blast it to hell." Mr. Finn held his oar against the waves, forcing the boat to turn closer to the mooncusser.

"Hurry," Luke cried. "I'm drifting away."

"I'd let him drift to the bottom of the sea," Mr. Finn muttered, "except for the captain."

"He's not moving." Mary kept her gaze focused on Jack's form. Fear grabbed her heart. "What has happened to him?" she asked as they drew alongside the other craft.

"Hit his head." The mooncusser shrugged. "Think it might have killed him."

"Killed him!" Desperate, Mary scrutinized Jack's chest for the signs of breathing. At her elbow, she heard Mr. Finn swear.

"Stay back, Miss McNeal," Mr. Finn whispered. "The mooncusser might have the pistol. Hold the rifle on him."

"Grab hold of our boat's side," Mr. Finn directed Luke. "I'm taking the captain on first."

Mary looked down at the rifle at her feet. The waves had soaked it. The gunpowder was ruined. Picking it up, she prayed the mooncusser wouldn't notice.

Luke caught hold of the other vessel. His yellow eyes gleamed as he grabbed hold of the sides of the craft.

Mary tried to steady the weapon while she watched Mr. Finn scramble into the other boat and bend over Jack's still form.

"Is he alive?" Mary asked.

"He's breathing. I'm bringing him over."

"Hurry. My hands hurt from holding tight here." Luke removed a hand and flexed his fingers.

"Let go, and she'll shoot you." Mr. Finn nodded toward Mary. He gathered Jack in his arms and took a second to balance himself before leaping back. He landed with a grunt.

In the darkness a puff of white and the boom of the cannons announced another shot.

Mary screamed. Mr. Finn fell with Jack landing on top of him.

"Hold on little Missy, I'm coming aboard." Luke swung his body into the boat.

Mary tugged at Jack's dead weight.

From underneath, the sailmaker gave a muffled cry.

"Captain! Mr. Finn! Help me with them," she yelled at Luke.

"Afraid not," the mooncusser said, picking up the oars. "We got to move or get blown into fish bait."

Mary drew up the rifle and pointed it at his heart. "Help me now."

Luke dropped the oars into the boat and smiled. "Anything for a lady with a weapon." He scrambled forward. "I'll lift."

Mary eased Jack's head while the mooncusser rolled him off the sailmaker.

Rubbing his forehead, Mr. Finn sat up.

Mary pushed the musket into his arms.

"Sorry, Miss, I'll need you to hold the gun on that good-for-nothing while I row."

Clutching the weapon close, Mary laid a hand on Jack's pale face. Her fingers touched something sticky. "He's bleeding!" She looked past Mr. Finn to Luke. "What did you do to him?"

The mooncusser shrugged. "He fell and hit his head."

"You'll wish the cannonball landed on your head when we get back to the ship," Mr. Finn said, yanking on the oars.

The little ship bounced over a wave. How could Mr.

Finn locate the ship? Mary glanced at the spot where she'd last seen the mooncusser's craft. She could discern nothing except the whizzing of a cannonball that fell a short distance from them.

Mary traced Jack's features and found the pulse steadily beating in his throat. Stroking his hair, she bent and murmured a few words of assurance.

"A bump on the head won't hurt him," Luke grumbled.

"You were headed for Gaspar's ship," Mary said, daring him to deny it.

"Got confused." Luke narrowed his eyes at the musket. "You can put that down. It's two to one. I can't go anywhere."

"Keep it up high," Mr. Finn advised.

"Don't worry, Mr. Finn. He's as trustworthy as Gaspar himself. Thank goodness we caught him and rescued the captain."

"I wasn't going anywhere. All the shooting made me mixed up about the directions."

"I suppose you were confused when you threatened to throw me off a cliff."

"Now it was a joke. We only had ye cook, didn't we?"

Mary opened her mouth to retort when Jack groaned.

Relief flowed through her. She struggled to keep the musket aimed while she gave her attention to him. "It's me."

His eyes blinked open. "Mary?" He stirred restlessly.

"Lie still. We'll be on the *Goodspeed* in only a moment."

He closed his eyes. For a moment, Mary feared the worst. Her hand wandered across his chest and rested on his beating heart. Her own fears pounded in her head.

"He needs help, Mr. Finn. Does anyone aboard know about head injuries?"

"Cook might."

"I wish Mr. Beckett were here."

Another groan came from Jack.

"He's fine," Luke said. "Dead men don't make no noises. How about holding my head for a while?" He rubbed the back of his head. "A rock fell on mine when that captain of yers blew up the cave. Come on, little Missy, pat my head."

Mary opened her mouth to tell the obnoxious mooncusser she didn't have to worry about his hard head, when the *Goodspeed* rose up in front of them. "The ship!"

Mr. Finn's face almost broke into a smile. They drifted beside the old hull. "Daniel," the sailmaker yelled.

Faces and a lantern popped up on the deck. "Is that you, Finn? Where's the captain and Miss McNeal?"

"Here," Mary shouted. "The captain's injured."

In the lantern light, she discerned Daniel's worried face.

"I'll lower the ladder," the first mate called.

"We have a prisoner coming up first," Finn said, cupping his hands to his mouth. "Then lower the ropes to hoist up the boat. The captain can't climb."

Mary bent over Jack. "We're safe. When you've recovered, we'll put that pirate in his proper place."

Jack's hand brushed against hers.

"I think he's awake," Mary said, trying not to shout the news. "I'll stay in the boat with him."

"Better not, Miss," Mr. Finn said. "The shore boat won't be steady when they lift it. You could fall in the water. I'll stay with him. Besides, the captain wouldn't allow it. You can get Cook to inspect the captain when we're aboard."

Mary nodded in resignation and squeezed Jack's hand.

The rope ladder hit against the side and caught her attention.

"We're ready," Daniel shouted. "Send up the prisoner."

Mr. Finn pointed the oar like a sword at Luke. "Up."

"Don't know why you made me a prisoner. I'm only a messenger. I didn't want to sail with Gaspar. He forced me."

"Climb."

Luke ambled up the ladder.

Mary passed the rifle to Mr. Finn, who crawled toward her.

"I'll take care of him," the sailmaker said. "Don't worry. It'll take more than a crack on the head to stop the captain."

"He's not speaking. I know that's a bad sign. In Oyster River, Mr. Beanpot was kicked by a horse in the head and—"

"Where's Miss McNeal?" Daniel held the lantern over the side while he peered down at them.

"You'd best go," the sailmaker encouraged. "Then we can hoist up the captain."

Cautiously, Mary exchanged places with Mr. Finn. With a last look at Jack, Mary ascended to the *Goodspeed*.

The pain in Jack's head shot into all parts of his body. Tired. He was too tired to fight, yet he knew he must escape from his enemy's ship. Gaspar had him. Jack had to stay still and gather his strength before Gaspar's men realized he'd regained his senses. Pain stabbed him. He couldn't think. St. George prayed for unconsciousness to take him.

In the sputtering lantern light, Mary stared down at Jack's dark head. Over his temple, blood had matted his hair and streaked down his cheek.

"The blood has slowed," Cook said at her elbow. "His head needs sewing. Finn, you can do it."

The sailmaker took a hesitant step forward. "Me? I've never mended a man's head."

"Fetch your needle, thread, and hot water," Cook ordered.

"I have thread and a needle," Mary offered, hurrying to the trunk. She flung open the lid and removed the utensils.

Cook frowned at Mr. Finn, who appeared frozen. "I'll fetch the hot water. If you want anything done on a ship, you have to do it—" The door closed on his last words.

After laying the notions on the table, Mary crossed the floor to Jack. The gray blanket had been flung over him.

"I wish he'd wake," Mary whispered. "A head wound and unconsciousness mean trouble."

"He doesn't look good." Mr. Finn trembled slightly.

A knock disturbed Mary's bleak thoughts. Daniel entered. "The men want to know how he is. Any change?"

"Not much," Mary admitted. "Has Gaspar been spotted?"

Daniel shook his head. "Can't see anything in this fog, but we're weighing anchor."

"We're leaving?" Mary whirled about to face the first mate.

"With the captain laid up, we're not in any position to fight. It's best to give the pirate the slip in this weather."

"We've waited so long to get this close. And we're running away."

"We have one of Gaspar's men, Miss McNeal. He may be able to tell us Gaspar's direction and news of your father."

"True." Her gaze fell on Jack in his deathlike stillness.

"We need to consult a doctor. How long before we reach land?"

Daniel gave her a sheepish grin. "I'm afraid I can't tell much tonight. But we're not waiting for Gaspar to find us."

A thumping on the cabin door produced Cook with his pail of water. Hot steam rose from the open bucket.

"How much of the captain needs washing?" Daniel asked, watching the water slosh against the sides of the pail.

"I brought some for Miss McNeal."

Surprised, Mary saw everyone look at her. For the first time she realized that blood had seeped under her nails and across the back of her hand. Even her dress had stains.

"Thank you, Cook," she whispered.

Cook set the pail on the table. "Knew you'd want it. I'll wash the needle, and Finn can stitch up the captain."

Mary wandered to the bunk and whispered to Jack. "You're safe now. But we need you. Gaspar is out there nearby. Help us."

Behind her, she heard the splash of water, and Cook telling Mr. Finn to start sewing. A loud thud answered Cook.

Turning, Mary found the sailmaker sprawled upon the planks. "Oh, Mr. Finn!" Mary cried, darting to him.

"Stand aside," Cook shouted. He lugged the water next to the collapsed man and sprinkled a handful on him.

With a moan, Mr. Finn opened his eyes. "Did I miss a stitch?"

"Come on, man." Daniel pulled his friend to his feet.

"Sorry, I don't think I'm good with blood," Mr. Finn said, staggering.

"Pretend it's only red cloth," Cook advised.

The sailmaker ran a shaky hand over his face. "I don't think I'm that good a pretender."

"I'll do it." Mary held out her hand. "My stitches won't be as expert as Mr. Finn's."

"I don't think the captain will be admiring his stitches much." Cook dropped the needle into her palm and held out the thread.

Swaying gently on his feet, Mr. Finn smiled weakly. "Thanks, Miss McNeal."

Biting her lip, Mary took off her telescope and put it away in the trunk. Then she approached her work. Cook washed the wound, and Mary sewed. The room was tense with silence by the time Mary tied the last stitch.

"Quick as a stitch," she said, trying to lighten the mood.

The men all nodded and stood about, looking helpless.

Time to take charge, Mary thought. "He needs his rest. I'll sleep in the captain's new quarters."

"I'm afraid you can't." Daniel sent her an uneasy look. "The prisoner has been placed in there."

How could she have forgotten Luke. "I'd like to speak to him. Mr. Finn, can you stay with the captain? When he regains consciousness, he'll have lots of questions."

"Sorry, Miss McNeal," Daniel said, "but I can't allow anyone near the prisoner. It's too dangerous. I can't even allow you in the cabin next to him. It's not safe. I'll string up a hammock for you in here. Then you can nurse the captain."

Without waiting for a response, Daniel headed for the door.

"In here?" Mary looked doubtfully at the captain. "Perhaps it's suitable if I'm to tend him."

"You've missed your meal," Cook reminded. "I'll scrape something together for you and Finn."

The sailmaker shook his head. "My stomach's not feeling right yet."

"Thank you, Cook," Mary said quickly. "But I couldn't eat a bit after all the excitement."

Cook scowled at his rejected offer. "Just a plate for the captain. He'll be hungry when he wakes."

"Yes, he will," Mary agreed, dipping her hands into the lukewarm water. She closed her eyes and imagined soaking in a large tub of scented bath water.

"When do you think he'll wake up?" the sailmaker asked.

Mr. Finn's voice brought Mary back to the cool room. She glanced at Jack lying beneath the short gray blanket. "Soon. Can you get him a better cover?"

"I will," Mr. Finn agreed. He spun on his heel toward the door. "The bottom is gone from that one. I wonder how that happened."

Alone, Mary crept closer. She remembered Mr. Finn's words to her in the boat. Jack had put her life above his own.

Feelings of fear and love flooded her. "Jack, please wake up. I know I didn't do a very satisfactory job as your navigator, but I'll do better. Please. I need you." With the tips of her fingers, she gently traced around the wounded area.

At least his skin felt warm. But he was so deathly still. What would she do if he never awoke. Panic gripped her. She must think of a way to reach him and bring him back. How? Bending close to his ear, Mary whispered, "I love you."

Jack felt warm breath on his face. A rat, he thought. *They filled the bowels of Gaspar's ship. He must get up*

*before it bit him. He didn't need the plague. He raised
his head and saw the flicker of a light.*

*Gaspar had sent a man to bring him on deck. Jack
didn't know how much more he could take. Wearily, he
opened an eye. Mary McNeal floated toward him, a candle gripped in her hand.*

"Mary?" He pushed himself up on his elbows.

She held out a hand. "I've come for you."

He couldn't believe it. "Why?"

*"I love you. Come back with me." Mary motioned with
her hand. "Hurry, they're almost here."*

Footsteps echoed from the far end.

"Run, Mary. Hide."

The light went out.

Jack's groan startled Mary. She drew back and waited.
Nothing. Had he heard her? Her heart pounded loudly in
her ears while she waited for him to speak.

A light rap on the door tore her attention away from
him. She ran across the floor and found Daniel at the
door. A rope hammock was folded in his arms.

"Think you'll be comfortable in this, Miss? I'll string
it up for you."

On his heels, Mr. Finn appeared with the promised
blanket. Mary noted that it was identical, except for
length, to Jack's own.

Mr. Finn shook out the covering and laid it on top of
the other blanket.

"I'm worried," Mary said, approaching the sailmaker.
"He should have regained consciousness by now. He
needs a doctor."

"I agree," Daniel called, pausing to test the end of the
hammock hanging from the beam near the desk.

Unclasping and clasping her hands, Mary continued. "Since you're in charge, Daniel, and I'm the navigator, we should discuss our course. We want one that will bring us to a doctor."

"Our only course now is escape. We're sailing, but slowly in this fog. It's more like drifting."

"Aimless drifting," Mary noted. She trudged to the desk and pulled open the drawer. Her fingers folded around the map.

Opening it upon the desk, she peered closely at the paper. Only a few hours ago, she'd looked at this chart with hope and joy, convinced she'd found her father.

Now Jack lay injured, perhaps dying. They'd not found her father, and Gaspar hovered nearby waiting to kill them all.

"What do you think?" Daniel stepped up behind her.

Mary tried to gather her scattered thoughts. Pointing to what she assumed was their present location, she shoved her worries deep inside. She scanned the map for the closest civilized landform.

"Here!" She indicated with her index finger. "We'll sail for Nova Scotia. A doctor should reside there."

The sailmaker came up beside her. "Let's hope the captain doesn't come to. He'd never agree to running away from Gaspar because of a bump."

"True," Mary said. "He's rather hard-headed, and I doubt a knock on the skull will bring him to his senses about his health. Daniel, I wish you'd reconsider my speaking with Luke. You can stay in the cabin with me."

Daniel's hand on the rope stilled. "The captain wouldn't approve. He'd want to talk to the prisoner first. It's how he runs his ship, and I have to follow his orders."

"You don't want to wait for the captain to regain consciousness, and you won't want to bother him right away with pressing problems. He'll require time to recuperate. There's only one solution. We will interrogate the prisoner ourselves."

"With all due respect, Miss McNeal, the captain wouldn't want you near the man. I can't imagine he'd let you speak to him, and after that time in Bath, I promised the captain to be careful with you."

Mary folded her arms across her chest. "I'm not a thing. Besides, I'm part of the crew. I'm the navigator. Mr. Finn will also accompany us. Besides, how dangerous can it be with both of you guarding him?"

"I think I'll stay with the captain," Mr. Finn said, settling himself into the desk chair.

Traitor, Mary thought. She pressed on with Daniel. "You'll have the musket. The prisoner will have none."

"In the shore boat, the captain had his pistol and Luke had none," Mr. Finn reasoned. "Look what happened."

"Very well," Mary said, whirling about to the desk. "Mr. Finn, I'll stay with the captain. You and Daniel shall question the mooncusser."

She searched the desk for writing paper. Finding none, she yanked a sheet from the log.

"Miss McNeal," Daniel said in an urgent tone. "You can't rip up the log book. The captain won't forgive you."

"I'm listing the questions for the prisoner. We need to know what he used to hit the captain." The pen flew across the paper as her ideas spilled onto it. "I'll write a complete description of my father." Finished, she held out the sheet.

Daniel took it and scanned the paper. His brows rose in surprise. "Often uses the expression, 'Bless my lucky stars'?"

"One person's physical description doesn't always match another's perception, and my father uses the saying frequently. A trait is more noticeable and helpful in tracing others."

"Don't worry, Miss McNeal. If that mooncusser has seen your father, we'll get it out of him. Come along, Finn."

"Good luck," Mary called, toting the footstool to the bunk.

Sinking down onto it, she surveyed Jack's pale face. "I know you wouldn't approve of them questioning Luke for me, but you'll forgive us."

"Mary?" His eyes blinked open.

Mary covered her mouth with her hand to stifle the cry.

"Are you safe?" Rolling onto his side, he winced. "They didn't get you?"

"Don't move." She jumped up from the stool. "Don't talk."

"That's what I tell you," Jack said in a tired voice. "Where's Gaspar?"

"He's far away. You're on the *Goodspeed*. Do you remember anything?"

Jack ran a hand over his eyes as though clearing his mind. "We're on the ship? I thought you spoke to me and—" He broke off and stared at her.

Why did he look at her so strangely? Suddenly she remembered her confession of love. Heavens, what if he'd heard her? Her face heated. She almost wished he'd remained unconscious. "You suffered a blow to the head," she explained rapidly. "It must have jarred your imagination. Don't worry. Cook inspected your wound."

"Cook!" He struggled to push himself up with his elbows. "He only knows about heads of cabbage."

"Careful," Mary warned, trying to help him sit up. "You could split your stitches."

"I've stitches?" He touched his wound and flinched. "Great Blackbeard's Ghost!" He closed and opened his eyes in disbelief. "Who sewed me? Not Finn."

"Well, he tried," Mary confessed, wondering how to calm him and hoping he wouldn't remember those three little words she'd said to him. "But Mr. Finn learned that mending cloth and your head were not the same. He couldn't do it."

"Thank God." He eyed her curiously. "Who put me back together?"

"I did." She bit her lip, waiting for his condemnation.

Instead, he slid down into his bunk. "That's better." He closed his eyes. "I'm tired."

"Of course you are." Mary fought the urge to draw the blanket up around his chin. "The best you can do is rest. I'll stay here in case you want anything."

"My ship," he whispered.

"No cause for worry. Daniel has taken charge. He's an excellent leader. You've taught him well. He's thought of nothing but our safety and following your rules. He hasn't done anything to cause alarm."

The door banged open, causing Mary to jump. Daniel and Mr. Finn strode into the room. The first mate's eyes gleamed with excitement. "Miss McNeal, Luke knows your father."

Fifteen

Mary ran to Daniel. "What did Luke say? Does he know where my father is?" In the back of her mind, she heard Jack mumbling in a gruff voice.

"Captain?" Daniel stared at St. George. "You're alive?"

"Yes." St. George drew a ragged breath. "Although, I understand while I lay unconscious," he drew in another labored breath, "all the crew examined me. I'm surprised you didn't invite Gaspar, too."

"How ridiculous," Mary said, stepping to his bedside. "You mustn't exhaust yourself speaking like this."

"If you're about to say my head will ache," he caught her gaze, "for once you're right."

"Rest," Mary ordered, feeling flustered by his praise. She glanced at the first mate and nodded at the door.

"Don't leave," Jack said. "I want to hear Daniel's report."

"You can discuss business later." Mary felt Jack's forehead.

He reached out and laced his fingers through hers, holding her still beside him.

Stunned by his public action, Mary stood immobile.

"Daniel, what lies did that mooncusser tell you?" Jack asked.

Mary tensed and turned her attention to the first mate. "Is my father on Gaspar's ship?"

"No, the mooncusser hasn't seen your father. He just heard about him."

Disappointed, tears clogged her throat and cut off Mary's questions.

"Go on," Jack encouraged.

"The mooncusser joined Gaspar after he met you, Miss McNeal. When he got on the ship, everyone on board talked about this huge treasure and how Gaspar has buried it."

"I don't understand," Mary said, sitting on the edge of the bunk and aware that Jack hadn't let go of her hand.

"The gold is surrounded by traps that will kill any man trying to dig up the money. The man who thought up all these tricks was your father."

"Where is he?" Mary held her breath while Jack squeezed her hand.

"The last time anyone saw him, he was on the island with the money."

"We have to go back to Queen's Island," Mary said to Jack.

"No, Miss," Daniel explained. "It's not that island. Luke told us it wasn't. He didn't know the name of the spot with the treasure, and there's another problem. Luke said that the crew who did know where to find the money were disappearing from the ship. No one left aboard wanted to say the name of the island for fear they'd be next to vanish."

Mary's hope faded with her fears. "Why would people disappear? Are they trying to get to the treasure first?"

"No, Mary," Jack answered in a quiet voice. "I know Gaspar. He is killing any man who reveals his hiding place."

How would they ever find her father? Unexpectedly, a tear trickled down her face. *How annoying,* she thought. She pulled her hand away and brushed at the tear. "But what clues will we use to find my father?" Her voice sounded thick and not like her own.

"Need a drink, Miss McNeal?" Mr. Finn asked, stepping forward with worry on his brow.

"No." Mary shook her head. "I knew he was alive."

"Daniel and Finn," Jack rasped. "Go on deck and see if there's been any sighting of Gaspar."

Throwing her sympathetic looks, the first mate and the sailmaker left.

"Don't put your faith in that mooncusser," Jack said. "He's a liar."

"I have to believe my father is alive."

"Believe it if you must, but don't base your faith on the word of that scoundrel. Remember what happened in Maine."

Mary blinked back the tears that refused to stop burning her eyes. Jack's face blurred, but she could distinguish a glimmer of pain in his eyes. "He hurt you, didn't he?" Gingerly, she reached out and lightly touched his cheek.

"I can't remember. We were together in the shore boat and—" He shrugged. "Nothing else is clear."

"He says you fell backward when Gaspar fired on you."

"I'll talk to him when my head clears."

Mary jumped to her feet. "I can interrogate him. The longer we wait, the more time he has to invent a story."

"I doubt the man could create a convincing white lie. Listen, you wanted me to help you because of my skills. It's time you let me. I know how to deal with prisoners."

Mary looked at him doubtfully. The reasonable part of her told her he made sense, yet being logical meant waiting for Jack to recover. "You shouldn't be out of bed for at least a week."

"Tomorrow morning."

"That's too soon. I know. We'll have Luke brought in here. You can interrogate him from your bed. I can be present too."

He looked about to refuse when his gaze flickered to the hammock strung near his desk.

"It's mine. You need to be kept under observation." Heat rushed to her cheeks as she remembered them together in bed.

"Yours?"

"You don't want Cook or Mr. Finn, do you?"

"Is that a threat, Miss McNeal?"

"Let's consider it a compromise. I shall wait until morning for news of my father, and you'll confine yourself to your bed."

"About tomorrow, Mary—"

"We'll discuss it later. I want to speak with Daniel. He may have forgotten an important fact that Luke mentioned. Promise you'll try to sleep while I'm gone."

"Give me your word that you won't speak to the mooncusser no matter what you imagine about your father."

"Captain, I'm a librarian. I deal with facts, not fancies." She leaned down and kissed his forehead. His arm came up about her waist, and he lightly held her, hovering above him. Startled, she looked down into his eyes. She saw the familiar spark of light that lit his gaze during their kisses. A shiver of anticipation ran through her. Then her common sense grasped hold of her. The man had nearly been killed. Most likely it was the fever simmering in his eyes. He didn't need kisses or his imagination carrying him away.

Mary pulled back and strode to the door. It closed be-

hind her before she remembered to say good-bye. Outside
the cabin, she took a deep breath and smoothed her skirt.
She had to concentrate on her father, not Jack. Her composure collected, she headed for the deck to jar Daniel's
memory.

Mary had barely emerged upon deck when Daniel
called out to her in a loud whisper. In the darkness, she
tried to make him out. The wind stirred, and her wet
clothes clung to her. Mary realized the fog and the waves
had soaked her dress. She'd have to change. Oh well,
she'd worry about new clothes later. She peered closer at
the first mate, who was now standing in front of her.

"Daniel?"

"Sorry, I ordered all lights out. We don't want to give
away our position to Gaspar."

"We'd be lucky to know our own position," Mary said,
squinting into the darkness.

"Since you're our navigator, where are we headed?"

"The compass is below, but I don't want the captain
to worry and think we're lost. I'll fetch it after he's had
a chance to fall asleep. Otherwise, he'll never stay in bed.
Please do not disturb him, Daniel."

"Will he still need a doctor?"

"A head injury is very serious. I've had many an oc-
casion to read about them, especially last fall when Mrs.
Harrison's horse kicked poor Mr. Beanpot. He suffered
headaches for eons. No Daniel, we must ignore the captain's wishes and chart a course to bring him to a physi-
cian."

"I don't think the captain will want much doctoring."

"We'll keep our plan a secret."

"The captain doesn't like secrets, and he might not like
the ship's direction."

"Don't worry, Daniel. I shall take care of it. Now repeat everything the prisoner told you. There may be an important detail you've forgotten."

"God's truth, Miss McNeal, he didn't say much. Mr. Finn told him your father's description from your piece of paper, and the mooncusser laughed and said, 'You mean the Star Master?' "

"Star Master!" Excitement rushed through her. "See, he does know my father. What a perfect description of him. Please, Daniel, what else did he say?"

"Like I said before, the prisoner has never seen or met your father. He heard talk that Gaspar had left him on an island with a chest of gold."

Mary clasped her hands tightly together, trying to contain her excitement. "Did he say anything about my father's health?"

"Don't think so. He didn't want to say much. Finn had to threaten to tie him to the mast to learn that much."

"Thank you for trying, Daniel. I'll get the compass for you." Mary whirled around on her heel. Her mind spun with questions and ideas she wanted to ask Luke.

She tiptoed into the cabin. Jack lay on the bunk with his eyes closed and his breathing steady. Mary snatched the key from the drawer and seized the compass from its velvet box. For a moment, she stood mesmerized by the arrow pointing north. In her mind, she saw the night sky with Cassiopeia. Had it all been a wild chase? Jack had almost died because of her obsession to follow a star, and Gaspar hovered nearby in the dark. How close was he? Mary's gaze went to the porthole, and she shivered.

Slanting a glance at Jack, her heart beat faster. How many men would have listened and given her an opportunity to pursue this course? Now she had to get them away from Gaspar.

Quietly, she returned to Daniel. The first mate took the

compass with a brief thanks and disappeared. Mary decided to take a quick nap and awake fresh and ready to help question Luke. Back in the cabin, Mary retrieved her telescope from the trunk and strung it around her neck. She paused with her hand on the trunk. Jack's shirt stared up at her. She did need to take off her stained dress.

Pulling out the shirt, the pink material caught her eye. Well, she didn't have time to sew a gown, but she'd improvise. Mary turned down the lantern. In the dim light, she shed her soiled clothing. Then she donned Jack's shirt, which hung to her knees. Underneath the shirt, she wrapped the pink material around her waist, letting the rest fall to her ankles as a skirt, and knotted the ends. Done at last, she tumbled into the hammock.

Mary stretched out and grabbed hold of the moving bed as it careened from side to side. Gradually, she relaxed and snuggled down into the depth of her rope berth. In only a few hours, she'd know the truth about her father. Jack would force the truth from the mooncusser.

Jack awoke with a headache that made him want to jump overboard. Carefully, he swung his feet over the side of the bunk. At a streak of pain, he remembered the stitches in his head and thought about sinking under the covers.

He knew he had promised to do something this morning, but his mind clouded with misery. Sitting still, he waited for the ache to subside. Even the day after they celebrated the end of the war, his head hadn't hurt like this.

Inching off the bunk, he winced and took the final plunge. His feet touched the cool wooden planks. His

vision blurred and cleared. The hammock came into focus. What the blazes?

Jack ignored his throbbing head. He crept closer. A
small figure was curled inside. Mary. The librarian had
spent the night with him in his cabin.

"Damn," he whispered. They had been together all
night, and he'd spent it sleeping. The gods of the seven
seas were against him.

He moved closer. He recognized his shirt and the pink
cloth that covered her legs. Her chestnut hair had loosened and lay around her face like a halo, while her full
lips were relaxed into a curve that made her look like she
was smiling. "Dreaming of a good book, my little librarian?" he whispered. He longed to bend down and kiss
her awake.

Great Blackbeard's Ghost! Hadn't he vowed on
Queen's Island to send her to safety? Here he was thinking about seducing her. Despite his conscience's warning,
he nudged closer and recognized that she clutched her
telescope in her sleep.

Tonight, he'd go back to his miserable, cramped cabin.
Wait, he didn't have to return. *This* was his cabin. Mary
could play nursemaid all she wanted. He wouldn't utter
a complaint about her presence. Besides, he'd been injured. The idea of Mary flitting near his bed brought a
smile to his face.

Running his hand through his hair, he winced. Stitches.
He closed his eyes and willed the pain away. Now what
had he planned for today? Ah yes, he needed to interrogate the mooncusser. Mary had wanted to accompany
him. All the more reason to question the man before she
awoke. He could imagine her technique for getting information from a prisoner. She'd probably lecture Jack on
using please and thank you.

He grabbed his coat and headed for the door.

"Jack?"

He stopped and whirled around to her hammock. "Good morning, Mary. Don't bother getting up. It's not daylight yet."

She blinked her eyes and jumped from her berth. It swung behind her. "You shouldn't be out of bed."

"I've only taken ten steps. Lovely clothes."

She glanced down at her newly fashioned skirt and blushed. "I didn't have time to sew." Drawing closer, she studied his face. "You're not well."

"Don't tell me. You can read people's faces like you do the night sky."

"You think you're quite witty, but this is very serious. A head injury requires a doctor's care. You may think you've recovered, but you haven't."

"I don't understand what you said, but it sounds like you. What happened to Gaspar?"

"What?"

"Last night, Gaspar shot at us. I don't remember what happened afterwards. Is he tailing us?"

"I–I don't know." Mary bit her lip and looked uncomfortable.

"Why is the map on the desk?" he asked, striding to it.

"I left it out last night. Sorry. I'm a bit disorganized."

"A strange quality for a librarian. How do you keep all those books in place?" He picked up the map.

"I manage. I'll get your breakfast."

Jack glanced up from the chart. "Good idea. Send Daniel here."

"Certainly." Mary scurried to the door. Once it clicked shut behind her, Jack sat at his desk and spread the map. He found their last position. Where and how far had they sailed? Yet another problem nagged at his mind. Gaspar.

Hearing the familiar short rap on the door, Jack knew Daniel had arrived. The librarian was fast. He'd have to work quickly. If only his blasted head would stop aching. He called for Daniel to enter. "Any sign of another ship?"

"None, but I've added a man to each watch."

"Good, I want us to head for land. We need to get Miss McNeal settled safely on shore before we're attacked again. A battle is not the place for a librarian."

"You think Gaspar will attack soon, Captain?"

"The only question is when, Daniel. Don't mention my plan to Miss McNeal."

"No, Captain She's worried about you. She insists that you need a doctor."

The door creaked. "Here's your breakfast," Mary said brightly, nudging the door open with one arm. In the other hand, she carried a bowl.

Jack gave Daniel a look commanding silence. To Mary he said, "I've never had a more helpful nurse." He glanced at the pasty, gray conglomeration in the bowl. "Is this some kind of headache remedy?"

"No, this food is nourishment. You must take care. Your body has suffered a shock. You can't expect it to return to normal overnight."

He opened his mouth to protest when a thought struck him. "You're right, Miss McNeal. I should rest." He shoved the bowl across the table. "I don't think I'm strong enough to eat yet. I'll take a nap."

Out of the corner of his eye, Jack saw Daniel's jaw drop open.

"I'm glad you're being reasonable." Mary picked up the bowl and peered down at the contents. "I can ask Cook for something else."

"Don't bother." Assuming a sickly role, he hobbled toward the bunk. "I'll sleep a while."

"What happened to your leg?"

Jack's hand snapped to his leg. "Ah, it's stiff. A little rest and I'll be fine. It's probably all that body shock you mentioned."

Mary nodded. "I'll take the food back to the galley. Daniel, don't you want to come?"

"Daniel can stay for a few minutes. I want to speak with him."

Mary hesitated. "Only a few minutes. You don't want to overdo it. I think I'll take my sewing with me."

Jack placed his hand over his heart. "You have my solemn word he'll stay but a moment. I will talk quickly."

"Why does your promise sound strange?" Mary raised a brow of doubt.

"Because he's tired?" Daniel offered hopefully.

Mary tilted her head as if assessing the situation. "He should be. I don't know why you want me to leave, Captain, but as long as you rest I won't complain. I'll bring back your *headache medicine* later." She paused. "I have to get my sewing." Quickly, she gathered her needle, shears, and thread.

After the door shut, Daniel approached St. George. "I don't think she believed you, Captain."

"At least it saved me from eating that gruel. Cook's talents never end." He clapped his hands together. "Daniel, your job is to keep her busy while I question the prisoner. She has a strange idea that she should be present."

"Yes, Captain."

"I know. Get her to sew for you."

"Maybe she'll make me another shirt," Daniel said hopefully.

"That's a good idea. Give her more work than she can

handle. I'll leave it to you." Jack strode to his cabinet and removed his last pistol. "Now I'll speak to our prisoner."

"Do you want me to come with you?"

"No. Do your job with Miss McNeal. Besides, I doubt that our prisoner would offer her any information that she could use." He struggled into his coat and shoved his pistol inside his coat pocket. "We'll speak later."

Inside his cabin, Luke looked up lazily from his bunk. "Too early for a visit."

"Sorry, Luke, this is part of the torture."

"How about some food? I've had nothing since I got here. This cabin is worse than the cave in Maine."

"Really? This was my cabin for a while." Jack leaned against the wall with folded arms. "I can make an exchange. You answer my questions, and I'll give you food."

Luke swung his feet onto the floor and stood. "Does that lady friend of yers know how ye treat people? First, ye tie up me and Morley. Then you try to blow us up, and now ye starve me."

"As I remember, you were going to kill Miss McNeal."

"Naw, we decided to be nice. We were willing to give her back to ye." His eyes gleamed with speculation. "For the right price."

"Enough." Jack strode toward the man standing in the middle of the cramped room. "How long did Gaspar plan to follow my ship?"

Luke shrugged. "Didn't know we were chasing ye. Gaspar didn't exactly discuss his plans with me."

"What did he say when you met in Maine?"

Luke grinned. "He said, 'Sail with me and ye can fix that Johnny St. George for leaving ye in a cave to die.' "

"What a coincidence Gaspar should happen along and save you. He's a *hero.*"

The mooncusser fingered his red beard. "People used to call ye one, too."

The words struck Jack like a slap. Anger boiled within him. "When you have something to tell me, we'll talk again." He marched across the floor. His hand touched the handle.

"Don't ye want to know about the little missy's father?"

Jack swung around and faced him. "What about him?"

"What ye got to eat?"

Impatience surged through Jack. "I'll have my own breakfast brought to you."

"Swear to it."

"On Neptune's tomb."

"He's with the money."

"What do you mean?" Jack asked. "Where?"

"Gone. Buried. Gaspar said, 'He's gone to the heavens.' Where's my food?"

Jack debated pressing further. Finally, he decided he'd question the mooncusser later. Dinnertime came to his mind. Luke would be good and hungry and might be easier to persuade. "I'll have your breakfast sent immediately."

"Have the Star Mistress bring it."

"Who?" St. George asked.

"The little missy. Gaspar always called her the Star Mistress."

Fear prickled the back of Jack's neck. "Gaspar knows Mary?"

Luke shrugged. "He knows everyone."

Sixteen

Jack sat on a stool in the galley, trying to force the gray soup down his throat while the throbbing in his temple refused to stop.

He stared into the gray soup bowl, but in his mind, he saw Mary McNeal. The scent of lavender rose up and filled the air. She held a flickering candle and whispered, "I love you."

He pushed away from the table. Had he dreamt these words?

In his cabin, Jack fell into his bunk where a restless sleep overtook him. A pounding in his head became the padding of footsteps. *He searched the darkness of Gaspar's hold. "Mary? It's safe. Come out."*

Only the creaks of the ship answered him. He raised himself up onto his elbows. Pain shot through him, and he was overcome with dizziness. He fell backward onto the wet slop in the bottom of Gaspar's ship. Inside his head, Mary's three words beat with the pain. "I love you. I love you. I love you."

Jack woke slowly. He stared at his built-in writing desk and cabinet. His gaze wandered to the unfamiliar hammock. Mary. He sat up straight in his bunk. Had she confessed that she loved him? When? Had it all been a dream?

He concentrated harder. What had he seen in her eyes?

Embarrassment? Was she afraid that he was ill, or was the concern for something else? He rubbed his temple, and the notion struck him. Mary was worried he'd heard her.

"Great Blackbeard's Ghost!" She had said she loved him.

A sudden urge filled him to grab her and make her say it again while he was conscious. But how? Women usually only said these things when they wanted something from a man. What did Mary want? Marriage? Damn, she'd gotten rid of that banking fellow and wanted someone new. He wasn't about to play that game, but he'd like to see how far she'd play out her hand.

The door creaked open, and the librarian tiptoed inside.

"You can move about like a normal person, Mary."

"I am a normal person."

He let her feeble joke pass. "What's happening on deck?"

"Above?" She shrugged and turned quickly away from him. "Everyday happenings. Cook is cooking. Daniel is first mating." She flung open the trunk and hid her face behind the chest lid.

"Why won't you look at me? Am I that ugly?"

"I don't want to disturb you. I'll simply take my telescope and leave. Have a nice nap."

"Stop!"

Mary whirled around to him. Irritation was written on her face. "You expect to regain your health by chitchatting?"

"I've never chitchatted in my life. Why do you need your telescope? Has the fog lifted?" His gaze flickered to the porthole. The light did seem brighter.

"Or are you giving one of those astronomy lessons that

Finn spoke to me about?" he asked, raising himself to a sitting position.

"Something rather like that." She twisted the scope's cord.

Mary was up to something. He decided to see how far she'd go to hide it from him. "You should include Beckett's crew. They need all the help they can get. What are you discussing?"

"I could talk about the Greeks and their celestial discoveries." She brightened. "In fact, I could practice my speech on you. Who is the father of astronomy?"

Despite his suspicions, his head ached, and he wanted to end their useless discussion. "Never mind, Miss McNeal. I'm sure my new crew will remember every word you say. Go ahead."

"Thank you, Captain." She spun about to leave and stopped.

"Is something wrong?" Jack asked.

"No." She strode to his side. Without a word, Mary bent and lightly kissed his lips. "For luck." She smiled shyly.

Before he could muster a sound, she flew from the cabin. He put a finger to his lips, warm from her kiss. Her behavior was strange even for Mary. Gritting his teeth, he threw the blanket aside.

She was planning something, and if he didn't stop her, she'd soon have his ship in chaos. Before the day ended, he'd have her confined in his cabin, alone, where he could get her to make her confession of love without any concession on his part. He grinned.

Emerging into the fresh spring air, Jack saw that the fog had cleared. Clouds clung to the sky. Over by the rail, Mary and Daniel stood closely together conversing while they looked out to sea. Absorbed in their conversation, they didn't see him. He should have realized Daniel would be involved. "Women are dangerous," he muttered. "They're like the weather: unpredictable."

Mary could see the yellow, round shape of the sun through the haze. She squinted her left eye and looked through the scope at the daytime star.

"Discovering a Greek celestial, Miss McNeal? Daniel, which one of the Greeks is your favorite?"

Mary and Daniel whirled toward Jack.

Daniel swallowed audibly. "I'm not sure."

Mary dropped her scope. It bounced on its cord. "Captain, you should be resting, not roaming about the ship."

"What? Lie abed and miss your lesson? I'd never forgive myself. Now where's the rest of the crew? They'll want to hear this. Daniel?"

"What?" the first mate asked in a small voice.

"Ignore the captain," Mary said to Daniel with resignation. "There's no astronomy lesson, but the captain already knows."

"Daniel, leave. Miss McNeal, ignoring your captain is an offense on a ship. Come below, and I'll decide your punishment."

The first mate stepped in front of Mary. "She didn't mean any harm. I take full responsibility."

"Stand aside, Daniel. You need to train the crew. None of them know the first thing about sailing. I'll attend to Mary."

With a look of apology, the first mate slowly moved away. He threw the librarian a wary glance over his shoulder.

"Captain," Mary said. "I have a surprise for you."

"Below, Miss McNeal. Now."

Mary folded her arms over her chest. "Ask like a gentleman, and I might consider it."

"What?"

"I know you've been ill, but sickness is no excuse for rudeness."

Jack ran his hand through his hair. Then his irritation faded, replaced by a gleam in his eyes. "I apologize. Please come below."

Mary's arms dropped slowly to her sides while she studied him suspiciously. He'd agreed too quickly. "What will you do in the cabin? Reprimand me?"

"You can nurse me."

Unease drifted through her. "I'm not sure what that means," she said, taking in his unusually happy countenance. "But I want to talk about our course. You need to know where we're headed."

He took her by the arm and led her toward the stairs. "Anywhere you've plotted is fine with me."

Stunned by his reaction, Mary followed. Outside the cabin, she stopped. She hoped he remembered their disagreement when they agreed not to be together again.

"I believe I have a fever." He opened the door, reached for her palm, and placed it on his forehead.

The warmth from his skin flowed into her hand. Excitement stirred within her while a warning sounded in her mind.

"What do you think?" He gave her a speculative look.

She couldn't think with him looking at her this closely. Self-conscious, she removed her hand. Heavens, the man was weak. "I think we should go inside. There's a draft here."

Jack stood back for her to proceed first.

Get control of yourself, Mary thought. *It's time to confess they were headed for land and not out to sea to locate*

Gaspar. His mood would change quickly. "Captain, I've spoken with—"

A strong rap sounded on the door.

"One moment," he said, striding to the door.

"Good day, Captain." The sailmaker peered into the room.

"Finn, do you have a reason for your interruption, or did you come here to stare at us?"

"Sorry, Captain." He scanned their faces again. "Daniel thought, so I thought, uh, are you all right, Miss McNeal?"

"She's fine." Impatience rang in his voice.

"Oh, Mr. Finn, can you take these caps to the men?" Mary swept up the white hats from the table. "Please give them to the new crewmen first. I'll make more for everyone later."

Mary suppressed the urge to run her hand over her hair. Why did he look at her so strangely? She watched the sailmaker disappear without another word.

Jack smiled. "I remember we were talking about my health."

"I'm glad you mentioned it. I think that given the severity of your injuries you should consult a doctor." She held her breath, waiting for his objections.

"Do you?" he asked in a quiet voice. His boots thudded across the wooden planks as he paced to her. *"I don't agree."*

"Please be reasonable. You've suffered a cruel blow."

"I do agree that I need nursing. But I want you." He raised a brow, and she saw a bright gleam in his eyes. The one he wore when he wanted to kiss her.

Her breath caught in her throat. She took a deep breath, trying to collect herself. "What did you say?"

"When I was ill, you took care of me." He gave her an innocent smile. "I felt much better afterwards."

She was imagining that look in his eye. What was wrong with her? *She* hadn't been hit in the head. "I'm glad you approve."

Mary had to move away from him. Being close to him confused her. She wandered to the bunk and sank down upon the edge.

Jack followed her.

With her hands folded together in her lap, Mary asked innocently, "Was there something else?"

"I wanted to compliment you on your skills. Most people don't handle emergencies well and know how to speak to the sickly."

She shrugged. "You were unconscious most of the time."

"Not all of it." He looked at her expectantly.

What did he want her to say? He couldn't . . . no, he couldn't have heard her speak to him. Heat rushed into her face. He'd been unconscious when she'd whispered those three words!

Apprehension gripped her. "I don't know what you remember, but while you were unconscious I said very little to you."

"Very little?"

"Captain," Mary said, bracing herself for his reaction. "I do have to speak to you about our destination."

He sighed. "Go ahead, but don't report that we're headed back to Queen's Island."

"We're not. Let me get the map." She sped to the desk. What would he say when she reported they were headed for land? A place where a doctor would treat him. Taking a seat at the desk, she removed the chart. Uncertain, her hands trembled.

Jack stood behind her. His canvas scent filled her senses.

Mary did her best to ignore him. "We're here, and we're headed there." She pointed and waited.

"Nova Scotia. Was there any reason for this choice?"

"It was closest."

"The ocean is the closest."

"Captain, you need time to mend, not sail about the sea."

He bent closer. His breath tickled the back of her neck. Lightly, he ran a fingertip down the side of her face. "I'm willing to put myself entirely in your hands."

"You are?" She couldn't think any more.

"Mary, I understand you set our course while I was ill."

"That's true." Mary searched his features, looking for a clue as to where the conversation was leading. He had become very unpredictable since his accident.

"You've proved yourself a good navigator, Miss McNeal. We're almost where you want us to be."

An uneasy feeling drifted through her. "At the doctor's?"

"Nova Scotia."

Seventeen

Mary focused her telescope on Venus and tightened the sash of her new pink gown. The planet shone brightly in the early twilight. She dropped her scope and scanned the darkening heavens. A few persistent stars had pushed their way into the early night sky.

Time was fleeing, and she was no closer to finding her father. Was he still alive? Fear streaked through her, and she shivered.

"Cold, Miss McNeal?" Jack's coat came down about her shoulders before she had time to gather her startled thoughts.

"Thank you," she finally managed to whisper.

He leaned a hip against the railing. "Are you taking note of the time the stars come out?"

She smiled at him and studied his now familiar face. For a change, his cheeks contained color. Maybe he wouldn't need a doctor. Peering into his gray eyes, she noted they no longer appeared shadowed and troubled. Instead, they were clear and bright. The demons that had plagued him had disappeared, at least for a while.

"You caught me woolgathering. I'm sure it's not proper for a true navigator."

"Mary, no one could have plotted a better course. As for your stories, Beckett's crew is used to storytelling."

He reached out and skimmed his fingertip along her cheek.

Mary fought the urge to reach out and take his hand in an attempt to seek reassurance that everything in her life would be all right. She clasped her hands together, fighting the temptation.

"Look!" Jack pointed over her head to the heavens.

Mary gazed at the light shining through the darkening sky.

"What is it?" he asked. "A falling star?"

"I don't believe so." She tilted her head and considered the sky. "It looks like a comet. See? The tail has a white streak behind it."

He stepped closer and slipped his arm around her back. The nearness of him made her mind spin as though the ship were darting across the sea like a shooting star.

"What do you think?" he asked in a warm voice. "Does this comet mean I'll have good luck?"

Mary forced herself to stare at the sky and not at the man beside her. She tried to collect herself. Concentrate. Comets.

"As I recall, men have believed that comets are signs of warning. They forecast famine, war, or the ruin of great leaders. Take Napoleon, for example."

"A comet warned Napoleon he'd lose the war?" He gave her a skeptical look.

"Many people think he'd have been wise to have paid attention to his night sky. A year before the war ended, a great comet appeared in the heavens. If Napoleon had noticed and heeded it, he'd not have lost his great army in Russia. Even Julius Caesar's murder was followed by the appearance of a comet."

"His murder," Jack repeated, his voice hoarse.

"I'm sorry," Mary said quickly. "I'm sure this omen is not meant for you. Most likely, it's a sign for Gaspar."

"No, it's not for me." Confidence laced his voice. "Come below. I have something for you, and I'd like a little privacy."

Uncertain, she hesitated to steal a glance at the bright light once more. "I hope I haven't disturbed you."

He laid a finger under her chin and tilted it upward. "In many ways. Come with me."

Without waiting for her agreement, he turned on his heel and left. Why did he want solitude to speak with her? His gentleness and her own curiosity overcame her question. She whirled about, clutching his coat close to her.

Jack already held the whale lantern when she reached him. Holding it high, he led the way through the damp passage. He threw open the cabin door and waited for her to enter first.

Mary examined the room for her surprise and saw nothing striking.

Jack crossed the floor to the table and grabbed a bottle. It looked like one of Cook's carafes. Uncorking it, he poured liquid into two glasses that sat on the table. He gave her one.

"Are we celebrating?" she asked, her heart beating faster in anticipation.

"Today, I realized that I never thanked you for saving my life. You would say I was rude," he said with a knowing expression.

She bit her lip and dropped her gaze to her cup. "Any of your crew would have done the same."

"No, not anyone would have faced Gaspar's guns to rescue me." He clinked his cup against hers. "Here's to you, Mary."

Embarrassed, she suggested, "We'd better drink to Mr. Finn, too. He helped."

He raised his cup. "To Mr. Finn."

She took a sip. Sweet liquid filled her mouth and flowed smoothly down her throat.

He lowered his drink. "We'll have more with the fish."

Her gaze traveled to the table. On it, two plates rested. Jack and she would eat together, alone. A part of her warned it was a bad idea, but she was tired, and she wanted to grasp onto the strange lightness that took possession of her mind.

"First," he took her chipped cup, "I have a present for you. Close your eyes."

Obediently, she did and nervously yanked on the cuff of her sleeve. "I'm surprised you didn't tell me to sit down first."

What could Jack have for her? Excitement surged through her. Would he present her with another navigational tool? Surely, not more material for a dress. The sound of his footsteps came back toward her. He took her hands and placed an object in it. She recognized the smooth texture and weight immediately. Her eyes flew open.

In her hands, she held the familiar black cover. "Your log book." She swallowed nervously. "What do you want me to do with it?"

"Keep it. It's yours. My present."

"Mine? But you said the log was your personal property."

"It's my thank you."

Mary clutched the book tightly against her chest, and her eyes burned with tears of gladness. Tilting her head up, she tried to keep the tears from spilling down her cheeks. She couldn't remember the last time she'd felt happy.

Jack shifted uneasily before her. "Don't you like it?"

"I love it," she whispered in a strained voice. She blinked her eyes to clear them. A few drops of moisture fell on the log cover. She had to thank him. Quickly, she darted forward and threw her arms about him. Her mouth found his. His lips had parted in surprise, and she felt their smoothness against hers.

Suddenly, his hands came down upon her arms and pushed her back as quickly as she'd rushed forward.

"What's wrong?" Mary asked, her voice shaking with fear that she'd repulsed him with her forwardness.

A grim determination lit his eyes. "I want more than kisses from you. Do you understand?"

"Yes." She ran a finger over the log cover, remembering her request that he stay away from her. She shouldn't have kissed him.

He ran a shaking hand through his hair and released a sigh of frustration. "I want to kiss you, but when I do, I like it so much I want more. I want more from you, Mary McNeal, than to have you as my navigator, nurse, or librarian. I want—" He frowned and looked into her eyes as though he were searching for something. "I want you." The look on his face left no doubt as to his meaning.

"You *do?*"

"And afterwards, I won't forget it or pretend it didn't happen. I can't do that. No. If we make love again, it happened. What do you have to say about it?" He waited, his body tense.

Happiness soared through her. Jack cared for her. He wanted to be with her forever. She could barely breathe.

"I didn't give you my log book to bribe you. It's a gift. You don't owe me anything in return. What do you say?"

It wasn't the formal marriage proposal of Oliver's, but she didn't care. "I accept." She stepped back into his arms. For a moment he seemed uncertain, his hands at his sides. Then he wrapped his arms about her.

The stubble from his chin scraped against her chin. Under his prodding, her mouth opened again, and his tongue swept inside hers, capturing and retreating.

Beneath his hands, Mary trembled, remembering their last time.

He paused and looked into her eyes.

"I'm afraid I'm not a good navigator in this situation," she confessed, feeling awkward.

"I am. I promise to take you on a voyage you won't forget." His fingers began to coax and stroke while he kissed her again. An aching sensation in the pit of her stomach began to grow and spread. Her mind reeled with sensations until she clung to him. She wasn't certain how she breathed. In her ear, he whispered words that made her face heat.

His hand skimmed down until he cupped her breast. She gave a small cry of astonishment that was lost in their kiss.

In one sweeping motion, Jack lifted her into his arms and began to carry her across the floor.

"Wait? Where are we going?"

He didn't stop. "To your bedroom, madam."

"Oh!" Apprehension grabbed hold of her. She'd experienced the fleeting pleasure once. Next came the frustration over the quickness.

He laid her upon the bunk and stood back to remove his shirt. His back and chest were bronze like his face. Under his tanned skin were smooth muscles and scattered scars. He unbuckled his belt and his pants slid to his feet. Her gaze traveled down his chest, sprinkled with dark hairs, to his flat stomach. She felt the heat in her cheeks as she dared to look further. But she had no time to finish her study as he joined her on the bed.

She stiffened and pressed her arms to her sides.

"What are you doing?" he asked.

"I'm ready." Mary closed her eyes. She was ready for the pleasure and the frustration that followed.

"I've set sail too quickly." He ran a hand over his chin. "Our trip has just begun."

Mary couldn't answer. His mouth closed over hers while his hands gently caressed. All the delightful feelings began to grow again. Her skin heated, and she pressed herself against him, seeking more. His hand caressed her calf and slid up her thigh while the feelings rippled over her. She began to float, higher and higher. He ran his hand down her back again and then broke away.

"What's wrong?" Had she done something to stop him?

"You've no buttons on your gown. I want it off this time." He rubbed his chin. "How do you get this garment off?"

"Off?" she asked in a weak voice. "Oh, yes."

He smiled in encouragement. "I just want to see you. All of you."

Mary cleared her throat in embarrassment over her own naivete. Of course it wasn't necessary. She glanced down at her gown. The sash was already missing.

"Pull," she suggested.

He only stared back at her. Mary pushed him aside and sat up. She removed her telescope and placed it on the floor beside the bunk. Then she pulled the pink gown over her head. With a flick of her hand, she flung it to the floor. She sat in her petticoat, feeling dubious. Maybe this wasn't a good idea.

"Beautiful," Jack murmured. He kissed her throat, and his mouth seared a trail down to her breasts.

She startled at his touch, but he whispered reassurances. Gradually, Mary relaxed. She had nothing to fear. The man was giving himself to her. He must love her. *Love* her. This was a moment in her life that she'd always dreamed would happen, and it was happening now. The realization made her bold, and Mary let all her doubts vanish in a sea of emotions.

"Jack," she managed to gasp. The urge to get closer grew and burned within her. She wanted more. She could give more.

"Too late, Mary. I'll accept no retreats, only surrender."

She pushed against the bunk with the heels of her hands, until she was half-sitting.

Jack's hands stilled, and he looked at her. "Mary, if you're changing your mind—"

She clutched the edges of her white cotton petticoat and pulled it over her head. For a moment, she held the white undergarment in her raised hand, forcing herself to stay brave.

He lifted a questioning brow.

"My white flag of surrender." Mary bit her lip, waiting for his answer.

Jack's face broke into a grin. "Did I ever tell you I like your way with words?"

Dropping the petticoat, she slipped back into his arms before any uncertainty resurfaced. The heat from his body burned like a hot star. His legs tangled with her own while a wild fervor stormed inside of her. This was love, she thought. She had not made a mistake.

He came down on top of her. She wanted him closer still. Without thought, her hips rose against his body. Waves of pleasure rippled through her. He surged to meet her, and there was no time for words.

Mary woke with a cramp in her leg. Stretching, she touched Jack's leg. The short hairs on his limb tickled her foot.

He lay beside her. She stared at him. Last night had truly happened. Her dream that a brave and smart man like Jack would love her had come true. No, not any man. Captain Jack St. George. No more fairy tales or looking for men who weren't real. No more dreams of sailing into the stars. Last night, she'd sailed higher than ever. The frustration she'd felt the last time had not happened.

A tingling warning of pins and needles traveled down her arm. Goodness. She was falling apart. Mary sat up and massaged the area below her elbow. Beside her, Jack stirred. He looked at her through half-open eyes. "Good morning."

She glanced at the bottom of the bunk and spied the gray blanket. "Good morning," she answered, pulling the gray coverlet over her as she relaxed next to him.

He raised a brow and the edges of his mouth twisted upward. "It's a little late for modesty, Mary." He rolled on his side and faced her. "You know what I think after last night?"

Fear clutched at her heart. Would he tell her it was all a mistake? Mary wanted to duck under the blanket. She forced herself to ask, "What?"

"I think you're more ferocious than the French navy. I'd better check that I'm unharmed."

Mary heated with the memory of the night. "Did I hurt you?"

Jack gave a short laugh. "I believe the man is supposed to ask the woman that question."

He tucked his arm around her, drawing her tight to him. He placed hot kisses on her neck.

She sighed and relaxed into his arms until a notion struck her. "What did you mean last night when you said you wouldn't deny we'd been together?"

"Hmm?" He continued his attack.

"Tell me." She nudged him with her elbow.

He brushed a lock of hair from his forehead. "What's wrong?"

"Last night you said you wouldn't lie about us being together. What did you mean?"

"I didn't want you to have regrets like last time. I know I'm not exactly the type of man you'd want. I mean, you're a librarian, and I'm not exactly a scholar."

"I'd have no other." She struggled to sit up.

He only tightened his grip on her. "What about Mr. Bank? You were engaged."

"Oliver? I liked the way he talked to me," she admitted, looking at the gray blanket. "Most of the men who came to our house were whalers. They had my father make charts for their voyages, and they weren't interested in talking with me unless I knew about fish. Oliver was different. He came to the library and talked to me about books. He's very well-read. But after we became engaged, I knew something was missing. I didn't know what until now. I didn't love Oliver. 'There is safety in reserve, but no attraction.' "

When he remained silent, she risked looking into his gray eyes, wishing he'd say, 'Forget your Oliver, Mary. I can give you what you missed. I love you. Marry me today.'

"I don't know much about quotes from your books," he finally admitted. "I've read mostly military tomes."

"Don't worry, you've plenty of time to read." Forcing her wish from her mind, Mary snuggled into his side, enjoying his warmth.

"About the time we have together." His arm loosened from around her, and he drew away, leaving her chilled.

"We can talk books later."

He swung his legs over the side of the bunk. "I have to go above before Daniel comes looking for me in here. We'll talk when I get back."

Startled by his abruptness, she watched him pull on his pants and button his shirt.

"Don't go anywhere," he said lightly.

Mary lay still while he crossed the floor. He paused at the door and gave her a halfhearted smile. His gray eyes clouded. His smile faded, and he left.

Clutching the blanket, Mary sat upright. Something was wrong. She had seen it in his eyes. Was it the ship? Jumping out of bed, she climbed onto the trunk. The blue of the water glinted in the bright sun, greeting her.

Could it be Gaspar? Did he think she'd leave him after finding her father? Yes, of course, he thought she'd leave him when their trip ended. How foolish. Hadn't she shown him how much she loved him last night? She'd set him right. Grabbing her petticoat, Mary yanked it over her head. She scooped up her pink dress, hurried to the door, struggled into the gown, and opened the door.

In the dim corridor, she ran into Daniel. Stepping back, she asked, "Have you seen the captain?"

Daniel looked her up and down.

Under his scrutiny, Mary warmed, and her hand went

to her tangled hair. Could he guess about her night from her appearance? "It's about my leaving," she blurted, hoping to distract his thoughts.

Surprise flashed across the first mate's face. "The captain told you?" He shook his head. "We'll miss you, Miss McNeal, but you'll be safer."

"I will?"

"The captain is worried about you since you're a woman. He only wants you off the ship immediately because it's dangerous."

Jack still wanted her off the *Goodspeed*? Her voice wavered as she asked, "When did he talk to you about this?"

"Yesterday, I think. Sooner or later we'll get Gaspar, and the captain doesn't want you on board for the battle."

He didn't want her? He had told Daniel. A pain in her stomach made her flinch. She reached out for the wall.

"Miss McNeal, are you sick? Shall I fetch the captain?"

She forced a smile on her face and backed toward the cabin. "I need breakfast. Don't worry, I'm fine. Excuse me, I forgot to get, umm, something, umm, in my cabin. I'll just get it."

He followed at her elbow. "I can bring food for you."

"Don't bother," she said, desperate to get away. She opened the door wide enough only for herself. She squeezed through the opening and shut the door in the first mate's face.

Shaking, Mary leaned back against the door frame and breathed deeply, trying to will away the nausea. Jack had intended to get rid of her all along. That's why he'd acted strangely when she'd said they had a long time together. Last night had been a good-bye. There was no more time.

Everyone knew she was to leave except for her. What a fool she'd been.

She thought he cared for her and had changed his mind. She was simply a conquest. The rumpled blanket on the bed was a reminder of her night of stupidity. Mary wandered across the floor and sank onto the bunk. Wrapping her arms about her waist, she tried to warm herself against the chill spreading through her.

All the gossip she'd heard about Captain Jack St. George had been true. He was a pirate. He'd taken her most valuable possession and abused it. Her heart.

Lost in her misery, Mary sat on the bunk trying to understand everything. She couldn't stop her tears. Over and over, she saw the night in her mind, and it ended with the revelation. He didn't love her. Finally, a loud thud from the above deck brought her back to her senses.

She wiped her eyes. What would she do? Wait for him to throw her off the ship? No, she had her pride. She forced the feelings of anger and resentment to replace her pain. She'd leave of her own volition. *Where? What about her father?*

Beckett. Beckett would help her. Mary found her log book on the desk and flung open the cover. Flipping through the pages, she recognized dates and places. She pushed her hair from her face and ripped a blank page from the book.

Rummaging through the drawer, she found writing utensils. Immediately, Mary plunged into a brief message. She paused when she reached the part naming their meeting place. Well, she'd have to wait to talk to Jack about their destination.

No. She'd not let *him* decide her fate. From the desk, she gathered the map and smoothed it on top.

The door opened, and Jack strode across the cabin. He

stopped by the desk. "I'll have breakfast brought here." In a low, seductive voice he added, "We can spend the morning together."

Mary raised the map in front of her face. She summoned up all her courage. "No thank you. I'm anxious to go ashore. By my calculations, we're in Mahone Bay. How soon can we leave for the town?"

When he didn't answer, she peeked over the map.

Confusion glittered in his gray eyes. "We can wait till noon." He stepped closer to her. "I'd like for us to spend this time together." His hand slid to her shoulder and down her arm.

She dredged up her resolve. Once they landed, he'd send her away. *Be strong and refuse him.* "What about Gaspar?"

His hand stilled. "You're right. I'm worried about your safety."

She jumped out of her seat, breaking their contact. "I have to go ashore." Her voice sounded desperate even to herself.

He stared at her. The worry line between his brows deepened as he seemed to work out her declaration in his mind.

"After I know it's safe, I'll bring you ashore."

"Good. I'll be ready." Trying to busy her shaking hands that betrayed her turmoil, she began to braid her hair.

He studied her. "Is something wrong? Something about last night?" He shifted uncomfortably and added, "You seem nervous."

She shrugged. "Do I? It's only that I'd like a little private time while I—" Her voice trailed away.

A light of understanding dawned in his eyes. "I'll give you time to get yourself ready for the morning. Keep your flag close."

She saw the teasing light in his eyes before he left.

In the cabin, Mary wrote to Beckett, asking him to meet her in Mahone Bay. She'd send the note ashore with one of the men.

The letter done, she dropped her hands to her sides. Upon the floor, she spied a forgotten shard from the snuff box. How ironic, now she was just like the box. Shattered. What a fool she'd been not to recognize that the omen of the comet had been for her.

Eighteen

An hour later, a firm knock on the door tore her attention away from her musings. Squaring her shoulders, she opened the door. It was Jack. In his eyes, she recognized the dark clouds of trouble. Her faint hope that he'd come to speak words of love faded. She wouldn't show him her hurt.

He brushed past her arm, sending those familiar tingles through her. Clasping her damp hands together, she prayed her voice wouldn't waver when she spoke.

"I realized I didn't report that I've spoken to the prisoner."

"You didn't wait for me to join you? I should have known. I need to speak to him immediately. I plan to leave soon."

"Leave!" His mouth opened and closed and only a few sputters emerged.

"Ah, yes." She raised her chin. "You can forget you ever knew me."

Confusion, then anger, flared in his gaze. "What should I do? Erase you like a misspelled word, Miss Librarian?"

"You're an overbearing brute! I don't know why I speak to you."

"I guess I won't bother to remind you Gaspar is dangerous, and you can lose your life following a cockeyed scheme!"

"I'm perfectly capable of caring for myself. I've done so for many years."

"We need to talk." He began to pace. "I want to know you're safe. I know you'd run off with Gaspar if he promised to take you to your father."

Anger surged through her. "I'm sure he has more manners than you do."

"You're right. Gaspar always says sorry you can't stay longer before he plunges a knife through your heart."

Mary fought her ire. "Captain, what do you want?"

He ran his hand through his hair. "I want to strike a bargain with you."

She looked at him suspiciously. "I'm listening."

"Supposedly, your father is on an island with the treasure. I'll sail to the nearby Pine Island and look for him."

"You will?" she gasped.

"Wait." He held up a hand. "You must promise to stay here and go nowhere else. Do we have an agreement?"

She didn't hesitate. With relief flooding through her, she thrust out her hand to seal their agreement.

He engulfed her hand in his larger one. For a second, she allowed herself to enjoy the warmth and security that she always felt with him. Then she pulled away from his grasp. She had no time for dreams of Jack. Those illusions were over.

She stared at her black shoe. It was better than looking at him and remembering what a fool she'd been. Firmly, she pushed aside her feelings and searched through her mind for something appropriate to say. "Do you intend to investigate yourself?"

"I'll do it differently this time. I don't intend to have a repeat of Queen's Island. A midnight visit will be safest."

"You may run into Gaspar." Unbidden, the image of his blood-colored ship rose up in her mind. Goose bumps broke out on her arms, and she shivered.

"Don't worry, Miss McNeal." He leaned closer. "I'll remember my manners."

"I'm serious. Your plan sounds dangerous."

"Chasing a pirate is no game. I've been trying to explain that to you." He shook his head. "Cook has food for you."

"At least one gentleman is aboard." She skirted round him and left.

Running a hand through his hair, Jack sank into the chair. On the desk, the map lay open. The island's name and an inlet caught his attention. The words "Star Cove" stared up at him. Apprehension crawled up his spine, and he bent closer. "Great Blackbeard's Ghost! I'm glad Miss McNeal isn't here to read this."

His mind spun. This was too much of a coincidence. First there was Mary and her belief in this star design on the snuff box, then the constellation, and now Star Cove. Mary would argue that it was a sign that her father was on the island.

He didn't like any of it, but he'd leave her safe on his ship.

For the rest of the day, he avoided Mary and any discussion of her joining him in his search. At midnight he slipped over the side of the ship. He headed to the Star Cove.

Mary stood at the rail, until Jack's shore boat blended into the darkness. With heavy feet, she trudged to her cabin. She wished Jack had taken her with him. She reached for the knob.

"Going somewhere, little Missy?"

Luke! Mary whirled about to face the mooncusser when a pain streaked through her head. She stumbled to her knees.

The first hint of daylight broke through the clouds. The slight protection of dusk would disappear soon. Jack had to hurry.

At the top of the incline, he paused to decide his next move. A few feet away on the knoll stood a gnarled oak tree. Upon the limb, dangled a form he recognized, a boat wrench. *Why in Neptune had a boat wrench been tied to a tree on a hill?*

He started forward and caught a glimpse of a dark form shadowing him. His instinct had been right. Jack dodged behind a large pine and sought his weapon. Laying his hand over the pistol handle, he whipped it out and aimed at the shadow.

"Come out, I know you're there." Jack tensed.

The shaggy-haired, bearded man stepped out of the trees. "My stars, are you looking for me?"

"Who are you?" Jack asked.

"I'm Professor Marcus McNeal, a man of science, of Oyster River, New Hampshire, in the United States of America."

"By God, that was a long introduction. You must be McNeal." Jack lowered his pistol and extended a hand. "I'm Captain St. George, a friend of your daughter, and I'm here to bring you back to her."

The professor took Jack's hand. "Where is Mary?"

Mary whirled around at the sound of the metal door latch to see Luke enter with a lantern. He smiled at her like a fox who had cornered his lunch. Behind him, a blond-haired man gracefully strode into the cabin. He was dressed in biscuit-colored breeches and wore a frilled, white shirt. From his left hand dangled a cheroot. The white smoke curled up around his manicured hand, and Mary recognized the sweet scent from the fragrance on the ghost ship.

"Mademoiselle," his lips twisted into a smirk. "Good day. I'm glad you have risen from your nap."

Mary fought the desire to cringe while a realization clicked in her mind. "You are Gaspar?"

"I'm pleased you know me." His lips curled upward. " 'Too oft is a smile but the hypocrite's.' "

"You quote Byron. How lovely. Who shall you quote when I'm finished with you? The devil comes to mind." He turned to Luke. "Bring her on deck. Our fun is about to begin."

Mary avoided Luke's grasp. "Wait, where is my father?"

"He met with an unfortunate accident while burying my gold."

"No!" She fought Luke as he dragged her from the cabin.

By noon, Jack and his new visitor reached the *Goodspeed*. Daniel met them by the rail. He wet his lips and blinked nervously. "Captain, Miss McNeal has disappeared."

Jack fisted his hands in frustration. "Did you check with Finn and Cook? How long has she been missing?"

"No one has seen her, and it's been about an hour," the first mate said, glancing uncomfortably at the men knotted about them. "Luke's guard was found unconscious in front of his cabin. The prisoner appears to have escaped. I think he has Mary."

Apprehension strangled Jack's voice. He could only nod.

The professor stepped forward. "I don't mean to intrude upon your conversation, but are you speaking about my daughter?"

"Who is he?" The first mate whispered.

"Sorry, Daniel. Allow me to introduce Professor Marcus McNeal. This is Miss McNeal's father."

The men standing by uttered exclamations. Jack stood aside while the crew crowded around their new visitor. The pain of the realization was crushing him. Mary wasn't here.

Fears pounded in Jack's mind. *Why had he ever left her? He should have locked her in his cabin. Where was she? Was she hurt?*

"Captain St. George?"

At the sound of Professor McNeal speaking to him, Jack focused on his present situation.

Marcus squared his shoulders. "What's happened to my daughter?"

Jack's throat tightened, and he paused to force out his confession. "She's been kidnapped."

"My stars!" The man put out his hand as if to ward off the truth. Jack hurried to his side.

Slipping an arm under the older man's elbow, Jack supported the professor. "We'll get you to the galley. Daniel, take him to Cook."

Marcus straightened. "Wait. What shall we do about Mary?"

Jack met the man's gaze. "Rescue her."

Nineteen

"Captain," Daniel shouted. "I see a sail."

Peering into the fog, Jack tamped down on the fear flooding through him. "Gaspar! Damn, let me be wrong. Mary can't be on that ship. Let her be anywhere but there."

The first mate brought him Mary's scope, and Jack scanned the ocean. Ghosts of mist danced before him. Then in a break through the whiteness, he recognized *LeDefenseur*'s stern.

Jack gripped the telescope tightly, and as he watched, Gaspar wrapped his arm around Mary's pink form.

As suddenly as the fog had opened, the clouds of white closed around the ship, blocking Jack's view. Splinters dug into his palm as he clutched the rail.

His arm with the scope fell to his side. He could barely say the words. "He has her. Gaspar has Mary."

"How can you tell?" Daniel asked, squinting out at the sea.

"I saw her pink dress." Jack whirled with the impact of the truth. How could he save her? He knew only one answer. "We give him what he wants. Me."

Daniel stepped in front of St. George. "He could shoot you as soon as you're near his ship. He could shoot Miss McNeal."

"What do you propose, Daniel?"

Determination burned in the first mate's eyes. "We fight to get Miss McNeal back. We've been chasing that devil for over a year. I'll not let him sail away without a chance to get back at him for my brother's death."

"Is this a mutiny, Daniel?" Jack asked sarcastically.

"I vote to fight. The men are ready, Captain. You only have to say the word."

"I can't imagine a battle in this soup." Jack looked at the resolution on his first mate's face and made his decision.

"First, I want everyone off this ship who can't fight."

"But, Captain, we need every man for the battle."

"Enough. I won't have their deaths on my conscience. Send them off. Now."

"Yes, Captain. But how can we fight without all of our crew?"

Jack closed his eyes, not wanting to face the truth: Only death awaited them in such an unfair battle. "I'll figure something out. Stand aside, Daniel." His voice grew weary with the weight of responsibility.

On *LeDefenseur*'s deck, Gaspar held Mary's wrists pinned to her back with a smooth, cold hand. The wind whipped the strands of her hair into her eyes. She twisted, trying to avert her gaze from the stinging sea breeze that whipped across the ocean.

She strained against Gaspar's hold, and her captor tightened his grip on her arms and pulled painfully. She cried out.

"A little louder, my *cherie*. St. George can't hear you."

Defiantly, Mary bit down on her lip to smother her distress.

"Too bad your captain cannot see you through the fog.

We could entertain him." Gaspar lightly ran a chilly finger down her cheek.

Mary fought against the queasiness that surged through her.

"Later, I promise." He released her. "I want to enjoy watching St. George squirm in my trap."

Mary looked up into Gaspar's ice blue eyes. She hoped he couldn't see the fear in her own. "Captain St. George has been waiting for you. His men are highly skilled. They've drilled day and night. Turn your ship around while you have a chance."

"They will fight to the death, you think?" Gaspar strode closer to the railing and peered outward. "Too bad I won't face your gallant men. It looks like they're abandoning ship."

He pointed to a break in the fog.

Mary squinted against the whiteness. Tied to the *Goodspeed*'s hull, a shore boat was rapidly loading with men. The crew was leaving! Panic welled up into her throat.

It must be a mistake. Jack couldn't fight without his men! As the fog rolled back and hid the scene, Mary swallowed the salty taste of fear. The *Goodspeed*'s sailors may have given up, but she wouldn't. She willed up her courage and faced Gaspar.

"Captain St. George doesn't need a large crew. He's a war hero. He'll force you to surrender. You'd better leave while you can escape. He's come back to take you to the authorities."

"You think, *cherie?* I think your St. George will raise a white flag and surrender." He smiled in smug satisfaction.

Mary peered into the fog. She could see nothing. "Never."

"It's quite simple, Mademoiselle. St. George knows he

can't fight me and win. He thinks he can bargain with me under a flag."

"But I want one thing. To blow your captain to the deepest, darkest hole in hell. No one deserts me and lives. Watch carefully. When St. George and his men come aboard to talk truce, I will cut him down and wash my deck with his blood."

"No!" Mary screamed and ran to the rail, waving her arms frantically. "Jack, it's a trick. Go back. Go back."

Grabbing her hair, Gaspar dragged her away from the side.

She dug her nails into his hands, but he held fast and smiled when she cried out in pain.

"Take her below," Gaspar shoved her toward the mooncusser. "I'll deal with her later, after I've killed St. George."

"I won't go."

Gaspar struck her before she had time to flinch. A roar sounded in her ears, and Mary fought the blackness creeping over her. Blindly, she held out her hand to steady herself and felt Luke gather her and toss her over his shoulder.

He was carrying her to the cabin below. Only death—or worse—awaited her there. They reached the cabin door.

Without warning, the ship lurched. Luke screamed as he pitched forward. Free, Mary slid across the deck. With a moan of pain, she landed a few feet away from Luke. Ignoring the pains shooting through her arms and legs, Mary sat up.

Her gaze fell upon rows of barrels against the rail. Mary crawled the short distance and squeezed between two large wooden barrels. Trembling, she tried to slow her breathing.

If only she could make herself invisible. She braced her hands against the rough wood and drew her feet up under her chin. A sticky brown substance from the barrel side clung to her fingers, and a sweet odor rose up to greet her. Molasses. Barrels of molasses. Gaspar's main ingredient for switchel.

She heard a moan. Luke staggered into view, rubbing the back of his head. He squinted and headed to the barrels. Within moments, he reached for her.

Mary drew back her hand and struck him full in the face.

With a shout of pain, he released her.

Frantic, Mary searched for a way to escape. But there was nowhere to go. Another barrel jabbed her back, and an idea sprang to life.

"This is for you, little Missy." His eyes gleamed with evil delight as he balled his fist.

With all her strength, Mary grabbed hold of the edge of the keg and pushed it into the mooncusser's path. It wobbled for a moment, then toppled to the deck. Molasses ran onto the deck and specks splattered herself and the mooncusser.

Inspired, Mary scrambled to overturn the next barrel. It tumbled to the deck and landed with a crack. The brown substance oozed out.

"Stop it!" Luke took a threatening step toward her and stopped at the edge of the molasses. With a grumble of frustration, he lunged at her. His feet slipped from underneath him, and his arms shot up into the air. He landed with a plunk in the brown pool.

Mary pulled down the next barrel. Three down already.

"Mademoiselle," Gaspar's cool voice stopped her. "A guest does not treat her host's ship in this manner.

Mary froze as she saw him a few feet from her. She

stared into his ice blue eyes. These were the eyes of the man who had killed her father. Anger surged through her. "She does if her host is a murderer."

"I fear I have no more patience. This is the end. We will not wait for St. George. Instead, I will take great delight in showing him your body. My men will enjoy you first, but I promise you will not enjoy them."

"Captain!" a deck hand screamed. "Captain! She comes!"

Mary jerked her head to the blanket of white surrounding them. Beyond, something lurked like a giant shadow, and the smell of danger floated on the stillness of the air. Goose bumps prickled her arms.

The *Goodspeed* broke through the fog like an angry sea monster coming to swallow them. Upon the quarterdeck, Captain Jack St. George stood. His dark blue navy coat gleamed in the whiteness. Determination was written on his face as he rode his ship straight into the enemy. With fear mixed with pride, Mary realized that the *Goodspeed* was sailing into them!

Around her, men screamed in panic. Many ran to the rail and jumped overboard. But it was too late for the rest of them. Mary heard the sickening sound of wood ramming wood. The ship lurched sideways, and the deck of *LeDefenseur* disappeared from beneath her feet.

Mary fell and somersaulted down the tilted deck. She was hurled toward the side and prayed for a quick death in the frigid water. With a thud, she stopped. Mary glanced about in confusion, until she realized that she'd hit the rail.

Leaning on its side, the ship threatened to drop her into the deadly sea. Beneath her, the dark waters swirled, promising a swift end. They were sinking. She shook and took deep, quivering breaths.

Shaking, Mary scrambled to her feet. Her clothes were covered with molasses. She had to get to the shore boats. It was her only hope. Mary fought for balance on the uneven deck.

"Leaving?"

Mary halted at the familiar, refined voice. Gaspar stood a few feet from her, a pistol in his hand. A pistol aimed at her heart.

"Don't!" Mary gasped.

"Mary!"

Her attention swiveled to the quarterdeck and the familiar voice. "Jack!"

He stood with a sword gripped in his hand. Relief shone in his gray eyes.

Gaspar's aim whirled toward his new victim, Jack.

"No!" Mary screamed. With all her strength, she sprang at Gaspar's outstretched arm. Pain shot through her chest as she hit him, and they continued to roll together across the deck, down, down into the blackness of the ocean.

Jack dashed to the side. Below, he saw Gaspar thrashing about in the water, and no sign of Mary.

"Help me," Gaspar gasped.

The man Jack had chased for more than a year was within his reach. No time to waste. He plunged into the water.

Mary lifted one eyelid and recognized a blue quilt covering her. She turned her head to the side and saw a man resembling her father sitting in a wooden chair. He dozed over a book opened on his lap.

Mary closed her eyes. She didn't want to ruin the dream, yet she couldn't resist looking again. "Father, Father?"

He sat up with a start. "Mary?"

"It's you! You're alive?"

"My stars, everyone was asking the same question about you." He leaned over and enveloped her in his arms. His book hit the floor with a thump.

Tears rolled down her cheeks and made it impossible for her to speak. For an eternity, she lay in his embrace. Pressed against his shabby white shirt, she caught the scent of pine and snuggled closer. Finally, she pulled away and whispered, "How did you get here?"

"Captain St. George rescued me from Pine Island. We met at Star Cove. Now we're in Mahone Bay in Nova Scotia."

"He saved you?" She wiped away the tears. "How did I get here?"

"Captain St. George rescued you from drowning. You were in the water quite a while before we pulled you both out. We had to pry you away from him. The man takes his job as captain very seriously."

A shiver of delight went through her. "Do you know what happened to his other men? Daniel?"

"He's safe. Everyone is safe."

"Thank goodness. Were you on the *Goodspeed* when you hit Gaspar's ship?"

"The captain ordered me and a few of the men off the ship before the battle. We were in a shore boat. I'm afraid I calculated the speed for the hit a little too high, but you're safe now, and Gaspar has disappeared."

Mary leaned back against a feather pillow. "I feel very tired." A fuzzy feeling floated through her as her father whispered reassuring words. "Wait!" She popped up in the bed. "Has the captain left?"

"No, he won't be going anywhere. He no longer has a ship."

She reached out and touched her father's hand that rested on the quilt. "You're alive. That's all that matters."

"Take a nap. We'll speak later."

Mary relaxed against the down mattress. Everything was well. Jack was safe. Her father was safe. They could go home. *Home.* She allowed the warm drowsiness to carry her off to sleep.

When she woke, the gray evening light flowed into the room. She was alone. At a knock on the door, she sat up. "Come in."

Jack opened the door and hesitated in the doorway. "Is it safe for me to come into your room?"

Mary glanced about the bedroom. "No pirates here."

He strode slowly forward, studying her face. The white sleeves of his shirt had been rolled up to his arms as if he were prepared to work. "I've been trying to get in here all day."

"You have?" Pleasure surged through her at his confession.

He nodded, stopping beside her bed. "We're at the local pastor's home. He has had the door guarded." He sat on the edge of the bed. Crease lines formed between his dark brows as he spoke. "How are you, Mary? You gave me a scare out there."

"I'm fit as a librarian can be." She tried to smile, but her lips trembled.

He reached out and touched her cheek. "Gaspar will never hurt you again."

For a second, she closed her eyes at the familiar sensations that spread through her at his touch. Opening her eyes, Mary gathered her composure. "I'm sorry about your ship. It meant everything to you."

"You're wrong, Mary. My ship once meant everything to me."

"Captain!"

Mary's attention turned to a young boy of about ten standing in the doorway.

"The guard," Jack whispered to Mary. "He's the reverend's son. His name is Jeremy. He's tough."

"I can see why you had trouble getting inside the room." Mary agreed with a knowing nod.

"Captain," Jeremy said. "My father wants you downstairs. He says it's an emergency. There's a man here who says he'll report us to the President of the United States of America if you don't come and talk to him."

From the open doorway, heavy footsteps sounded on the stairs.

A man could be heard shouting up the stairs. "You can't search my house. I don't give my permission."

Beckett, dressed in his crisp white clothes, burst past Jeremy. "Jack! And Miss McNeal! No wonder no one could find you, Jack, and I've been searching. I couldn't sit around Bath any longer. Mary, I heard about your terrible accident. I hope you're improving."

"Excuse me, young man." Professor McNeal barged into the room, followed by a man who must have been the pastor. "My daughter is not well."

"It's all right, Father. This is a friend."

"Father?" Beckett grabbed Marcus's hand and pumped it. "Allow me to introduce myself. I'm Thomas T. Beckett, the owner of the once beautiful yacht the *Helen of Troy*. It still isn't fixed, and I had to buy the first available vessel from a man in the harbor. It's named the *New Moon* but it should be called the *Desolate Moon*."

Mary jolted in surprise. It must have been the moon-cusser's ship. "Did you buy it from a man named Morley?"

"You know him?" Beckett asked in surprise.

"We met in Maine," Mary answered. She caught Jack's gaze. "Captain, whatever happened to Luke?"

"We fished him out of the sea, and he's locked up in the jail."

"Who's Luke?" Beckett asked.

"Please, gentlemen," the pastor interrupted. "We should take this conversation to the parlor."

"I agree." Beckett grasped Mary's hand. "Now that your father's here, allow me the pleasure of bringing you both home."

Mary slid a glance from Beckett's hovering face to Jack's, hoping he'd offer to take them.

"Thank you, we accept," Professor McNeal answered.

"Please, let's go downstairs," the pastor pleaded again. "This is not proper, entertaining in a lady's bedroom."

"Of course," Beckett agreed, straightening. "Jack, lead the way. I want to hear about my treasure."

"Treasure?" Jeremy asked with delight shining in his eyes.

"A treasure no one will ever recover," Marcus said, following. "I devised a plan that will fool the most scientific of men when they attempt to uncover the small fortune on Pine Island."

"I'll come back," Jack called to Mary over his shoulder.

With a heavy heart, Mary watched him leave. She knew the truth. Their adventure together had ended. She brushed a tear from her eye.

" 'I bid thee now a last farewell,' " she whispered.

* * *

A full moon rose in the night sky. On the library widow's walk, Mary put the telescope to her eye and searched for the first star. From the open doorway, she heard the fall of footsteps on the stairs. Her breath caught in her throat, and she turned to face the newcomer.

Jack appeared at the top of the stairs. He wore a new blue pea coat with shiny brass buttons. Slowly, he strode forward. His clear gray eyes fastened on her.

Mary's heart beat furiously, and she resisted the urge to smooth her blue muslin gown and her upswept topknot. Gathering herself, she spoke, "Good evening, Captain. I thought you'd arrive today."

"Did you get my message?"

"Beckett stopped here on his way to New Bedford and told me about your letter."

She clasped her hands together in front of her and recited, "He said Gaspar's body had been found, and the authorities in Mahone Bay had written you a letter of commendation. You would stop in Oyster River on your way home to see your mother and father." She smiled at him. "Your parents will be proud."

"I gave Beckett a letter for you." Jack stepped onto the roof beside her. "I should have known Beckett would keep it. I'm sorry I've agreed to become his partner, although he did back my new ship."

"Thomas couldn't have a better partner than you. Are you staying long? My father will want to see you. The observatory in our house is nearly finished. Would you like to see it?"

"I'd like to talk to you first. I never could speak to you alone at the reverend's. There was always someone in your room."

Mary felt her stomach flutter. "What would you like to discuss? Your ship? Gaspar?" Nervously, she gestured to the sky. "The night? 'In stars adorn the vault of heaven.' "

He caught her hand in his. "Us."

"Oh!" Her mind spun wildly, and she couldn't think of another word to utter.

"I've thought about you a lot."

"You have?" She bit her lip, waiting.

"I never thought I'd say this, but you helped me, Mary, more than anyone."

"Well, there you are. Women *can* be useful." Her gaze wavered to his worn Hessian boots. "I have an apology myself." She looked up into his intense gaze. "I'd like to apologize for thinking that you were an uneducated . . ."

"Brute?" he suggested with a smile.

Her cheeks warmed, and she nodded. "Sailing was quite an education for me."

He ran his hand through his black hair. "I have my own piece to say, but it isn't easy. When we met, a part of me was . . . missing. Does that make sense?"

"Yes, you'd lost your good name," Mary said carefully.

"No. Damn it, Mary, if I learned anything, it's that a man makes his own reputation."

"Oh!"

"If I ever doubt it again, I just have to look into your eyes."

Her breath caught in her throat. She could barely speak. "What . . . what are you trying to say?"

"My heart."

"I don't understand."

"When I met you, my heart was missing." He shook his head and smiled grimly. "I must sound like one of those poets you read."

"Better," Mary said, tears burning in her eyes. "No one has ever spoken such beautiful words to me."

The tense lines about his mouth relaxed. "They haven't?" He smiled mischievously. " 'She walks in Beauty, like the night.' "

"Byron!" she gasped.

" 'Of cloudless climes and starry skies;' "

"You memorized Byron? For me?"

"Only for you." Abruptly, he dropped to one knee. "Mary McNeal, will you do me the honor of becoming my wife?"

Tears slid down her cheek and clogged her throat. "Your wife?"

He stood. His gray eyes clouded. "I didn't do it right, and I wanted to do it perfect."

"Yes, you did. It was lovely."

"No, I forgot the most important part."

"You did?"

He pulled her gently to him. "I love you, Mary McNeal. From the first time I saw you standing here. I was just too bullheaded to admit it."

A rush of warm feelings flooded through her. "I love you too!"

"I know," he said with a devilish smile. "You told me when I was ill."

"You heard me!" She attempted to draw away, but he held her.

"You're forgetting to answer my question."

She wiped her tears and took a deep breath. "I'd be honored to become your wife."

"Tomorrow," he whispered. "I can't wait any longer."

"Yes. Though I don't know much about being a captain's wife. Perhaps I can find a few references in the library. I hope—"

Jack silenced her with a kiss.